Merde at the Paris Olympics

Stephen Clarke

pAf

A pAf paperback

ISBN: 978-2-9585663-2-6

COVER DESIGN BY RUTH MURRAY

MORE BOOKS BY STEPHEN CLARKE

Fiction
A Year in the Merde
Merde Actually (US edition: In the Merde for Love)
Merde Happens
Dial M for Merde
The Merde Factor
Merde in Europe
A Brief History of the Future
Death Goes Viral (previously published as Who Killed Beano)
The Spy Who Inspired Me

Non-Fiction
1,000 Years of Annoying the French
Dirty Bertie, an English King Made in France
How the French Won Waterloo (or Think They Did)
The French Revolution & What Went Wrong
Talk to the Snail : the Ten Commandments for Understanding
  the French
Paris Revealed : the Secret Life of a City
Château d'Hardelot, a Souvenir Guide
The British Invasion (with co-author Valli)
I Did It My Ways (with co-author D'yan Forest)
The Golden Treasure of the Entente Cordiale (chapter on
  Edward VII's diplomacy)
Elizabeth II, Queen of Laughs

ABOUT THE AUTHOR

Stephen Clarke is a British author living in Paris, where he divides his time between writing and not writing.

His books have been translated into 20-odd languages. His best-known novels are the worldwide bestselling *Merde* series, including *A Year in the Merde* (which has sold well over a million copies worldwide) and *Merde Actually* (a number-one bestseller in the UK).

He has also written several non-fiction books, including *1,000 Years of Annoying the French* which was a number-one bestseller in the UK, in both hardback and paperback, and was shortlisted for a French history prize, the Prix du Guesclin.

1,000 Years of Annoying the French inspired the permanent collection at a French museum, which Clarke curated. It is the Centre Culturel de l'Entente Cordiale at the Château d'Hardelot in northern France.

He has written two stage shows based on his books – an adaptation of his novel *The Merde Factor*, and a words-and-music show in French called *L'Entente Cordiale en Paroles et Musique*.

He also writes jokes for stand-up comedians and lyrics for singers, and has co-written a French radio sitcom and a radio play. He occasionally performs his own material in music and comedy clubs – but mainly for fun (his own rather than the audience's).

www.stephenclarkewriter.com   @sclarkewriter

THANKS

To my ever-present, never-failing support group.

This novel is based on a true story.
But then again, so is what we call reality.

1

"Monsieur Paul West?"

"Yes."

Well, in fact the woman had said something like "Pull Vest", but I've been in France long enough to say yes to anything that sounds even vaguely like my name.

"We want your 'ead."

"My head?"

"Yes, monsieur."

Everything about the person who wanted to decapitate me said "young French career woman". Her trouser suit was chic but not too chic, her blond hair styled and yet un-styled, her lipstick red but not too red, her spoken English self-assured but of unmistakably French origin.

She was accompanied by what looked like a French peasant who'd got lost in Paris during a protest march about dung prices. He was 60-ish and bald, with a huge grey moustache and a stomach that seemed to contain a whole roast pig.

"You want my head? But the French Revolution's over," I told them. "The guillotines are all out of action. Unless you've come to tell me it's started up again?"

The man raised his already creased forehead to a new level of wrinkliness.

"What you want to say, sir?" he asked, sounding like a Frenchman torturing the English language. Which was fair enough, because that was what he was.

"No, the question is," I said, "what do *you* want to say?"

The woman huffed impatiently.

"We want, we need your 'ead," she said.

This was beginning to sound like a bad Madonna song.

"We will pay you well," the woman added.

"I'm not sure I want to sell my head," I told her. "I use it quite a lot for eating and speaking."

They looked even more confused, but I was enjoying myself. Sometimes, when you're a Brit in France, it's fun to see how far a misunderstanding will go. How many avenues of nonsense can you explore? How far can you stretch a lack of communication before it snaps and someone French wants to punch you?

"Ah!" The woman raised her eyebrows, which were plucked but not too plucked. She seemed to be having a moment of revelation. "Not your 'ead. Your *id*."

"My id? You want to buy my personality?"

She groaned. The guy looked as though he was about to faint from linguistic exhaustion.

"Vous pouvez le dire en français," I said. You can say it in French.

Now the woman clearly wanted to punch me for wasting her time.

"Votre aide," she said, meaning my help. My *aid*. Which, I had to admit, was what I'd understood about two lines into our dialogue.

"My aid to do what?" I asked, risking English again.

The woman took a deep breath and told me.

"We want you to 'elp us to make pétanque a new Olympic sport."

Now that is a completely new avenue of nonsense, I thought. One that needs exploring.

"You'd better come into my meeting room," I said.

To be honest, it wasn't *my* meeting room. It was an empty office I'd booked when this same career woman had messaged me the previous day asking for a "rendez-vous to discuss a very delicate affair". Despite what people say about Paris, it's rare that I get messages from people offering me an affair, delicate or otherwise, so of course I invited her to come and see me at a start-up incubator where I was renting a part-share in a desk.

I didn't have an actual desk space of my own at the incubator. The idea was that you turned up and sat wherever was free. The incubator was a converted railway repair shop near the Gare du Nord, a brick-and-glass building that had been refitted with dozens of desks, as well as armchairs and sofas for slouchers like me. As a business address it wasn't exactly the Champs-Elysées, but it was cheap, equipped with unlimited coffee, and buzzing with ideas.

America's ex-President George W Bush got it doubly wrong when he said there's no French word for entrepreneur. Linguistically, of course, the poor old hick made an international idiot of himself. But sociologically, too. This place where I came to slouch was as bursting with innovations as a whole series of *Star Trek*.

Just chatting at the coffee machine in my first week there, I'd talked to two women who had worked out a convincing – to me anyway – method of making solar panels more efficient, more eco-friendly and more affordable. Another woman was working on a way of instantly fining every car that ran a red light. If that got through parliament, the fines dished out to Parisian drivers alone were going to repay France's whole national debt.

And these were just the projects I *understood*. Some young guy had tried to explain his new way of making rust-free, unbreakable hinges, but had given up when it turned out I'd mistaken the French word for hinge – *charnière* – for *chaumière*, a thatched cottage. By the time he'd understood why I was asking him how a cottage could bend in the middle, he was too exasperated to go on.

Next to these geniuses, my own business was a no-brainer. Translation, interpretation, negotiation, anything that helped French and English-speaking people to get along without resorting to mutual insults about Joan of Arc, Dunkirk and what language the world should be speaking.

I still owned a share of my English tearoom business, My Tea Is Rich, which had survived the worst periods of Covid lockdown by selling tea, sympathy and sausages from a takeaway counter in the shop doorway. But the business wasn't making enough money to employ me, or even pay me a dividend, so I'd set up online as a translator and now worked mostly from a phone and computer.

Although I constantly needed cash, there was one sort of work I always turned down. I never took written translation jobs – contracts, manuals and the like – for the simple reason that I'd once translated a contract and missed out the word "not" at a crucial moment, which had slightly altered the legal implications of the document.

But then what kind of idiot lawyer doesn't get someone to re-read a translated contract before it's signed? They couldn't really blame me, could they? Though they did.

So now the jobs I accepted consisted mostly of sitting in on meetings to help French people communicate with English speakers. Luckily very few of my meetings were about hinges. Anyway, it was often less a case of translating words than conveying differences in brain patterns.

French brains just aren't programmed like Anglo brains. A French mind might master the technical details of a thing but fail totally to understand that not everyone has a doctorate in engineering.

Meanwhile, Anglos might see only the short-term financial side of an idea, and be nervous about where to get funding, whereas the French have been programmed since birth to expect the state to back them financially – which it usually does.

So quite often my job was to translate a few sentences, then add on a long explanation as to *why* someone French might want to say such a thing.

Which was going to be the case today, if I agreed to work for my two visitors, the career woman and the pig swallower. Why, I urgently needed to know, would anyone think that the Olympic Committee might accept *pétanque* as an official event? Surely it was one of those beer-belly games like darts, poker and arm-wrestling that will never make it into the medal tables?

They introduced themselves. I already knew that the woman's name was Marjorie Daure. We'd exchanged details online, and I was surprised to see that she actually looked like her profile photo. It's rare. I hoped I didn't look too much like mine. My official mugshots always make me look as though I've just been arrested for stealing an old lady's life savings.

The peasant guy now explained that he was called something like A-lang F-yong. I quickly worked out that there was a southern French accent at play.

As soon as we were seated in our goldfish bowl, Marjorie launched into her pitch.

I would never have figured her for a *pétanque* player – she didn't have the look of someone who spent her spare time lobbing cannonballs around in sandpits. But I was wrong. She was, she told me, a keen *bouliste*, and regularly met a group of like-minded chums for a *pétanque* party by the canal in Paris's 19th arrondissement.

This was my current neighbourhood, so I'd often seen these hipsters chucking metal about. But I'd always assumed they were there for the alcohol and the laughter rather than the science of actually getting the *boule* nudging the *cochonnet*.

"We have a very serious club called Les Boules au Bassin," she said. This sounded like a sexual pun. *Boules* are balls, both the ones used for bowling and those usually hidden in a man's underwear, while *bassin* is a canal basin but is also the word for pelvis. "Our club will participate this year," she went on, "in the national ... championate?"

"Ship," I corrected her.

"No, it is true," she said.

Her peasant friend was watching us mutely, more lost than ever because of our exchange in English.

"Et vous, monsieur, vous êtes bouliste?" I asked him.

He nodded. "Président de la Fédération Unie des Clubs de Pétanque," he announced like a man who was very proud of his ball-tossing skills. "Fuck pet," he added unexpectedly. I'd heard of fuck buddies, but this was a new concept.

"It is the abréviation," his female colleague explained. She could see that I was confused.

The guy gave me his card, which introduced him as "Fillon,

Alain, Président, FUCPET". Typically for a French email address, I saw that his was endless, with lots of dots and underscores inserted in unnecessary places.

"How exactly can I help you?" I asked them. "Why do you need an Anglophone?"

"The Parisian committee Olympique have refuse to permit the pétanque at the games of two sousand twenty-four," Marjorie said.

"Une honte!" Alain added. The shame of it. He was as outraged as if a Frenchman had been unjustly accused of drinking tea with *bœuf bourguignon*.

"So we must lobby the committee international in Lausanne. In English, of course," Marjorie said.

"En anglais! Une honte!" Alain was outraged again, as are many Frenchmen who think the whole planet would be better off having the fiendish rules of French syntax beaten into them rather than muddling happily along in ungrammatical English.

"And you want me to come with you to Switzerland?" I asked, envisaging fondue, lake-swimming and unlimited chocolate.

"No, no. We will do this with Zoom," Marjorie declared, sounding as if she had moral objections to fondue. But then she added regretfully, "The budget, it is not so big." I deduced that she had nothing personal against melted cheese and was herself suffering because of the limited FUCPET kitty.

If there's one downside to the post-virus world, it's that people have learnt that it's much cheaper to hold their meetings online. The good old expense-account jaunt has become an endangered species. Now, instead of jetting to the Côte d'Azur for a sea-view lunch meeting, employers think you should sit at home talking to a blurred face on screen.

"But if you need to convince someone quickly about what is after all a *very* delicate affair," I said, "a single face-to-face meeting with the right person can be more efficient than a dozen Zoom conferences."

"What 'e say?" the president demanded. Marjorie explained in French and he nodded. He was clearly a fondue fan like me.

"If is vary urgent, maybe in fut-toor we 'av fee-nonce for meeting," he said in something like English.

"Good," I said. "After all, getting pétanque accepted as an Olympic sport will be correcting an historic injustice. Basketball, baseball and surfing are Olympic sports," (I was guessing) "and curling is a winter sport, so why shouldn't France's national game be accepted? Merde!" I added for good measure.

"Merde!" Alain agreed.

Marjorie nodded with a discreet smile, obviously realizing that I might help to increase *her* expenses bill, too.

"So Monsieur Vest, you give us 'ead?" Alain asked.

"With pleasure, monsieur le president."

I knew I was far from the first person to promise *that* to a French president.

2

I was en route to my next meeting of the day. It was the early summer, and Paris couldn't quite decide how the season was going to start. I had the choice: wear a jacket and sweat uncomfortably in the crowded *Métro*, or *not* wear a jacket and also sweat in the *Métro*, but then freeze if the Bretons or Normans sent us one of their damp westerly winds. So I decided to walk.

I'd opted for a light suit jacket that morning because of my business meeting, and I was feeling comfortable in the mild sunshine as I strolled from the Gare du Nord towards my least favourite square in Paris – Place Stalingrad.

The city has done its best to preserve the old stone roundhouse that used to be a toll station for canal traffic, but there's something profoundly wrong with Place Stalingrad. It's always been a haven for drug addicts and homeless people, and all the authorities ever seem to do about this is fence off areas of the square, inadvertently creating little no-go zones where druggies can crash out even more effectively.

The name, which was meant as a homage to the survivors of the World War Two siege of Stalingrad, only seems to encourage lasting conflict and squalor.

And yet literally yards away is one of the hippest areas of Paris, the Bassin de la Villette, with its Amsterdam-like canal banks and trendy cafés.

This was where Marjorie did her *pétanque*-ing and where I was due to meet my American friend Jake – the world's least fashionable dresser and most tasteless poet.

Jake was still eking out a living in Paris as an English teacher, even though he was increasingly incapable of speaking English. Or any recognized language, for that matter.

His tendency to mingle French words and English sentence structures at random meant that he was only understandable by a small bilingual community with an ear for accents. Both his English and French were coloured with a strong American twang.

We'd once done an American road trip[1] together, and it had been touching to see his ecstasy when he arrived in Louisiana and found Cajuns who mixed languages exactly the way he did. I think he would have stayed there forever if he hadn't suffered an overdose of Tabasco.

Now he was supplementing his income with online advertising. He had plenty of followers on social media, because he'd actually sold a poem.

At the height of the pandemic, one of Jake's most malodorous odes, a four-line verse of bludgeoning obscenity, had gone viral:

> "Ma chérie, you may have corona,
> But you can still give me a boner.
> And I know I'll maintain mon érection,
> If you sneeze in the other direction."

Inexplicably, this nonsense had convinced a French catering company to use Jake to attract young Anglo tourists to Paris. The reasoning, I suppose, was that everyone thinks Paris is intrinsically sexy, so why not confirm their impressions with some rhyming comedy filth?

What these caterers didn't know, of course, was that Jake takes his drivel seriously. When he realized they thought he was being funny, his initial reaction was to throw an artistic hissy fit, but he wasn't one to look a gift *cheval* in the *bouche*, and the upshot was that he now had a bit of money and a pocketful of vouchers to binge for free in a selection of French eateries.

---

[1] In the novel *Merde Happens*.

I went to meet him for lunch in what he described as a "*bistro bobo*", meaning a trendy little restaurant staffed by, and catering for, youngish people who want to eat traditional French food while maintaining their rebel bohemian image. There are tons of these places in Paris, run by people with plenty of tattoos and generally excellent culinary taste.

"Hey mec!" Jake called out from a table on the covered terrace of a small café near the canal basin. It was one of the lucky establishments that had actually prospered during Covid. In the long, masked-up summer of 2020 it had been allowed to extend its terrace right out into the road, gobbling up several parking spaces with tables that were occupied non-stop whenever the French government allowed us to eat and drink in public. Since then, thanks to the city's anti-car policy, all the new tables had stayed put, so that Jake was now sitting where previously there would have been a Renault or Peugeot blocking the view of the canal. It was currently one of northern Paris's coolest lunch tables.

As usual, Jake looked as though he'd got dressed after waking up in a charity shop's reject department. His shapeless, washed-out shirt should have been labelled "for immediate recycling", and from what I could see of his jeans, one leg was several centimetres shorter than the other.

But somehow he still looked enviably good. His face was Kurt Cobain with extra vitamins, his blond hair effortlessly surfer-godlike. And as always, he was grinning. He asked little from life other than a supply of cigarette papers and the prospect of imminent sex, both of which he seemed to obtain with little or no effort.

I joined him at the traditional Parisian marble-topped table that this hip restaurant had chosen as its décor. I wasn't complaining about the lack of innovation in their furniture. It's one of the best things about French culture of all sorts – the French, young and old, know when to keep things French.

"Let's command some vin," Jake said. "Cécile!"

He waved his hand towards a dark-haired girl in jeans and

crop top, the informally dressed waitress. She gave Jake a bright smile and came over to our table, bending down to kiss him on the cheeks. This might have been the über-trendy *bistro*'s way of greeting all its customers, but I supposed that Jake knew her already.

He asked a question about white wines, and Cécile reeled off a list like the sommelier in Paris's poshest restaurant, finally recommending an organic Chardonnay.

"We take a bottle à la ficelle?" Jake asked me. A *ficelle*, I knew, was a small, thin loaf of bread, half the dimensions of a baguette. So I guessed he was suggesting some kind of traditional workers' lunch – a hunk of baguette washed down with alcohol.

"Just bread?" I asked him. "Wouldn't you prefer a proper meal?"

Jake and his friend Cécile shared a chuckle. I'd obviously got things wrong.

"OK, une bouteille de Chardonnay à la ficelle, s'il te plaît," Jake ordered. "Alors, what's up with toi?" he asked me.

I began to explain my potential *pétanque* gig, and to my surprise, Jake nodded furiously.

"This is formidable," he said.

I thought he'd find the whole thing ludicrous, but he turned out to be a big *boules* fan, which was weird because I'd never seen him take an interest in any sport more vigorous than puffing a joint.

"A fantastic coincidence," he said when I had finished telling my story. "You know, I have a poem about this."

Oh shit, I thought. He cleared his throat and I prepared for the worst. Putting on his recital face (a supposedly intellectual frown that made him look as though he'd forgotten where he left his keys), he began.

"Ah pétanque pétanque, how I love the click click ... Of Frenchmen playing with their boules in public ... They juggle their balls and with a little luck ..."

"Right yes, thanks, Jake."

He wasn't insulted by the interruption. He was used to my allergy where his poetry was concerned.

11

"But both of us are now in the business de pétanque! It's karma, mec," he said. "Coincidental karma!" He was nodding even more enthusiastically.

Cécile arrived with a bottle of Chardonnay and two glasses. Jake tasted the wine and nodded again.

"Super," he said, and poured each of us a glass.

Cécile propped a large blackboard against a nearby empty table – these trendy places don't do printed menus – and left us to it.

"Where's the ficelle?" I asked, making dunking motions.

Jake guffawed and explained that there wasn't going to be any bread. Ordering *à la ficelle* was an old-fashioned way of drinking wine. You were entrusted with the whole bottle, but only paid for what you drank. This quantity was measured *à la ficelle*. *Ficelle* meant string – which was why the thin loaf of bread got its name, he said. In the past, it had referred to a measuring string dipped into the wine. Now it just meant what the waiter or waitress estimated that you'd drunk. It was, Jake said, *à la tête du client*, or how the customer looked. And Jake had a friendly-looking head, so I guessed he got undercharged in his regular watering holes.

The wine was pungently fruity. I don't know anything about wine, but this one tickled the tonsils pleasantly, so I was happy.

"I also am working on the Olympiques," he told me, pronouncing the last word in French. O-lamp-EEK.

"Really?" I couldn't imagine the Paris 2024 people employing Jake for anything except raking the long-jump sandpit. And even then, the jumpers would be in danger of landing on one of his discarded cigarette ends.

"Yes, I am contributing to the creation of new games."

Again, I was baffled. Was dressing badly to become an exhibition sport?

Before he could explain, Cécile came back to take our food order.

Jake opted for the *entrecôte frites* (basically steak and chips, as old-school French as you can get) and I ordered a sea bream fillet with mashed *topinambours* – Jerusalem artichokes, a vegetable straight out of the Second World War. Like I said, these supposed trendies are closet traditionalists.

I congratulated Cécile on the wine, and she more or less told me the producer's life story – a young *viticulteur* in Burgundy with three dogs, twenty hectares and a fondness for Baudelaire, or something like that. She knew her stuff.

When she'd gone, without writing down our food orders of course (in Paris, notepads are for amateurs), I asked Jake, keeping my incredulity at a minimum, how the holy hell he was involved with the Olympics.

"Alors," he said, pouring himself a fresh length of *ficelle*, "you know that the Jeux Olympiques are discrimina …" he searched his mind for a suffix "…tist? …tant? What I mean is, the Olympiques are only for talented, fast, fit people."

"Yes," I agreed, "that's why they have the Paralympics."

"Exactement!" Jake was delighted by my reply. "These Paralympics, they're also discriminatic. Some of those sprinters can run really fast on their false legs. There are people in wheelchairs who are great at ping-pong. And blind people can run marathons, man. It's discriminatism!"

"I don't understand."

He was looking very pleased with himself. I'd obviously fallen into his rhetorical trap.

"Alors! What about all of us who have zero talent?" he said. "All of us who have no fitness and can't run a hundred metres without stopping for a cigarette? All of us who have no motivation or ambition, who can't be bothered to get up off the couch? We are the excluded. We have no games. We need our Olympiques. The Nolympiques."

He was serious. He showed me a website, and reading its credo, I saw that there was a whole Nolympic movement out there, made up of talentless slobs who were demanding equal rights with athletes. They were proposing (with no apparent irony) the creation of events like the 24-hour couch potato endurance test and the burger-eating marathon.

"I personally am militating for another sport also," Jake explained. "Cigarette rolling. OK, this may be defined as a talent, so maybe it shouldn't qualify for the Nolympiques, but it's not recognized by the real Olympiques, n'est-ce pas?"

"No, you're right Jake, even though they do accept gymnasts rolling about on mats."

"C'est une honte," Jake said, sounding eerily like my new friend Alang.

"So are you proposing to hold your Nolympics during the real Paris Olympics?" I asked.

Jake shrugged very Frenchly.

"Oh, I don't know. We're not pressed. It doesn't *have* to be in 2024. It's a lot of organization, you know. So much effort."

The food came, and it looked and smelled mouth-watering.

"Bonne dégustation, messieurs," Cécile wished us – happy food-tasting. Then she crossed over to the other side of the narrow street and stood in the doorway of an old apartment building to puff on a quick joint.

"I like her," Jake said, cutting into his bloody steak. "But I think she would be difficile."

"Difficult? How?"

"Oh, she has a strong caractère," he said as if that might be a fault. "I think she would want, you know, respect and maybe even a true, what do we say in English, relation?"

"Relationship. Yes, she does sound a bit too demanding for you, Jake."

He chewed meditatively for a while, and I enjoyed a scoop of Jerusalem artichoke mash, which tasted like slightly over-enthusiastic potato.

"Maybe I should write a poem explaining what I would like to do with her?" Jake said. "And what I do *not* want après. Like fidelity and shit."

"Yes, I think that would be the merciful thing to do," I said. It would scare her away once and for all.

Jake took a mouthful of wine, and spent a few seconds in deep thought. I was worried he might start rhyming, but instead he hit me with a question.

"And you, Paul, you have largued your vegan?"

To translate for those unfamiliar with Jake's patois, *larguer* is a French verb meaning dump. The "vegan" was my current girlfriend, a shop assistant whose diet just happened to be entirely plant-based.

I groaned at his question, and Jake rightly took it for a no.

"You have to larg her, man. Why torture yourself? She is not for you."

That was unfair. It was more a case of me not being for her.

Her name was Nolwenn.

When I'd first met her, a few weeks earlier, all I'd seen was the blonde hair piled Bardot-like on top of a mischievous face, and the long green apron that was the uniform of the health-food shop where she was working.

There are several chains of these organic supermarkets in France. They're very expensive, and the veg is occasionally on the muddy or sandy side, but they can have excellent cheese counters. And it was while I was salivating over a display of creamy goats' offerings one morning that I began wondering whether anyone would actually come and serve me.

I turned around and saw this tall, apron-clad girl gazing out the shop window into the street, maybe wondering when the next delivery of gluten-free muesli would arrive.

"Bonjour!" I called out. In France, there's no point saying anything along the lines of "Hey, why aren't you serving your customers instead of watching the traffic?"

She turned and smiled.

"Bonjour," she said.

Usually, people working in shops understand the subliminal message: the customer is saying "Bonjour!" but what he or she really means is "Hey, why aren't you serving ... etc".

Not in this case, though. She didn't move.

"Could you serve me some goat's cheese, please?" I asked in my best French.

"No," she said, "sorry," smiling again, not at all sorry.

"Oh." I decided it wasn't worth opting for an ironic comment like "Isn't your cheese for sale, then?" or maybe "Are

15

you on a meditation break?"

"I'm vegan," she explained. "I don't serve animal products. Would you like some vegetables? Or bread?"

Given that there was no likelihood of getting my hands on anything dairy in the immediate future, I went over to the bread counter, and she sold me a large, dark brick of rye bread that was the weight (and price) of half a dozen baguettes.

As she bagged it up, I told her I thought it was good of her employers to allow her not to serve non-vegan products.

She hit me with another of her warm smiles.

"Yes, but it annoys some customers, you know."

"Not me," I assured her. "I mean, I would like some goats' cheese, but I'd prefer it to be served by someone who had no moral objections to it."

She squinted at me.

"You're not French, are you?" she asked.

I guessed that my last sentence had been a mite too complicated for my French syntax.

"Anglais," I told her.

"Ah yes, there are lots of English vegans, and nobody is against *them*. England is more tolerant."

"Right," I said, conveniently ignoring the bloodrush of public outrage in the UK when a mainstream British bakery chain started selling vegan sausage rolls. "Everyone in England has vegan friends, and when I was a student I had a vegan girlfriend. Oh sorry," I added quickly, "that sounded like …" I didn't know the French for "a pathetic come-on".

"No problem," she said, smiling again. "I have nothing against going out with non-vegans."

That, I thought, sounded even more like a come-on.

"Well," I said, summoning up my carnivorous courage, "perhaps you would like to come with me for a drink this evening? Is wine vegan?"

"Yes," she said. "Unless it has been filtered through bone charcoal."

I started to laugh, but she was being serious.

"And yes, I will have a drink with you," she added. "If you

agree to buy olive tapenade instead of goat's cheese." She pointed at a nearby stack of glass jars containing an oil-black pâté.

Like a horny coward (the worst kind of coward), I gave in.

"You have to larg her," Jake now repeated, as he sliced into his oozing steak. "She's bad for your santé," meaning my health. "You're losing kilos. You're pale as a Norwegian's ass." He was probably comparing from memory.

This was nonsense. I'd been out with Nolwenn a few times, and so far we'd spent two nights together at her place. And as long as she wasn't actually present to disapprove of a specific meal, I was still merrily eating whatever I wanted. I felt fine.

"Come on, haven't you ever dated a vegan, Jake?" He has made a life's mission of dating, or at least sleeping with, women of every nationality, religion and ethnic origin, so I expected a bit more tolerance.

"How do I know, man? Anyway, no one tells me what to eat or not eat, what to do or not do."

This, I guessed, was true. Jake's moral code, if you could call it that, bore no traces of outside influence.

"And the problem is, this girl Nolwenn thinks only of food, n'est-ce pas?" he asked. "I parry that you ... Parry?"

"Bet." I assumed he was aiming for the French verb *parier*.

"Merci. I bet that next time you see her it will be to eat, n'est-ce pas?" I didn't answer. "I knew it!" He rewarded himself with yet another measure of Chardonnay.

I was due to see Nolwenn that very evening – at a vegan restaurant. Despite what she'd said about dating non-vegans, she only ever ate out at vegan restaurants because, as she put it, all the others were "colonized" by animal products. This was to be our first actual dinner together. Before that we'd only done drinks and lunch. Going out for a formal French evening meal felt like a big occasion. We were moving ahead.

"That is your erreur, Paul. You are going on to her moral territory. And I parry she does not know you are eating fish, huh?"

I looked guiltily down at what was left of my mutilated sea bream.

Jake laughed, but it was no joke. Although in reality I ate what I wanted, I had managed to convince her that I now embraced a full-time life of vegetables.

"I agree with her on lots of things," I said. "About not cutting down the Amazon rainforest to turn it into grazing for animals, and the cruelty of foie gras, and intensive pig farming that causes algae blooms in Brittany …"

"Oui, oui," Jake interrupted me. "But this French bœuf I'm eating was farmed by a little guy in Auvergne with ten hectares and a donkey called Françoise. You ask Cécile." Jake pointed a bloody fork across the street at her. "Hey, forget your vegan, man. You are free tomorrow in the soirée?" he asked. "You must come to our Nolympique meeting."

"You have meetings?"

"Well, most of us won't turn up, but yeah. And I'm le president of the Paris comité."

Suddenly Paris was overflowing with presidents.

3

After lunch, I went back to what I was currently calling home. In French it was cosily termed a *foyer*. This did not imply that I was living in an entrance lobby. *Foyer* is a word that has its roots in the family fireside, but which in French has now come to mean any building in which people are crammed to live cheaply. *Foyers* are what Paris calls its overcrowded refugee centres, outside which you often see groups of young men wondering whether they'll ever see a cosy family fireside again.

For the last couple of years, I'd been living in a much more luxurious *foyer*, a new building in the northeast of Paris designed for students. Which I was, by the way. I had become a fully card-carrying *étudiant*. In France, further education is practically free, so I had enrolled at a university just outside Paris, paying under 200 euros in tuition fees to become a degree student of English and Business (or to give the course its French name, "Anglais et Business"). I thereby qualified for generously subsidized student accommodation, even if I didn't attend a single lecture.

The French university system is based on the supposedly democratic principle of accepting everyone with a *baccalauréat* (high-school diploma) or its equivalent, and then hoping that most of them will drop out quickly so that classes won't be too crowded. Non-attendance by people like me actually helps the system.

My room was a self-contained studio with a tiny shower and loo, a cuisinette, a microwave oven and, being intended for French students, a double bed. Very sporting of the university authorities, I thought.

Everything in the building felt brand-new – the staircase

smelled faintly of paint, my toilet still had plumber's instructions taped to the U-bend, and the lift worked. The only thing that showed signs of wear was the cycle rack outside, which seemed to have been targeted since day one by thieves with spanners and bolt cutters. Half the rack was taken up by lone padlocked wheels and stripped frames.

The neighbourhood's petty criminals had also homed in the wall of letter boxes in the entrance hall. All the locks on the little red doors were broken. But this didn't bother me – these days, who receives anything in an envelope but junk mail?

The double-glazed window of my room looked out over a disused railway line. That may sound grungy, but Paris's old *petite ceinture* ("little belt"), a 19th-century line encircling the city, is gradually being converted into walkways and urban gardens, and the view from my window was of young trees and bushes poking out of freshly tilled soil. The train tracks were overgrown, and a gravel pathway was being laid.

Even now, the summery air was abuzz with the twittering of birds, including young sparrows, who are becoming an endangered species in Paris. Apparently, they like to nest in the cracks in building façades, and as the city gentrifies, these cracks are getting too rare for all the sparrows to find nesting space. Luckily, the gardens outside my window were still home to some of the little grey-and-brown flutterers. I occasionally sprinkled sunflower seeds along my window ledge and watched the more courageous fledglings come to peck up high-energy snacks. Organic, of course.

Strangely, the inside of my students' *foyer* was as tranquil as outside.

When I was at university in England, the halls of residence were like squats, and every night there would usually be four or five sound systems competing for musical supremacy. But the Parisian students in my building were much more docile (when they were not rioting in street protests, of course). As far as I could gather, most of them went home to *maman* and *papa* at weekends, or whenever they needed a decent meal. Personally, I didn't see the point of being a student if you weren't keeping away from your parents as much as possible, but now it meant that I was living in relative peace.

I decided to spend the afternoon in my room, mugging up on the campaign to get *pétanque* elected as an Olympic event. I opened my window, stretched out on my bed and began browsing through the bumph that Marjorie had given me.

First there was the history of the sport, if it could be called one. The name, according to FUCPET, was derived from a Provençal term meaning "with both feet firmly on the ground". In the physical sense, that is – after a few glasses of pastis, I suspect that most Provençal *pétanque* players are flying pretty high.

I learned that *pétanque* was invented by the Ancient Gauls, presumably when they were looking for something useful to do with the bronze they'd just invented. And the game was mentioned in the first-ever French encyclopaedia, published in the 18th century. This, according to FUCPET, proved that *pétanque* was an integral part of the French Enlightenment. I could just imagine Voltaire and his fellow luminaries discussing the true meaning of the cosmos whilst lobbing miniature planets around the Tuileries.

Alain Fillon and his friends admitted that *pétanque* didn't actually have fixed rules until 1910, when Jules Hugue, a man from La Ciotat, near Marseille, invented the modern version of the game, with the immobile feet. FUCPET's historians confessed that this Jules only started playing with his "*pieds tanqués*" because rheumatism prevented him taking a run-up. So in a way it was like inventing the low-jump or the slow-motion sprint. Not very sporty at all.

Nevertheless, in 2005, France's Ministry of Youth and Sport declared *pétanque* a "high-level sport", despite the fact that a whole *pétanque* tournament involves about the same physical exertion as two minutes of basketball.

And FUCPET were now demanding to know why a French high-level sport would *not* be included in the Paris Olympic Games. After all, they argued, there was the shot putt, which was just throwing a lead weight where the hell you wanted.

I could see FUCPET's point. Just as the French had taken the humble swimsuit and elevated it to the art of the bikini, so they had perfected the aimless shot putt by adding accuracy, thereby creating *pétanque*.

I began to think that maybe after all I was being hired to support a just cause.

Until then, I'd taken the cynic's view that *pétanque* was merely an excuse for men in the south of France to avoid having to cook dinner. But now I sensed that the cause went far deeper than sport. It was about recognizing France's genius for technical innovation.

So how come the Paris 2024 committee had rejected *pétanque*'s plea for recognition?

I scrolled to a summary of the fateful meeting, which had taken place just a few days earlier.

First there was Alain's opening speech, which gave the history of the sport, mentioning that the first official *pétanque* association had been founded in 1942, during Nazi Occupation. In his view, this made the game part of the Resistance – though I'd have said it made it part of collaboration. He said that there had been World *Pétanque* Championships since 1959, involving teams from more than 20 countries, many of which had never been French colonies. The championship, he said, was so open that a British team had once been allowed to win a bronze medal.

After the history lesson, Alain's speech got a little aggressive, and began bashing recent additions to the Olympic catalogue such as mountain biking, skateboarding and breakdancing. These were all blatantly American activities, he said, so why was Paris allowing them? And was breakdancing even a game?

Next we got down to the Paris committee's response, which was detailed, understanding and totally negative. They cited lack of time, lack of space, an official list of events already prepared, voting already closed, etc, etc.

But reading between the lines, it seemed to come down to one central problem: *pétanque* wasn't cool. Neither, one could argue, are the shot putt or some of the flouncier kinds of gymnastics, but instead of getting rid of those, it looked as if the Paris Olympic committee wanted to acquire a more modern image by tacking on trendy new events. They quoted the International Olympic Committee's desire to see "gender-balanced and youth-based sports". And I had to agree that when you close your eyes and think of *pétanque*, all you see is a crowd of old male boozers.

It seemed to me that FUCPET's only hope was to spearhead their campaign with a new form of beach *pétanque* featuring fit young players in swimwear. It had worked for volleyball.

And in a way, Marjorie seemed to agree with me, because from the bumph she sent me, I saw that her new battle plan was centred on proving that in fact *pétanque* was increasingly young and mixed-gender. She was a living example of this, as seen in some photos she'd included of herself and friends playing by the canal. She'd photoshopped out the cigarettes, joints and alcohol that usually accompanied these evening matches. Good idea, I thought, because the Olympics has suffered enough doping scandals already.

Marjorie had also added a page with a single-line question in bold capitals, which read "PARISIANISME?"

I wondered what this meant.

Before I had a chance to think further, I was interrupted by a knock on my door.

"Monsieur Pol!" a breathless voice said.

I recognized it as Madalena, the concierge, whose main job was the heroic ordeal of getting up at six every single morning including Sundays to roll out the heavy bins. It was a task made even more onerous because French students, despite their renowned gift for technical subjects, seemed to be incapable of understanding how bins worked.

There were explanatory notices taped to the wall of our courtyard, but the future geniuses occupying the students' residence had failed to learn that rubbish had to be placed *inside* the large, wheeled containers, not beside or on top of them.

Furthermore, even I, a foreigner, had grasped that the *jaune* (yellow) lidded bin was for recyclable materials like the ones helpfully depicted on the lid itself – packaging, paper, cardboard boxes, plastic bottles and the like. Half-eaten hamburgers did not therefore belong in this bin and would need to be picked out and disposed of properly by the eternally vigilant Madalena, otherwise the bin men would refuse to empty it.

She had written a note to this effect and pinned it up in the entrance hall, but its only effect was to provoke an outbreak of pedantry amongst the residents, who corrected all her spelling and grammar mistakes.

Madalena liked me because I'd immediately offered to help her type up a corrected version of her notice (using Google translate, of course). Sadly, it didn't have much effect on bin usage, so she now took revenge before dawn every day by slamming the building's front doors after she'd reclassified the mess she found in the bins, and then having loud conversations with the bin men above the noise of their truck.

Anyway, hence her breathless voice. That and constantly vaping what smelled like essence of burning tyre.

I opened the door to find Madalena waving a large envelope at me. As thanks for my solidarity, she always brought me anything that looked important from my mailbox with the broken lock.

"Vous avez une lettre," she informed me. She always addressed me with the formal *vous*, probably because she had noticed that I was a few years older than most of the other students.

"Merci, Madalena."

She grinned at me from below her unnaturally black helmet of hair. When she wasn't wearing her nylon overall, she usually looked as though she was just off to church. Neat blouse, carefully ironed skirt, glowing hair.

Now she was expectant, as if waiting for the first line of Mass. I guessed why.

"You think it's about my nationality?" I asked her, in French of course.

"You think?" she chanted back at me.

I ripped open the large brown envelope and read the first few lines of the letter inside.

"Not yet," I said.

"Not yet? It will come."

"Let us pray it does."

"Yes, let us pray."

She smiled and went vaping off along the corridor.

Perhaps I should explain. The nationality we were referring to was French, and I was in the process of applying for it.

I lack Frenchness in so many ways – I have always been allergic to a national anthem that talks about "impure blood"; there are lots of French pop songs whose words and/or music cause me physical pain; and I've always thought that the vast majority of the accents in written French are a waste of time. For example, what is the point of the added squiggles in *fenêtre*, *pâtisserie* or even *pétanque*? No one would go without croissants if the only shop they could see was called a *patisserie*, without the accent.

But despite all this, I'd decided to become French. Or try to, anyway.

Predictably, it was Brexit that made my mind up.

After years of being able to live and work in France without admin hassle of any kind, I was suddenly required to pay 200 euros to apply for a residence permit whose only function was to ensure that I wouldn't be deported from what had long become my hometown. It was beyond absurd. It was like salmon suddenly being told they needed a permit to swim.

And applying for residence meant forms, queues, waiting, stress. Just so I could continue living where I was already allowed to live.

Ever since the Brexit referendum, the British Embassy in Paris had been continually tweeting about its service to advise expats who wanted to stay on in France, offering us a potential stay of execution.

The problem for me was that the Embassy website talked

about financial thresholds for EU citizens wanting to live in the UK, which might logically inspire France to impose the same conditions. And right now, my own financial threshold was a battered doormat.

Times were tough and I didn't have a regular salary, so I was more or less on the same level as some poor potato picker from Moldova who has been invited to help out on a farm in Suffolk, but who gets turned back at Dover because he doesn't have a degree in agronomy or a bank account in the Caymans.

In short, I'd quickly realized that if France felt like it, instead of giving me a residence permit, it could grant me a farewell kick up the backside.

Then, rooting about online, I discovered that because I'd been in Paris for five years already, I could apply for a different card that would ensure I could live in France for ever if I felt so inclined, as well as being free to travel and work in Berlin, Prague, Dublin, or anywhere else in the whole of the EU that offered decent beer as part of the lifestyle. It wouldn't matter if I was poor, because I'd be a poor Frenchman, a poor member of the single market. And to cap it all, this permanent French ID card would cost only 90 euros instead of 200 for the residence permit.

So requesting French nationality rather than residence was a no-brainer. The only problem was that both temporary and permanent options entailed bashing my head against the Bastille that is French bureaucracy.

This letter I'd just received was a new salvo from the people behind the ramparts. I'd followed all the instructions online, or so I thought, but was now being told that my application could not be considered because a new online form had been published, whereas I'd used the old one.

I didn't even take time out to groan or swear. It's like one of those medieval battles between soldiers wielding iron cudgels. You don't stop to say "ouch" if someone bashes you on the helmet. You hit back.

So if France wanted a new application form, it would get one. Two could play at the helmet-bashing game of bureaucracy.

But I didn't have the time or energy to organize my riposte just yet.

First, for the next hour or so, I had to go through the ritual cleansing to prepare for my meeting with Nolwenn. I suspected that this time, after two nights at her place, she might want to come back to mine.

Did my cupboard contain any biscuits or snacks with animal products in the ingredients list? If so, they had to be relocated to the green-lidded bin, and their empty packets to the yellow.

Because if Nolwenn opted to come back to my room after dinner and caught so much as a whiff of my lie about being a vegan, it would be proof that I was a double agent in the war against animal exploitation, and therefore unworthy of sex.

And like any healthy human, the last thing I want in life is to be deemed unworthy of sex.

4

Out in the Parisian evening, I decided to walk to the restaurant, to stretch both my legs and my mind.

Paris's long series of lockdowns had taken their toll on me, like they had on everyone. For months on end during the pandemic, I'd been "confined" as the French put it, alone in my student room, allowed no visitors and restricted to exploring only the square kilometre around my address. I'd come to know the neighbourhood, and myself, pretty well.

Fortunately, I could do my interpretation work on screen, even if it did mean staring up my clients' noses for hours on end.

I'd also got into cooking, using lots of herbs and spices to take comfort food to unheard-of heights of complexity. My poached egg on toast "*à la* Covid" became a legend in my own household (which was where it stayed, of course). At the peak of its sophistication, it consisted of a slice of toast coated in butter that had been liberally laced with crushed fresh garlic (who was I going to breathe on?), on top of which stood a poached egg that had been delicately encrusted in a mixture of turmeric, fine-ground green pepper, chipotle flakes and curry powder. It took two cans of Parisian-brewed IPA to cool my tongue down afterwards, but then alcohol is sometimes what puts the "comfort" in comfort food.

Talking of a different kind of "comfort", I made the mistake of being single when Parisian lockdown set in, so my immediate future looked as sexless as that of a monk on a mountaintop.

Luckily, one of the well-known dating apps proved its worth. Less than a kilometre away from my student residence, I found a woman who practised socially distanced sex. And not just online. We could meet physically, she said, and she would do everything to guarantee that we would both stay Covid-free. I envisaged some kind of strategically holed diving suit.

Her profile claimed she was "under 40", and her photo definitely was. She was called, she said, "Fleur" and preferred never to chat via Zoom or Skype. I guessed she was either much older than her photo, or married, or maybe even a Russian bot, but after a few weeks of lockdown I really didn't care.

To evade the rule against visiting other households, she proposed that we meet in her car, which was parked in the basement of her apartment building.

I raised the predictable objections: How do you stay a metre apart in a car? What if other residents should come into the garage while we're at it? And who in their right mind agrees to meet in a stranger's basement?

But she had it all worked out. We'd stay masked, she replied, and meet at 3am when no one would come down into the garage. And in case I was scared of kidnap or worse, I could tell all my friends her address. Just come and check it out one night, she said, and if I felt unsafe, we'd forget the whole thing.

The main problem I foresaw was what the French authorities called the *attestation*. This was the form you had to sign, on paper or online, stating your reason for going out during lockdown. You had to take it with you every time you left the house in case you were stopped by a policeman. So, according to the instructions, I needed to decide whether visiting Fleur was to "attend a place of education or training" (I was sure she could teach me a thing or two), "assist vulnerable persons" (meaning myself – who is more vulnerable than someone who hasn't got laid in ages?), a "medical examination or consultation" (you could call it sex therapy, surely?), to make "essential purchases" (if I stopped off for condoms, maybe), or a "brief outing linked to physical exercise". I plumped for the last option, even though it specified "individual exercise". But then again, I told myself, the French are a nation of existentialists who believe each individual person is alone in the infinite universe. I just hoped the gendarmes would be in a philosophical mood.

One dark, silent night I stepped out into the deserted streets, and ten minutes later, on the damp second level of Fleur's underground garage, in the middle of a row of empty vehicles, I found a large, dark-grey, seven-seater Renault. Inside was a silhouette with bushy hair.

"Ici, Pol," she whispered. I'd used my real name on the app.

A door opened, the car's interior light went on and I saw that all the rear seats of the Renault were folded down. Squatting yoga-style on a plaid blanket was an olive-skinned woman wearing a blue surgical mask, above which her eyes seemed to be smiling at me.

"Merci d'être venu, Pol," she said. Thanks for coming.

"Merci pour l'invitation, Fleur," I replied.

She explained, very matter-of-fact, that she would be facing away from me, breathing in untainted air from an open window. I was to kneel behind her and stick my head out of the open sunroof.

"D'accord?" she asked. Did I agree?

I said a rapid "oui."

For the next few minutes (it had been a long time), my head stared at the dust on the roof of a nearby Peugeot 308 while my body enjoyed much more pleasurable experiences.

I then backed out of the car, and Fleur returned to her yoga position. Her eyes were still smiling.

"Same time next week?" she asked.

"Oui."

"Merci d'être venu, Pol."

"Merci pour l'invitation, Fleur."

And that was it. As soon as the first lockdown ended, "Fleur" disappeared. But she was one of the many reasons why you can never let anyone try to tell you the French aren't efficient when they want to be.

As well as my nocturnal strolls, I did a lot of daytime walking during that first, highly localized, lockdown. And I made some cool discoveries.

On a stretch of canal bank behind the gardeners' sheds in the nearby Villette park, I found a row of massive fig trees. All through the spring and early summer I watched the fruits growing and darkening on the curved branches, hidden amongst bright leaves that gave off a rich, oily scent every time they caught the sun. At last, one of the figs looked fat and soft enough to eat, so I pulled it off the tree. Peeling back its thick green skin, bruised with purple, and sucking up the sticky white seeds gifted me a few sweet moments of victory over the virus.

And then there was all the street art, which covered every spare expanse of wall in my neighbourhood. I sent photos of the paintings to friends back in England, who unfailingly raved along the lines of "OMG you live right near a [insert name of artist I'd never heard of but who was apparently mega-famous] mural!?"

Now, on my way to meet Nolwenn for dinner, I passed a canal bridge decorated with what looked like a multi-coloured Aztec mask with jade eyes and jet-black lips, then a shuttered shopfront from which a leopard-skinned Nefertiti was emerging after buying an armful of nuclear missiles (I think some street artists seek inspiration in mind-altering substances).

Along the canal basin, a session of live painting was going on. An empty brick building, once a lock-keeper's hut, was encased in low scaffolding. A woman was standing six feet off the ground, putting the finishing touches to a giant penguin that was playing an electric guitar (see the above note about substances).

A few yards further on, on the side of a two-storeyed stone building that had been converted into a café, three kids in hoodies were spraying semi-abstract swirls around a giant figure "19", the number of the *arrondissement*, urged on by a sound system that was making the ground vibrate as I walked by.

Not that anyone was going to complain about the noise, because all this artistic activity was openly sanctioned by the powers that be. Hanging from lampposts all along the canal were banners bearing the logo of the city of Paris (a ship pretending that it's not afraid of sinking) and a graffiti-style slogan: *Place à la Muralité*. This was a verbal pun, like most of French culture – it meant "make room for murality", presumably an adaptation of some famous proverb about morals.

So Paris was subsidizing all this. It was street art turned establishment. A bit disappointing, I thought. Street art was meant to be subversive, anarchic. But then it was very French to take something rebellious and make it an institution. Like nuclear power. All that raw explosive energy and they turn it into their biggest national business.

Just beyond this evening art show, I came to a wide expanse of canal bank where several *pétanque* games were in full swing. I stopped to watch.

During the day, these areas of gravel were often occupied by groups of older guys, plus a few women, playing intensely competitive *pétanque* – silently measuring exact distances to see who'd won, demanding second opinions, and then victoriously or resignedly retrieving their *boules* from the gravel with magnets on strings. It was serious stuff.

By evening, though, younger players had taken over and the alcohol had kicked in. Men and women were laughing and chatting as they played, a *boule* in one hand, a drink in the other. On nearby benches stood skittle-like rows of beer and wine bottles, the evening's refreshment. Dogs and a few kids had been brought along, and they were occasionally allowed to disrupt play by chasing after *boules*.

But despite the generally relaxed atmosphere, there were still groups of these hipsters who were obviously playing to win, advising their teammates on whether to go for stealth or strength, groaning or high-fiving according to where the shot landed. Some of them might well have been potential Olympic champions in the making. Though not all of them would have passed the dope test.

Anyway, it gave me plenty to think about as I left the canal basin and strode on towards my date at the restaurant. This mass *pétanque*-ing couldn't just be a Parisian phenomenon, I thought. There had to be similar scenes going on all over France.

I decided that Marjorie and Alain ought to get out here and interview both sets of players, daytime and evening, young and old. Film some vox pops to support their case.

I took out my phone and noted the exact time. I was going to bill them for this personal brainstorming session.

5

I arrived at the restaurant a few minutes early.

It was called Végé-Table, a typically French name, even if their word for vegetable is *légume*. It was typically French because their favourite puns are the ones that include English words. This was why they'd enjoyed what I had originally thought was a stupid name for my own tearoom in Paris – My Tea Is Rich. My French colleagues who came up with the English name assured me that it was hilarious because it punned on a phrase from their old English school manuals – "my tailor is rich". It was a bit like calling a French bakery in London Où Est la Baguette de Ma Tante?

Everywhere you go in France, you bump into painful examples of this French fetish for joking around with English. This is especially true of shopfronts. I've seen a hairdresser's called Plein Hair (a pun on *plein air* – open air), a record store called Just Do Hit, and worst of all, a shopping mall near my student residence was called Vill'up, a joke so twisted that I'm sure no one gets it. The neighbourhood is called La Villette, and when you go shopping, you "fill up". Get it? I didn't for months. But no doubt the French creative team thought it was genius.

Végé-Table was set in a refurbished industrial building in the 10th *arrondissement*, on the northern edge of the old garment district. The restaurant had presumably replaced the workshops of sewing machinists whose jobs had emigrated to Asia.

A massive plate-glass façade had been opened up, allowing passers-by to gaze into a forest of tall exotic plants. Not all of them were for use in the kitchen, I hoped. Some of those leaves looked chewy and toxic.

I went in and was greeted at a bamboo lectern by a tall woman in a floaty dress. One of her arms was tattooed all over with dark swirls, while the other was totally virgin flesh. It looked a bit spooky, as though her body was slowly being afflicted with a decorative form of gangrene.

"Bonsoir. Vous avez réservé?" she asked, although the restaurant was half-empty.

"Bonsoir. Oui, au nom de West," I answered.

She looked down the list and shook her head at me. Maybe I was exuding whiffs of sea bream.

"C'est votre nom de famille?" she asked. Was that my family name?

"Oui."

"Et votre prénom?" What was my first name? This place was too cool for family names.

"Paul," I said, then "Pol" just in case.

She checked the list again, and it reminded me of when I used to try and blag my way into VIP guest nights in London. Back then, though, the aim was to drink free champagne. Tonight, all I was asking for was the chance to pay for a vegetable or two.

"Ah oui," she finally said. "Pol. Deux personnes."

She eyed me suspiciously, correctly surmising that I didn't have the second diner concealed in my back pocket.

"Elle arrive," I said. She was on her way.

The tall woman took a few seconds to decide whether she believed me, then told me to wait until someone escorted me to my table. Maybe they had a history of diners getting lost amongst the indoor shrubs.

I was left standing alone beside a young banana plant.

Finally a guy arrived, dressed the same colour as most of the foliage. Luckily he didn't have green hair, so above the shoulders he stood out against the leaves.

He asked me politely to follow him, and we successfully made our way through the jungle to a table by the wall. This table and the chair either side of it looked to have been hewn from solid teak – sustainable, I hoped. Ah yes, I noticed as I sat down, on the tabletop there was a note explaining the furniture's impeccable provenance and offering me the chance to buy similar models at prices that seemed to include the cost of new accommodation for a whole subspecies of displaced orang-utan.

I ordered "une IPA" (the French are really into American-style ale) and checked my phone to see whether Nolwenn had left any messages about running late.

She had written to me, saying "J'arrive", the message French people send when they're going to be anything between two minutes and two hours late.

The male waiter arrived with my beer, into which someone had accidentally spilled a fruit of some kind. At least, that's what I had to assume. No one deliberately adds fruit to beer, do they?

There was a QR code on the table and I pointed my phone at it. The menu popped up, revealing the reason for the ambient snobbery. Ignoring the actual dishes, my eye was instantly drawn to the numbers in the right-hand column. Just one starter would have bought two main courses and half of Jake's *ficelle* bottle at lunchtime. And I'd always thought veg was cheap.

I was still staring open-mouthed at the menu when Nolwenn arrived.

"You found something that makes your mouth water?" she asked me.

"My eyes, you mean," I wanted to answer, but I just stood up, wished her "bonsoir" and kissed her. My philosophy is, once you're sitting in the restaurant, it's too late. If it's going to cost a fortune, just make sure you eat and drink something tasty. You've got to be like Edith Piaf: "Je ne regrette rien". But then, other people probably used to pay for Edith's meals.

Nolwenn was looking very edible. Her hair was piled high to reveal her mischievous face, the blond strands picking out the gold nuggets that flecked her hazel eyes. She smelled lemony, like a young white wine.

I asked how her day had gone and she shrugged. The only highlight, she told me, was when she had a brief argument with her boss, who was still refusing to remove the real sausages and cooked meats from the cold cabinets. In France, organic shops feel no obligation to stop serving dead animals, and this annoyed

Nolwenn. Three of her colleagues were supporting her campaign, she said. It sounded as if her boss was about to experience another French Revolution.

We ordered wine – we didn't get the maker's life story this time – and began to peruse the menu together. Apart from the prices, some of it looked very appetizing. There was an aubergine curry, a Malaysian-style fried rice and a seasonal veg *pot au feu*, dishes that really don't need anything animal.

I was a bit worried, though, to read that their bread was made with "dehydrated linen". Was it healthy, I wondered, to eat an ingredient more often used to make baggy trousers?

I said I would go for a samosa followed by the curry. But Nolwenn disapproved.

"Il faut manger cru," she said. You need to eat raw.

"Humans have been cooking since we discovered fire," I said. "Don't you think we've evolved enough to be able to eat cooked food?"

"We have also evolved enough to poison our planet," she riposted, smiling but deadly serious.

I promised to compromise by ordering mashed mushrooms as a starter. Like I said, I'm a horny coward.

"All cooking is processing," she went on. "It is essentially industrial."

So is mashing mushrooms, I wanted to answer, but didn't dare.

It struck me that Jake was right – almost all my conversations with Nolwenn were about food, and mostly about things she refused to eat. Sometimes it was exhausting. I mean, who wants to talk non-stop about music they hate? Or all the sexual things they *don't* want to do?

As she rattled on about how heating carrots turns them into radioactive time bombs, I mused on my core mistake.

The Parisian girls I'd previously been out with were all typical French eaters who would snaffle down an obese goose's undercooked liver without drawing breath. They were extreme omnivores. Nolwenn was extreme in the other direction. And the problem wasn't that she was vegan. She was a *French* vegan.

A Fregan, as they ought to be labelled.

When I first met her, I assumed that a French vegan would be like a British one.

I'd once had a vegan girlfriend in London, and with her it was simple: she was anti-meat because it truly disgusted her, and anti-dairy on principle, but she wouldn't have chucked me out of bed for confessing to a cheese and pickle sandwich. She was also keen to prove to herself and the rest of the world that you can make tasty custard with oat milk. She lived her veganism joyfully, sensually, and made me want to join in.

Now I was increasingly realizing to my cost that Nolwenn wasn't the same. Like everything in France, her veganism seemed to be more rational and technical. Nolwenn could prove mathematically that eating Camembert would ultimately flood Normandy.

In short, to my London ex-girlfriend, veganism was all about the positive side of not needing animal proteins. To Nolwenn, food was a series of minus signs.

I should have been forewarned.

Until very recently, if you said "I'm vegan" in France, most people thought you were claiming to come from outer space. They had a French word, *végétalien*, but that just made it sound as if the person was actually made of vegetables, and very few French people had heard the word anyway. Meanwhile, saying "je suis végétarien" or "I don't eat meat" would elicit questions like "what about chicken and ham?".

This had to be why now, people like Nolwenn were making the most of their new recognition, revelling in their radicalism.

Before I met Nolwenn, I went to a newly-opened vegan café in Paris, and it was full of wannabe supermodels sipping herbal tea between colonic irrigations. A place of joy and plenty it was not.

The French have a word that has no real translation in English – *gourmandise*. Some people say it means greed or gluttony, but it doesn't. It expresses the pleasure of eating. If a French person says "*tu es gourmand*" it is likely to be a compliment

– they're acknowledging that you know what you like, and they're pleased that you want more. The Nolwenn school of eating seemed to be *anti-gourmand* – you know what you don't want, and you don't want anyone else to have any more of it.

Our starters came. My mashed mushrooms looked like something my mum's cat would leave on the carpet, but they turned out to be very truffly, and extremely tasty when spread on to a thin slice of the baggy-trouser bread.

Nolwenn, I noticed, wasn't so happy. She'd ordered fake sushi. Every so-called Japanese restaurant serves vegan rolls stuffed with cucumber, avocado or radish, but this was real fake sushi, a blob of rice topped with a slice of imitation flesh. I didn't want to ask what it was made of.

"Not good?" I asked.

She shook her head. "It's not a good idea to try to replace meaty or fishy textures. Why be an imitation meat-eater?"

I sympathized but couldn't stop myself asking her why she hadn't ordered something she actually wanted to eat.

"Fais-toi plaisir," I said. Pleasure yourself. In a general way, that is.

She grunted assent, but bit into another piece of fake sushi and grimaced. Weirdly, the fact that she didn't enjoy it seemed to make her almost glad.

"Are you liking *not* liking that?" I asked, stretching my French to its limit. "It's almost as if you're against pleasure," I went on. Now I was the one grimacing. Was there a stupider thing to say to a girl on a date?

She goggled at me in surprise and then laughed.

"Oh no," she said, "I'm not against pleasure." And the mischievous look came back to her face. I felt reprieved. Luckily for me, she seemed to keep her appetites for food and *amour* strictly separate.

6

Overall, the rest of the meal went well despite Nolwenn's tendency to predict the destruction of all known life on Earth if humans carried on eating yoghurt. She even suggested we move on to somewhere "more private".

I quickly got the bill, slimmed down my bank account by several kilos, and we were off.

During the taxi ride to my place, we made the most of the back seat by letting our hands do the walking. At last, the evening had stopped being political and become promisingly physical.

We were kissing as we slinked past my building's bicycle park, where not a single saddle remained, and if the residence had had fifty floors instead of five, we might well have made love in the lift before reaching the roof level.

Inside my room, which smelled of a breezy forest thanks to Nolwenn's shop's cleaning fluid, probably made from vegan pine trees, we performed a mouth-to-mouth tango as far as my bed, and fell headlong, tugging at each other's clothing.

"Un instant," Nolwenn whispered. She pointed over her shoulder with a questioning finger. I guessed she meant what the French often call "*le pipi-room*".

"The door on the right," I told her.

She kissed me and jumped up, apparently keen to return to the bed as soon as possible.

Then she let out a short, sharp scream.

Fearing that one of the bicycle rack vandals had broken into my shower room to steal the loo paper, I leapt to her rescue. I found her standing outside the bathroom, gazing downwards.

There was an alcove in the tiny corridor that led to my front door, and on the floor of this stood my small but costly collection of shoes.

I usually walk around in comfortable sneakers, but I also possess four pairs of top-quality footwear that I bought when I had more money. Two pairs of black, two of brown. They are the English-made type of shoe that will last for ever if you resole them regularly and keep them well polished. And polished they definitely were, because what else was there to do during lockdown other than polish your shoes? And no, that's not a euphemism.

So there at our feet stood eight shoes, propped up with their heels on the floor, toes against the wall, looking like a row of miniature condemned men waiting for Nolwenn to give the firing squad its fatal order.

She pointed at them.

"Berk!" she said, a French word for "yuk".

"What's the problem?" I asked. I wondered if there was dog poo encrusted somewhere, even though the shoes hadn't been out walking for weeks.

"Queer!" she squeaked, which surprised me. But it quickly struck me that she was speaking French, saying either "*cuire*", the verb to cook, or "*cuir*", meaning leather. I guessed it was the latter, even though together they seemed to sum up two of her hatreds at once: cooked food and animal by-products.

I stared down at the offending shoes. I had to admit that they looked very leathery.

"But you're wearing leather too," I argued. Her sandals were definitely not plastic.

"They're made by a company in the Cévennes which uses skins from animals that died of natural causes," she said.

I didn't dare ask if the cows or sheep had actually signed a will saying they agreed to be skinned and worn on people's feet rather than getting a more dignified burial.

"At the restaurant I was wearing baskets that are leather," I said. "*Basket*" is the French word for sneaker – apparently the first French sports-shoe importer didn't speak English.

"I did not notice," she said. "But now I see that you are a true fan of leather!"

She pointed yet again at my neat row of shoes, which, it was true, did look a bit like a collector's or fetishist's exhibition.

"I've had them for years," I said. "You don't want me to throw them away?"

She did a shrug with raised eyebrows and jutting chin, a very French gesture which means something along the lines of, "Well, now you mention it, your ironic, impractical suggestion is actually a good idea." French gestures are so eloquent.

"I inherited them from my grandfather," I said. As someone once told me, if you're going to lie, *lie*.

"Là, tu me prends vraiment pour une conne," she snapped. This is one of the ultimate French female putdowns which, if spoken in a meeting where I was interpreting, I would translate as "You must think I'm a real brainless twat."

If there had been any remaining sexual tension in the room – though I prefer to think of it as sexual relaxation – it had evaporated.

My biscuit and snack clear-out had been a waste of time. Nolwenn shook her head at me, opened the front door and stormed out.

Hoping that there was still a chance of salvaging the evening if I came over all French and crushed her in a passionate, wordless kiss, I went after her. She was moving fast, though, and strode straight past the lift.

She was soon stomping down the stairs, a dangerous place to try and grab a kiss, so I tried a verbal approach.

"You're the first real vegan I've ever known," I lied. "It's a shock." She ignored me and carried on stomping. I kept pace with her, a few steps behind. "A *good* shock," I added. "You make me think about my life."

At that precise moment, what I was thinking about my life was, why the hell am I running downstairs instead of kissing upstairs?

Nolwenn continued to ignore me, and opened the door to the ground floor.

The entrance hall, I thought, would be my best chance of attempting a bit of wordless passion.

But as I emerged from the stairwell, I saw that we weren't going to be alone. A woman was trying to enter the building, carrying something big, flat and heavy, and struggling to get in.

Nolwenn accelerated to help her, pulling the door open before shooting me a murderous glance and heading for the street.

"Merci," the load-bearing woman said to Nolwenn. To me she said, "Oh, bonsoir," smiling as if she knew me. She did look familiar.

I returned her "bonsoir" and then combined holding the door open while calling after the retreating Nolwenn, who was almost out on the pavement.

"Wait!" I pleaded. I tried to think of a good reason why she should do so. "Didn't you want to do a pipi?"

Nolwenn half-turned to yell over her shoulder at me.

"Tu me fais chier!" This is a French insult meaning that you bore or annoy someone, but literally it means "you make me shit", so I thought I'd better explain all this toilet vocabulary to the woman for whom I was now holding the door open.

"We had a political disagreement," I said.

"T'es qu'un con de menteur éco-fasciste!" Nolwenn shouted back at me. Literally translated, she was accusing me of being a "lying, eco-fascist male twat".

"You disagree with her?" the woman at the door asked. She addressed me with the friendly, both-the-same-age, of equal status, "tu".

At first I wasn't intending to answer, but it was beginning to dawn on me that Nolwenn probably wasn't going to stop and allow herself to be kissed, or even ask to pay a farewell visit to my loo.

"Well, I'm not a fascist," I replied.

"You are male, though," the woman said, smiling. She moved towards the stairs and looked at me enquiringly. She wasn't going to be able to open that door either, so I resigned myself to a fate worse than Nolwenn, and went to help.

And it was as I was wondering about the rectangular package the woman was carrying that I recognized her. She was one of the solar-panel duo from my start-up incubator. I'd only ever seen her in presentation-giving mode, in a business suit, with her black hair tied back. Now she was in jeans, her long locks hanging down into her eyes. Her skin was dark brown, and she was wearing lipstick that was the colour of coal.

"Are you a student as well as an inventor?" I asked.

"I'm doing a doctorate in electronics," she said.

I nodded. There's nothing witty you can say to that at eleven at night in an entrance hall where the lights are functioning normally.

"And if you're not an eco-fascist," she went on, "maybe you would open this door so that I can carry my revolutionary new solar panel upstairs?"

"Sorry." I grabbed the door handle. "And no, I'm definitely not an eco-fascist. I'll even carry it for you if you want."

"So you are a bit sexist," she said.

"I'm only trying to help."

"Would you offer to carry a *man's* solar panel upstairs?" she asked, but I could sense that she was teasing.

"Maybe not," I admitted.

"Ah!" She had won her argument.

"Because he would probably be lazier than you and take the lift," I said. "Why don't you?"

"It makes too much noise. I don't like to disturb people at night."

"Wow," I said. "That is so kind."

"You think all French people are egomaniacs?"

"Not all of you," I conceded. "But that is the first time I've ever heard anyone say they would prefer to carry something upstairs instead of …" My French ran out on me, but she seemed to get the message.

"Well now this panel is getting heavy, and since it's your fault that you stopped me to talk in the entrance hall, maybe you could help me, after all?"

I held out my arms and she filled them with solar panel. It

weighed half a ton, even though most of its bulk seemed to be made up of bubble wrap. I did my best to resist the temptation to start popping bubbles as we walked upstairs.

She went first, and turned round to look at me. I thought maybe she was afraid I'd drop her precious panel. But she had something else on her mind.

"I'm not inviting you into my room," she said.

"No, no. Don't worry," I told her, "I'm not a Frenchman. I don't assume that every woman who talks to me wants to sleep with me."

"That's probably wise," she said, smiling again. It was a pleasantly mocking smile, flashing between her dark lips.

"It saves a lot of time," I agreed.

"And energy. All those stairs. Perhaps you should decide to speak to women only if you're in a lift."

"But then I wouldn't have got talking to you," I said.

She laughed.

"How long have you been in France, Englishman? You *talk* just like a Frenchman."

"I'll take that as an insult," I said.

She laughed again, and I thought that this was the most fun I'd had bantering with a French person for a long time.

We arrived on the fourth-floor landing.

"Voilà. Merci." She stopped outside a door and started unlocking it. Number 42.

"The meaning of life," I said.

She frowned at my *Hitchhiker's* reference. Not a sci-fi fan, perhaps. She was into *real* science.

"It's very late," she said, "let's save the meaning of life for another time. Merci."

She held out her arms and I gave her the solar panel.

"De rien," I replied, meaning it was nothing.

"In French, if someone says 'merci' you should not reply that it's nothing," she said.

"What should I say, then?"

"Je t'en prie," she said.

I'd heard this before but enjoyed the inherent sexiness of

getting a late-night French lesson.

"Je t'en prie," I repeated, earning another of her gently teasing smiles.

"Bonsoir," she said.

"Bonsoir," I replied and headed back downstairs, relieved for the first time in my life that I wasn't at that moment naked in bed with a vegan.

7

I filled out the new nationality form – which looked to be exactly the same as the old one except that it was called *nouveau* – before making sure that all the photocopies of my essential documents were still in the file that the bureaucrats had sent back to me.

Photos of passport pages, check.

Electricity bill as proof of address, check, though in France it's easy to get a utility bill – you just phone the provider and say you want to pay the bill for a specific address.

Income tax returns, check. They showed very meagre earnings, but apparently when applying for citizenship it was the thought that counted rather than the amount.

Proof that I'd been living in France for five years, check – a copy of my original work contract with Vian'Diffusion, a meat company. It was lucky Nolwenn had never seen that, even if I'd only been opening a tearoom after the boss decided to branch out from selling dead cows.

I'd also had to get my birth certificate translated into French by an officially recognized legal translator. This had cost me fifty euros, even though the only words really needing translation were my parents' professions.

Also in the file were a handwritten letter from a French person willing to attest that I wasn't a total bastard (my long-term ex-girlfriend Alexa had grudgingly consented); a *lettre de motivation* that the same ex-girlfriend assured me would have to be a bit longer than "Brexit, what else?"; and the bill from a restaurant proving that I'd once eaten snails. Well, that last one might be an exaggeration. After a while I stopped questioning anything, I just obtained the documents.

My only worry about the application to become French was the question on the form about having a criminal record. I'd ticked the "NON" box – or rather crossed it, because the French don't know about ticks, maybe because their over-strict schoolteachers never want to admit that their students might have got a question right.

However, in truth I had once had an official run-in with the French legal system, getting fined when I first opened my tearoom because my menu had been written in English only, a contravention of French language laws.

So now I just had to hope that failing to translate "cup of tea" into French was not regarded by the nationality department as an offence on the same level as say, robbing a bank.

Once I'd checked that everything was in the envelope, I decided that it was probably safer and quicker to deliver it myself rather than post it. French postal workers are often on strike, and French strikes often lead to riots, so you can never be sure that a truly vital letter won't end up getting set on fire and thrown at a policeman.

I looked up the relevant government office and found an address on the Île de la Cité, just behind Notre-Dame. There, according to the French government's website, was the office dealing with Paris-based applicants for both citizenship and residency.

Half an hour later I was outside a medieval building decorated with a plaque confirming that it was the Bureau de Naturalisation. The place looked so old and run down that I wondered whether this same address hadn't welcomed famous applicants for French residency in the past: Leonardo da Vinci, Oscar Wilde, Picasso, Hitler. (OK, true, Hitler didn't actually ask whether his soldiers could stay.)

Inside the shabby entrance hall were two bored security men, who didn't seem at all bothered when I set off the metal detector. They shrugged and told me "second floor" as soon as I showed them my envelope.

I climbed the stairs, thinking how prominent in my life stairwells had become in recent hours, and pushed open a battered door that led to a waiting room with half its seats occupied by a variety of people like myself. They were clearly from widely different parts of the world, but they all shared the same nervous look of someone wondering whether it's a good idea to become French.

Straight ahead of me was a cubicle protected by a Perspex screen. This was the *Accueil*, or reception desk. I began to walk towards it, but the woman sitting in there saw me coming and pointed at a notice taped to the wall on my left: *Prenez un ticket*.

I now saw that there was a ticket machine like the ones you sometimes get at French supermarket fish counters, and an electronic board displaying the number of the person being summoned to the receptionist's screen. The screen was showing 402. My ticket was number 421.

Oh *merde*, I thought, I should have brought along a couple of volumes of Proust.

I found a spare seat amongst the other applicants and settled down to wait. As the numbers clicked slowly by, a few people went up to the desk and were sent through to another room at the rear. I just hoped it didn't lead to an ejector chute.

I had plenty of time to read the notices decorating the walls. There was one about the need to wash your hands. It probably dated from Covid but should, I thought, have been there much earlier. Even before the pandemic, surely it was a bad idea for French bakers to squeeze baguettes with the same fingers that handle coins? And for waiters to fill bread baskets by hand when they were also picking up forks and spoons that had been inside other people's mouths?

Another poster explained the French government's decision to prolong the *Vigipirate* programme. This was the name of the scheme that placed security men and X-ray machines at the entrance to all public buildings as protection against terrorism. *Vigipirate*. A strangely flippant name, I'd always thought, as if France had to be vigilant about a threat from one-legged sailors with parrots on their shoulders. Maybe the French authorities felt the need to downplay danger. In 1940, they probably launched a programme called *Vigi-schnitzel*.

There was also a large poster edged with tricolour bands of red, white and blue, quoting the full text of France's founding document, the 1789 *Declaration of Human Rights*. I'd read the declaration before. It was a list of truly noble intentions, all about protecting individual freedoms but – the essential thing in my view – only those freedoms that "do no harm to others". The collective good was more important than individual whim. A fine principle.

It's just unfortunate that if you read the original declaration literally, French women have no rights at all. The French Revolution was all about the rights of *hommes*. Not a mention of *femmes*.

Then again, I thought, it probably wouldn't help my application for nationality if I mentioned this now.

When the ticket counter was on number 410, a young woman came in from the stairwell and marched straight towards the reception desk.

Without taking a ticket.

There was a collective intake of breath from everyone else in the room. We knew the system.

"Bonjour," the naïve young woman said, but we were all thinking, there's no point being polite. Without a ticket, you're doomed.

"J'avais rendez-vous à onze heures," the condemned woman went on. She had an appointment at eleven.

I thought the receptionist was just going to blank her and point to the ticket machine, but she seemed to be intrigued by the woman's conversational gambit.

"You had an appointment at eleven?" the receptionist asked.

"Oui," the woman confirmed.

"But it's not yet eleven o'clock," the receptionist said. "Are you saying that you *had* an appointment at eleven, but now you want to cancel it?"

"Oh non!" The woman looked horrified.

"Well then," the receptionist said, "you should have said, '*j'ai* rendez-vous à onze heures' not '*j'avais* rendez-vous à onze heures'. In the *present* tense. Do you see?"

"Oh oui, merci," the woman said.

"So you *have* an appointment at eleven o'clock?" the receptionist asked.

"Oh oui," the woman said, as if her life had just been saved by the last-minute injection of an antidote to cobra venom.

"Prenez un ticket," the receptionist said, pointing at the machine.

The woman almost curtsied as she went to obey.

I was tempted to applaud this masterly piece of waiting-room control. Not only had the receptionist put the newcomer in her place and enforced the first rule of waiting-room club (take a ticket), she had also dangled before all of us the tantalizing prospect that one day, if we became French, we too would be able to dominate and humiliate people by the use of grammar alone. It was like being offered a superpower.

I was interrupted in these musings by the buzz of my phone. The receptionist looked up to see who'd broken rule two of waiting-room club, as illustrated by the unmissable diagram next to the *Prenez un ticket* sign – a crossed-out mobile phone. The drawing was of an antique model circa 1995 with a little aerial, but I presumed the rule still applied, so I looked around innocently for the offender like everyone else.

As soon as all eyes were elsewhere, I slid my phone out of my pocket and, turning away while pretending to scratch my leg, I switched the phone to silent and took a peek at a message from Jake.

"How was le diner at le restaurant?" he had asked.

I quickly typed an answer, "Dix astéroïdes."

Mine was a French phone on autocorrect.

More slowly this time, I typed out "disastrous".

"And après diner?" Jake replied, with a winking smiley.

"Fuchsia œuf." Autocorrect again, but I didn't bother re-sending.

"Leave it with me Paul," he replied.

I had no idea what that meant, but didn't want to endanger

my nationality application by carrying on the exchange of messages in the waiting room. I switched off my phone.

Just before I went insane with boredom, there was an electronic ding and number 421 came up on the board.

I slid over to reception and displayed my winning ticket.

After examining it carefully on both sides to make sure it wasn't fake, the receptionist asked me what she could do for me.

"Teach me all the killer bits of French grammar," I wanted to say, but instead informed her that I had come to *déposer* (drop off) my *dossier de naturalisation*.

She looked surprised.

"Vous ne *déposez* pas un dossier de naturalisation," she said.

Oh *merde*, I thought. Wrong verb. My application for French citizenship was going to run aground on a reef of mistaken vocabulary. It's not only their grammar that is lethal.

Behind me, I could almost hear the room urging me to fight back. Do it for all of us, they were telling me telepathically. Show us the way.

What could the correct verb be, I wondered. If it wasn't *déposer*, could it be *livrer*, to deliver? Surely it wasn't simply *donner*, to give?

No, I had a better idea.

"I have come to 'soumettre' my dossier," I told her. I was submitting it. That sounded slavish enough to be correct.

"Ah non," she replied, her face expressing a curious mix of regret and delight.

I began to sweat. I'd exhausted my vocabulary. Behind me, I thought I heard whimpers of empathy from the waiting room.

"Non, monsieur." She was moving in for the *coup de grâce*. "Vous l'envoyez par la Poste." I had to send it in by post.

She smiled and handed me an address card, before advising me that it was probably best to send my application in a registered letter to be sure it would arrive safely.

"Merci," I managed to mumble, close to tears, feeling as though I had just been pulled back from the guillotine by a merciful Robespierre.

As I staggered for the door, some of my fellow applicants smiled at me, perhaps viewing my fate as a sign from the heavens that there was hope for all of us. Life had meaning, and that meaning could be obtained simply by sending a registered envelope.

Of course, once I was out in the street I began swearing at myself in fluent French – "Merde, con, éco-fasciste!" – for not reading the government website closely enough, for not noticing that I was the only person in the room clutching a large envelope, for wasting several hours of my life.

But like I said, in the battle with the bureaucrats, you can't hang around hurting. You have to hit back.

I googled the nearest post office and marched straight towards it, pitying anyone who tried to get between me and the front of the queue for the registered letter labels.

Now I just had to pray that there wouldn't be a postal strike within the next couple of weeks. Ah, the everyday suspense of French life.

8

Next morning I had a meeting with Marjorie the *pétanque* lobbyist. Just the two of us this time. She'd suggested a quick get-together to sign my contract and have what she called *un briefing*. French didn't seem to have a word for this.

We met at my start-up incubator. I hadn't reserved an office, so we lounged in armchairs, coffees in hand, in a casual corner of an open office space. As we talked, people flitted back and forth, half-listening as they passed. This seemed to be the spirit of the place: get your ideas out there in the public realm, see who will stop and ask questions. After five minutes, though, no one had skidded to a halt beside our armchairs and squealed, "Mon dieu! You *must* let me in on your mind-blowingly futuristic pétanque project!"

Marjorie was wearing a different business suit to last time – a deep purplish blue. She looked so chic and ironed that I spent the first three minutes of our conversation gazing into her eyes while trying to remember whether I'd put on fresh trousers that morning. Clean shirt, yes, as always, but what about my legs? Were they looking creased?

"Just between us," she was saying, in French, "our friend Alain would have no hope on his own. He represents everything that the Olympics hates. FUCPET ..." This time, we both sniggered at the name, "... is male-dominated, aging, alcoholic."

Wow, I thought, and she was supposed to be on his side.

"But," she added, raising an oratory finger, "pétanque itself has a chance. You know that the Paralympics already has a pétanque-style game?"

"Yes, boccia," I said. I'd discovered its existence the previous

54

day, on the Paris Olympics website. It's a kind of bowls that can be played from a wheelchair.

"Exactly. But Alain is against it," she said, tutting. "He says that the name pétanque contains the Provençal word for feet, so you can't play it from a wheelchair."

I had to flinch at this lack of political correctness. "I hope he didn't say that to the Paris Olympic committee," I said.

She grimaced and nodded.

"But the existence of boccia opens the way for us," she went on. "If they have a Paralympic version of pétanque, why not the real thing? And we can also attack them for discrimination."

I was reminded of the word she'd scrawled on the last page of her notes.

"Parisianisme?" I asked.

"Yes. Pétanque is a sport from the south," she said, "from the provinces. We can accuse the committee of anti-regionalism, of being elitist Parisians."

I thought about this and began to imagine rival claims from all sorts of French regional sports. There was probably a federation in Auvergne for cow jumping, a Breton committee for oyster racing.

"I think your other argument is stronger," I told Marjorie. "Your idea that these days, pétanque is getting younger, less masculine, more *populaire*." This is an adjective that means "of the people" as well as "popular". "Your pétanque club, I'm sure it's mixed, n'est-ce pas?" She nodded. "Well, you're not the only ones," I went on. "I live near the canal, and I see young men and women playing pétanque there every night. Only when the weather's good, of course, but then this is the summer Olympics we're talking about, not the skiing season."

"Exactly," Marjorie said. "Curling is the winter pétanque, and how many people actually play that? Almost nobody. But it's an Olympic event. Whereas pétanque is the sport of the people!" She sounded as though she was willing to guillotine anyone who dared to contradict her.

A guy at the coffee machine turned around and stared. I guessed it wasn't very often that you heard sentences like "pétanque is the sport of the people" in start-up incubators.

"You ought to take along a camera next time you play," I said. "Interview people. Preferably young people, at least half of them female, of different origins …"

"Oui!" She bounced forward in her seat, slopping her coffee. Luckily none of it went on her smart suit, or on my probably-creased trousers. "We can make a film. We can prove that pétanque is for everyone. Yes we can!" she added in English, a phrase that the French picked up from Obama and haven't stopped using since. "You must come and play, too, Pol. Will you?"

She'd suddenly stopped calling me the formal "vous". I'd become a "tu". She noticed that I'd noticed.

"We can call each other 'tu', n'est-ce pas?" she said. "We're colleagues now."

"Of course," I agreed.

It crossed my mind, self-flatteringly, that she might have begun to wonder whether we could become something more. Her eyes were shining at me in a way that you more often see in someone who decides they might like a kiss, rather than during a conversation about *pétanque*. But then, I thought, it's been a long time since I was in a French business meeting where someone sounded as positive as Marjorie. I was much more used to coolness or plain negativity.

So I dismissed non-professional thoughts from my mind.

"When is your next pétanque game?" I asked.

"I don't know," she said. "I'll organize one. Are you free tomorrow evening?"

"Perfect."

I definitely had no more plans to meet up with Nolwenn.

I was just making sure that Marjorie's armchair was free of coffee stains after our meeting when I heard a cheerful "Bonjour!" aimed towards me.

I looked up to see my fourth-floor neighbour, the solar woman – whose name I still didn't know.

She was carrying the same bubble-wrapped rectangular

package as the previous evening. Now, though, she was in presentation mode again – hair tied back, lipstick a more conventional dark red, and wearing a black business suit.

"Bonjour," I replied. "If I'd known you were coming here this morning, I could have carried your ... thing." Overnight I seemed to have forgotten the word for solar panel. "Sorry, I need another French lesson."

She laughed. I hoped "French lesson" didn't have sexual overtones like it does in English.

"You need another *sexism* lesson," she said. "You still think I need a man to do all my heavy work for me?"

Fortunately, she was smiling as she said it.

"No," I said. "It's like you when you don't use the lift in our building at night. Sometimes I do kind things for no reason at all. I offer to carry things for people. I put sunflower seeds by my window for the sparrows. And not because I want to eat them."

She laughed again. Either I was being incredibly witty or she thought I was a clown. It occurred to me that I didn't mind which.

"Don't you know that it's illegal to feed Parisian wild birds?" she said.

"Even sparrows?"

"Well, mainly pigeons, but sparrows too."

"Oh well," I said, "sometimes I like to live dangerously." Maybe it was saying this, even as a joke, that gave me the nerve to come out with the next line. "Do you want to get some lunch together later? Roast pigeon maybe?"

This time she didn't laugh.

"I have no time for lunch," she said. "Sorry. We have to prepare a presentation."

"Of course, yes, I know it's very important, ecology, solar ... things." I realized I was rambling while my mind adjusted to her putdown.

"And now I really have to go and put this *thing* on a table somewhere," she said, smiling.

She set off towards the meeting rooms at the back of the building. But she didn't say goodbye, so I took it as a cue to continue the conversation, and followed her.

"Do you play pétanque?" I asked. It occurred to me as I said it that this must be some kind of ancient French chat-up line, along the lines of "Do you like snails?" and "Is that your guillotine or are you looking after it for a friend?"

"Pétanque," she repeated, nodding as though I had just confirmed some dark secret about myself.

"Yes, you must have seen all the people playing by the canal, near our foyer," I went on.

"Of course." She went into one of the meeting rooms and gently put her panel down on the large white table in the centre.

"I was wondering if you'd like to come for a game one evening. Tomorrow, for example?"

I saw that she was now paying much more attention to unwrapping her solar panel than she was to me.

"I don't have time –" she began.

"It would be after work of course," I interrupted.

She stopped unwrapping and looked me in the eye. Hers seemed to be drilling straight into my skull.

"You know, I heard what you said," she said.

"What I said?" I didn't get it.

"What you said to your colleague. I was passing just behind you and I heard what you said."

I shook my head. I was still lost.

"About needing to prove that pétanque is played by people of different origins," she said. She raised her hands to do a double finger point at her dark-skinned face, and then returned to unveiling her solar panel.

"What?" I said. "No. Merde. What? Merde. No." That last word, I decided, expressed the most important idea to get across. My mind was paralysed by the injustice of it all. And the unpleasantness. I'd simply thought it would be fun to meet up with her after work. It had nothing to do with origins or skin colour. How could she think that?

She was still mutely unpacking, carefully pulling bubble wrap from around a metal framework.

"Thanks for the invitation," she said, not looking at me.

"But –" was all I managed to splutter.

This was the first time, I'm glad to say, that a woman ever refused to meet up with me on the grounds that I might be a total bastard. To be honest, in the past a few women had called me that exact thing, but usually after some misunderstanding, like because I'd failed to notice it was our one-month anniversary, or because I'd assumed we'd broken up and had asked her friend out on a date.

She finished unwrapping her panel, which was sleek and black, like the top of a ceramic kitchen hob after two hours of cleaning and polishing.

"Panneau solaire," I said. The translation had suddenly come back to me. The panel was so perfect that I naturally wanted to touch it, but realized instinctively that I shouldn't. "It's beautiful," I said.

She stared at me for a couple of seconds, maybe wondering whether it was worth ever talking to me again, then seemed to come to a decision.

"More importantly, it's efficient," she said.

We stared down at this sleek, efficient object for a second.

"But listen," I went on. "This invitation. And what I said to my colleague. You misunderstood me. Really. I just thought that I would like to have lunch or a drink or a coffee or yes, a game of pétanque with you."

"Coincidentally."

"OK, I am working on a pétanque thing at the moment, and, yes, we want to interview people of all sorts. Male, female, students, workers, everyone, especially young people. But that has nothing to do with my invitation to you. Pétanque was just an excuse. I mean, I could be working on a project to transform, I don't know, the Eiffel Tower into a giant vibrator, and I would still – oh merde."

Not for the first time in my life, trying to improvise a jokey excuse had only plunged me deeper into the shit.

Stephen Clarke

But she was smiling, apparently enjoying my pain.

"A giant vibrator?" she asked. "Who would that be for?"

"Forget the vibrator, please," I said, with total sincerity. I really hoped she could. "And forget pétanque."

"That might be easier."

"What I'm saying is, if you get any free time for a drink, a coffee, a walk up the stairs, anything, just let me know. I'm Paul, by the way."

"Paaawwl," she said, clearly trying out the Englishness of it.

"Have you got time to tell me your name?" I asked.

She reached into her suit jacket pocket and pulled out a business card. She handed it to me. The logo on it read "Sol Mineur".

"Sol Mineur?" I asked.

"It's a pun," she said. I should have guessed. There must be a law obliging all French businesses to use puns when choosing a name. Though this one didn't seem to have any English in it, which was unusual. "Sol for sun, of course," she explained. "And mineur because the cost of our panels will be minor. And also it's a key in music. Mozart's sonata in sol mineur. You know, do ray mee far sol."

I counted up the scale.

"G," I said. "Gee!" It was meant to be a joke but clearly didn't translate. "Excellent." I looked back at the card. "But there are *two* founders' names."

"My associate and myself."

"Which one are you?"

"Find out," she said. "And now I'm sorry, but I have to prepare for this presentation."

I left her to it, feeling rejected but somehow encouraged.

She had no time for lunches, no time for fools either, but she seemed to have forgiven my unintended gaffe and decided she had time for a bit of flirty wordplay.

9

Of course, it took me approximately three seconds on Google to find out that she was Ambre Bonnet, pronounced presumably "bonnay", and was not Lara Zaoui, the other name on the card.

I was rewarded with some cute photos, too. There was Ambre, laughing on a beachside balcony whilst wearing a bikini. Laughing in a crowded nightclub whilst holding a champagne bottle. Laughing whilst laughing. Good news, I thought, that she did so much of it. I hoped she would have time for more.

I also checked out Sol Mineur and found some cool film of the two women giving a presentation during which Paris rooftops suddenly got decorated with black panels while ugly white wind turbines wilted like dead flowers and a coal-fired power station shrivelled into obsolescence. Those solar panels seemed to exude powerful magic. They were, I learned, made almost entirely from recycled materials, and were capable of harnessing solar energy even on cloudy days. To cap it all, they could produce electricity when it was *raining*.

Just a few minutes after receiving Sol Mineur's business card, I sent a message to the phone number, saying "Bonjour Ambre, ici Paaaaaauuul."

I didn't get an immediate reply, but at least I'd proved that I was interested.

It was early evening, and I was on my way to find out more about Jake's Nolympics project. The meeting was being held, for some reason, in a music school not far from my students' residence – again, a stone's throw from the canal. Practically my whole life seemed to be taking place in the same square kilometre. The post-lockdown effect maybe.

The music school was housed in a 1930s red-brick apartment complex, one of Paris's older low-rent housing blocks. The Parisians call them *HLM*, pronounced "ash-ell-em", which stands for *habitation à loyer modéré* (dwelling at a reasonable rent).

This block showed how the neighbourhood was changing. At street level, next to a dingy-looking office offering writing services for "all your letters and documents" was a freshly-painted black-and-white double door advertising an *École de Talent*. I wondered why Jake would choose this place to hold his meeting for the talentless.

And the first person I saw was surprisingly Olympic-looking – Cécile the waitress in a tracksuit. She pushed open the double doors and, turning around to see if it was safe to let them close behind her, spotted me a couple of yards away.

She held the doors open and smiled with half-recognition as I thanked her.

"Are you going to Jake's meeting?" I asked.

"Moi? Non," she said, grinning, and disappeared into the nearest room.

"Monsieur?" A man in a black suit was staring at me from a doorway just inside the entrance. In the past, it was probably the concierge's cubby hole, but had now been fitted with a wall of CCTV screens.

The security man seemed to have decided that I didn't have enough talent to be in the building.

"Vous cherchez quelqu'un?" he asked. Was I looking for someone?

Aren't we all, I thought.

"Le meeting Nolympique?" I replied.

"Ah oui." Apparently my *lack* of any talent needed no proof. "End of the corridor, door on the right."

The twenty yards or so of corridor walls were covered in fish-scale layers of event posters, presumably advertising shows by pupils. A hyperactive bunch.

The door at the end of the corridor was thick and heavy, as

wide as a wardrobe. Soundproof. Behind it I found a rehearsal room equipped with two large guitar amplifiers, a drumkit, several microphone stands and a mixing desk, but no Nolympic committee members.

Predictable, I decided. Being on time is a talent.

I sent Jake a message asking him if I was in the right place (subtext: Why aren't *you*?), and he replied, "En route", so there was some hope that he'd be there within a few hours.

The atmosphere in this empty rehearsal space contained about 50 per cent stale sweat, so I began looking for a switch to activate the overhead air vent.

I had just enjoyed the first rush of clean oxygen when the door was heaved open and in walked Jake.

He seemed to be wearing exactly the same clothes as the previous day. He was gripping an extinguished roll-up between his lips.

"Merde, man," he grumbled. "This is an école of musique and they won't let me smoke a joint?"

"I'm surprised at you Jake," I told him. "I'd have thought your very first priority when choosing a venue for your meeting would have been smoking allowed."

He looked sheepish.

"Oui, well, I forgot to réserver a place, and then Cécile has suggested ici."

"I saw her coming in just now."

"Yeah, she studies here. She will sing my poems."

It took a second or two for this to sink in.

"You're asking a *woman* to sing your poems?" I said. "That's like asking Aretha Franklin to sing in favour of disrespect, or getting Britney Spears to confess that she never did it again, or —"

Jake interrupted me. "Or Amy Winehouse finally going to rehab. Oui, I get the message Paul, je ne suis pas un moron."

"No. Sorry, Jake." It was just that he so often behaved like one. And he certainly wrote like one.

"I know, from a purely conventional moral point de vue, my

poems are …" Jake groped for the correct term. I was thinking, repulsive, vomit-inducing. "Unique," he decided. "But she is French."

"What difference does that make?"

"She doesn't understand all the words."

Lucky her, I thought.

"We can go out for a drink with her après the meeting," he said.

"Great."

"Because I know tonight you will not see la végane." He grinned at me.

"How did you guess?"

"I made sure for you."

"What do you mean?"

Grinning even more manically, he pulled out his phone and opened up a photo. It was of me, doing a clownish smile and pointing my knife and fork down at my sea bream. He'd taken it when we were lunching together.

"I have sent this to her," he told me.

I had to laugh. Now she'd know I was a leather-wearing, *fish-eating* eco-fascist.

"Anyway, you have met this pétanque woman, non?" he asked me. I must have mentioned Marjorie to him in passing.

"No, I'm not really interested in her. There's, er …"

I decided not to reveal anything to him about women bearing solar panels, but he wasn't going to stand for such blatant *confessius interruptus.*

"Oh oui ? There's une autre femme, Paul?" He pointed his joint at me accusingly.

Reluctantly, I told him about the meeting with Ambre on the staircase and the fruitless follow-up at the incubator.

"She is Française and she says she has no time for *lunch*? Impossible!" Jake was aghast. "But anyway, you spend way too much time eating with women, Paul. It only causes you problèmes. You don't need to eat with them, just –"

"Jake, please …"

I really didn't need his neolithic advice. I was actually

enjoying the flirtatiousness of things with Ambre. It was thrilling, a bit scary. It was old-school. It was wooing. Literally. If and when she replied to my email, I'd think, "Woo!"

"Listen, mon ami," Jake went on. "You have to play the cards in your hand, not the ones that haven't been dealt yet." Jake grew up in Las Vegas with a mother who was a part-time hooker, hence his view of life as a game of sexual poker. "Forget the too-busy solar woman. Play pétanque with this other woman, then invite her back to your apartment."

"Right, thanks, Jake." As usual, his version of life coaching had given me an instant headache.

"No problème, man. Alors, where are les autres?" he said. "They will never find us. We must go outside to wait."

Though judging by the way Jake was sucking on his unlit joint, he had other reasons for leaving the smoke-free zone.

Half an hour later, there was a committee of five in the rehearsal room, plus me the neutral observer. Unsurprisingly, almost all the Nolympians were male. Who else would mount a campaign in favour of inactivity?

Two of the guys were what we used to call "seriously overweight", or "Nolympic" as it would doubtless soon be known. One of them was a young, bearded French nerd in a plain beige T-shirt that seemed to feature drink stains and snack crumbs as a part of its design. The other was an older American guy with thick glasses and long straight hair that flopped down either side of his grey face. He was wearing a shirt and trousers that he had seemingly bought in the 1980s. The key word was polyester.

The third male was French and in his late teens. He was slumped on the floor, his head resting against the bass drum. He had a finger-sized joint in his shirt pocket and the general air of someone who spends most of his life with smoke coming out of his ears. I'd met his kind in Paris before, the kids of aging hipsters who think it's cool to let their offspring smoke dope like they do. Now the hipster parents were wondering why their kids did nothing with their lives except get high. I guessed that this lad had been brought here in a parent's car, just to get him out of the house.

The only female member of the committee was American. She was wearing a loose orange tracksuit and seemed much too energetic to be a Nolympian. She heaved the two guitar amplifiers into the centre of the room, followed by a chair and the drum stool, so that most of us would have a seat. I offered to sit on the floor and give her my amp, but she preferred to squat in a lotus position.

I didn't get anyone's names, because Jake, the chairman on his drum stool, didn't bother to announce them, if he even remembered them. And no one seemed particularly keen to know who I was, so we remained anonymous.

It took the committee several minutes to get down to matters strictly Nolympic.

"Why can't we meet in the centre of town?" the American guy complained, in French. "I never come this far north."

"Can't we at least *drink* in here?" the young pothead wanted to know, also in French.

"Non, but we can take a smoking pause in a minute," Jake sympathized, in his usual Franco-English cocktail.

"Parle français!" the American guy snapped at him. "Nous sommes en France." This is a view held by some American expats in Paris, who want to get the most out of the French experience, even if they can't actually speak decent French.

"No, let's speak English," the nerd objected, which is the view generally held by many young French nerds who, in their heads, live in California.

"Tu décides, monsieur le président," the American woman told Jake.

"I suggest that we parler français, out of politesse," Jake answered, confusing everyone.

He put it to a vote, and they elected to speak French, by three English-speakers to one French (the pothead didn't bother to raise his hand).

As an observer, I abstained, even though to me, it always feels perverse to speak French to a fellow English speaker.

Unless, of course, the conversation includes a French person who wouldn't understand English, which wasn't the case here.

So the English-speakers started practising their bad French at each other, while the French nerd scowled at them.

The American woman finally called the committee to order. "Nous choisons nouveaux sports," she suggested, ungrammatically. She looked expectantly at Jake, who just shrugged and allowed the proposal to rebound into the room.

"Striptease," the French nerd said, coincidentally a word that is the same in English and French.

The older American guy cheered, the woman groaned.

"Oui oui, tu mesures la vitesse," the older guy said. You measure the speed.

"Exactement! How fast can they striptease?" Jake said. "Femmes and hommes wear the same thing, shorts and a T-shirt Olympique."

"Nolympic," the French nerd corrected him.

"Oui," Jake agreed. "Nolympique T-shirt et shorts, striptease against the clock."

The woman said it sounded too much like a sport – unlike yoga, for example, which was her suggestion for a new Nolympic event.

"Combien long tu peux hold une position," she said.

"That also sounds like a real Olympic sport," the older guy said in French. "I couldn't do that. Nolympic events should be things that *everyone* can do, with zero talent, energy or physical coordination." His French was actually very fluent, even if it did have a New York accent.

The other men agreed with him, except for the young pothead who was now asleep. Dozing was definitely going to be one of the Nolympians' major events.

"C'est la question," Jake said. "What are talentless people good at?"

Everyone started to think.

"Just say your suggestions," Jake told them. "This is a brainstorming. No limits. Just name activities."

"And tell us how they will be judged," the young nerd added.

"Péter," the older guy said – farting. "Range, intensity, decibels."

Most people laughed, the woman groaned. She had a talent for groaning.

"Le pole dancing," she said.

"That's a real sport too," the old guy objected.

"Hey, no critiques, this is a brainstorming," Jake said.

"Shouting?" the nerd suggested.

This time the woman and I groaned together, though maybe for different reasons. She just thought the idea was stupid, whereas I was going insane.

"Come on, be serious," I begged, which surprised me. I'd come along expecting to take the piss, and had been given more than enough reasons to do just that.

But seeing that the woman – whatever her name was – genuinely seemed to want a tournament for people who were neither Olympic nor Paralympic, I'd realized that they really did have a genuine niche to occupy.

"You'd probably get a lot of public support if you proposed a Nolympic Games tournament with real sports," I said.

"Hey, parle français!" the American guy complained.

But I couldn't be bothered. Everyone here understood English.

"With a few serious suggestions," I went on, "you could get the general public behind a tournament that sits exactly between the Olympics and Paralympics. Totally inclusive sports that anyone can play but that will never be Olympic events. Tiddly winks, skittles, stuff like that."

For a second I toyed with the idea of suggesting that my *pétanqueurs* should join the Nolympians. After all, distributing small lumps of metal around a sandpit doesn't take Olympic strength or lung capacity. But I couldn't betray Alain and his dreams of authentic Olympic glory.

"Of course, if you want to have a laugh," I went on, "you can have fun versions of existing Olympic events like, I don't know, floating down some rapids in an inner tube or doing a bomb in a swimming pool."

"Hey, bonne idée, Paul," Jake congratulated me. "We measure how much water you displace. Fun *and* scientifique."

"Pathétique," the woman groaned.

"OK, but do you see what I mean?" I asked the room. "If you forget all this bollocks about shouting and farting, maybe you can offer a serious –"

I didn't get any farther.

"Non non non non non non non," the American guy recited, sounding very much like a French translation of the middle of "Bohemian Rhapsody". I expected him to continue with a "Mama mia" or two, but instead he asked me who I thought I was, and how skittles was in any way talentless, because to be any good you had to practise for hours a day, which was against the whole philosophy of Nolympianism.

So now it was a philosophical movement?

"Nous sommes pour l'anti-sport," the American guy concluded triumphantly.

"Ça, c'est exact, Paul. Sorry mon ami," Jake adjudicated. "Anyway, personally right now I need un peu de smoke, let's pause."

"Yeah, couldn't you get a room with *chairs*?" the French nerd moaned in English, rubbing his backside as he lifted himself up from a guitar amp. I didn't like to imagine the imprints in his buttocks made by the volume knobs.

The woman said she was going to stay and do some yoga, and stretched herself out on the floor.

"Tu es très *active*," the American guy grunted at her, painfully straightening his back.

We all filed out, except for the teenager who probably wasn't going to wake up for hours unless a drummer came in and started slamming out a beat.

In the street, the evening was livening up. It was still not dark, but groups of people were gathering on the canal bank for alcohol-based picnics. Just opposite the talent school, six or seven student types were squatting around an oasis of wine bottles. They had brought along a clutch of baguettes, and plastic containers of salad, cheese and sausage slices. They were even drinking out of proper glasses. It was all very civilized.

Further along, other groups were staking their claims. On fine evenings like this one, both canal banks would eventually be turned into a continuous string of picnics with singing, guitar-playing and, before the end of the night, deliberate and accidental swimming in the dark green waters where ducks pooped and rats took their baths.

Jake was filling his lungs with pungent smoke.

He and I were standing a few feet away from the two guys on his committee. I could hear them carrying on a bilingual conversation, the American speaking French, the Frenchman English, about the inherent stupidity of kicking, throwing or hitting a ball for sporting pleasure.

"Let's break," Jake suggested.

I didn't get it. "We *are* having a break."

"No, *break*. Cassons-nous."

He meant let's go. *Se casser*, to break oneself, is a French slang word for to leave.

"Can you just *leave*, Jake? You're president."

"It's the Nolympics. The idea is just say no."

"But they'll throw you off the committee."

He exhaled deeply, engulfing his head in a cloud.

"Non," he said when he emerged. "I have the most followers on social media. These days that's how we choose our presidents, n'est-ce pas?" He had a point.

He went to break the news to his two colleagues, who didn't seem bothered. From the way they were eyeing the nearby students, they seemed to have decided that boozing by the canal might be one sport they wanted to play.

"What about the other two inside?" I asked Jake.

He shrugged. "Oh, one is asleep, the other is in meditation. I'll send them a message. Come on, let's break ourselves."

It seemed that one sport Nolympians were especially bad at was human interaction.

Suddenly, the canal bank was flooded in coloured light as a time-switch activated the neon strips that were fitted to the street lamps. Picnickers now had green, red, blue or yellow food.

As Jake and I walked towards Stalingrad, I found myself staring into the pools of colour, looking for a familiar face. Would Ambre take time out to meet friends for a snack or a drink after dropping off her solar panel at the students' residence?

Jake saw me examining the drinkers and jumped to exactly the wrong conclusion. Not only that, he took exactly the most inappropriate action. Clutching me around the shoulder, he began to rap in his loudest voice.

"Mademoiselle Marjorie! Are you ici? Are you free?" he called out above the chatter and the clinking of bottle on glass.

"Shut up, Jake." I tried to wriggle loose.

"Oh Marjorie ... I won't commit parjory!"

"Parjory?"

"Es-tu ici? Marjorie!"

Now he was attracting the attention of a large group of drinkers under a bright yellow neon light, and I was praying that Ambre wasn't there in the pool of amber.

"For Christ's sake, Jake." Now even I was rhyming. "I told you. I'm not interested in Marjorie."

"Oh man." He slugged me on the back, almost knocking me into the canal. "You have to take opportunities. What is that Latin thing they say? Cave canem?"

"I think that means beware of the dog."

"Yeah, well that's true, too."

"You mean carpe diem," I said. "Seize the day."

"Oui, and seize the night. Let's go find you a drink."

"OK." Anything to shut him up. "Just one drink, though. I want to get up early tomorrow and work."

71

10

Someone was shining a high-powered torch in my face. Hot light was burning through my clenched eyelids. My skull seemed to be shrivelling, no doubt because of this heat source that was irradiating it.

With eyes still closed, I groped my way to the sink and clutched at the tap nozzle like a new-born goat taking its first urgent drink of mother's milk. Cold water gushed down my throat and spurted out of my nostrils, but after this bout of self-waterboarding I finally managed to open my eyes and take stock of the situation.

I saw sun outdoors, relentlessly trying to get indoors. This was obviously a morning. The morning after a night.

So far so good. Any more details in the memory bank?

Ah yes. Jake and red wine, *ficelle* after *ficelle*.

Not good. Had there been food?

Yes, I now recalled, but it had come much too late. First there had been wine. And then more wine.

Any regrets? Any flashbacks of drunken idiocy? I rebooted my brain and sifted through the diagnostics.

There was a conversation with a woman. A smoking woman. Jake's waitress friend, Cécile.

Yes – I was trying to explain to her that I wanted something. Comfort. No, comfort *food*. Blancmange, one of those French words that we English use but the French don't understand. Like "double entendre", which they never say. I told Cécile that I had a craving for blancmange. I tried to explain: it's *crème brûlée* without the *crème* or the *brûlée*. Simple. Could she get her chef to make some for me?

No, she couldn't, and at that point, if I remembered correctly, the consensus was that I ought to go home. Which I did, half-carried by Jake, who had annoyed me.

How had he done that? Why?

Ah yes. First, he had kissed Cécile goodbye, with tongues and hands and promises. This infuriated me. And made me envious. He was a 1950s sexist throwback, so why didn't these modern women hate him?

Then he wouldn't let me swim across the canal, although it looked so refreshing, and the route across the water was so direct compared to the long trek to the nearest bridge with its swaying, evasive stairs.

And that was all I remembered. There was a bit of noise, then sleep. Or unconsciousness. Until the painful awakening.

Back when I worked in London, I'd often go out drinking with my colleagues straight after work. I'd happily knock back a small army of pints, eating nothing until I grabbed something inedible on the way home. Even so, the next morning I'd be in the office more or less on time.

Now though, my body had become French. It was perfectly content to deal with wine at lunchtime, followed by an early evening *apéritif* and plenty more wine in the evening, but it now demanded solids at the same time as drink. Any attempt to spend most of the evening doing things the old, purely liquid, English way were severely punished next morning.

Fortunately for me, France is like a huge ambulance speeding you towards a cure. In Paris, there is approximately one pharmacy per inhabitant. Look down almost any street in the city and you will see an illuminated green cross shining at you like a new dawn.

I had slept fully dressed, so I staggered outdoors and wandered randomly around for only about two minutes before finding myself inside a pharmacy. It was as big as a supermarket and smelled of soap and creams and soothing plants.

A down-to-earth lady in a long white coat took one look at me and nodded. I hardly needed to say *"gueule de bois"*, the

French for hangover, which literally means "wooden gob". Very apt this morning.

This angel in an overall proceeded to fill a blindingly white, deafeningly loud, paper carrier bag with tubes and packets, telling me to take two effervescent tablets straight away (even the word "effervescent" started to make me feel better), followed by two more in the afternoon (she tactfully refrained from mentioning lunch), and then continuing with a week-long cure to "re-boost my intestinal flora" (she was right, I could feel that its petals had wilted) with stimulating digestive yeast. Ah yes, I thought gratefully, Paris the moveable yeast.

I went back to my room and washed all this medicinal goodness down with a bottle of France's most refreshing mineral water, Célestins, which sparkles, but subtly. After each swallow of Célestins, I could feel the water working its way through my digestive system, cleaning out impurities as it went, zapping anything indigestible with its large but gentle bubbles. It comes from Vichy, the town in central France where the collaborationist government was based during World War Two. I've always thought that they chose the town because it helped to wash away their daily dose of shame.

After a fistful of pills and a litre of Célestins, my own shame began to fade, and I felt fit enough to shower and get on with the day.

Needing air and exercise, I decided to go and look at Paris's Olympic venues (or building sites) in preparation for my appointment that evening to play *pétanque* with Marjorie and her friends. I sucked the final drops from my bottle of Célestins, checked my map and headed for the lift.

I was down in the foyer of my *foyer*, emptying my mailbox of pizza takeaway fliers and estate agents' offers to help me sell my rented room, when I heard the door to the stairway open behind me.

I felt a sudden involuntary burst of adrenaline that made my head fizz, and I realized that I was hoping to turn around and see Ambre. I hadn't heard from her since sending my last message.

This was what I meant about the thrill of old-school wooing. Did Jake ever care whether or not he bumped into a woman? For him, there was never any anticipation, so meeting any woman was nothing more than a "pourquoi pas?" Every woman on his "will I shag them?" list was in equal first place. Pole position.

But the person emerging from the stairway wasn't Ambre. It was a young guy carrying a fold-up scooter over his shoulder. I'd seen him around before. I said "Bonjour".

My adrenaline began to recede, or rather to ferment into disappointment. And envy of Jake's indifference. In his world, I thought bitterly, there weren't just plenty more fish in the sea. To a shark like him, the crabs, octopuses, even the plankton were all fair game.

I threw my junk mail in the recycle bin and headed out through the front gate into the street.

"Merci," someone said.

The voice behind me was feminine. I wheeled around and saw that I had just let the gate swing shut in front of Ambre. As usual, she had her hands full of technology.

She was looking miffed.

"Je m'excuse!" I said. Sorry. "I didn't see you."

Adrenaline kicked in again, accompanied by whatever enzyme makes you feel a bastard for slamming a gate in someone's face. I opened the gate for her.

"Merci," she repeated.

"Je t'en prie."

She gave me a smile so brief that it was only just detectable with the human eye, and then turned left, towards the nearest *Métro* station.

Was she ignoring me? I wondered if maybe my hangover was so bad that I had morphed into a completely different person. A notorious criminal, for example.

I jogged a few steps to catch up with her.

"Ça va?" I asked.

"Bien, merci," she answered, as if conversations were being taxed per syllable.

"Vraiment?" I asked. Really? "It looks to me as if ça ne va pas."

She stopped suddenly, forcing me to swerve into a parked Peugeot to avoid a collision with her. My knee hit a headlight head on.

"Yes, well maybe things would be better if I hadn't had a wake-up call at two in the morning," she said.

"A wake-up call? Oh no," I said, but suddenly my memory was saying "Oh yes," and the "you're a bastard" enzyme began to throb in my temples.

Ambre was striding off again. I followed, hobbling on my dented knee.

"Merde," I said. "Did I wake you up?"

Her lack of reply was all too eloquent.

"I'm so sorry," I said. "My friend Jake forced me to drink wine before dinner."

The combination of renewed hangover and limited French vocabulary was making me sound even stupider than I felt.

"*Forced* you?"

"No of course not. But I can't drink wine before dinner, I mean, without dinner. So I was drunk."

"And then you decided to come and bang on my door."

"Oh no," I groaned. "Did I do that?"

"Oui."

"Excuse-moi. I probably wanted to come and tell you I'd discovered your name."

She was walking so fast that it was hard to keep up.

"That's OK then," she said over her shoulder, "I really needed someone to wake me up in the middle of the night and remind me what my name is. Or rather, tell me how it sounds when mispronounced by a drunken Englishman."

"You mean I got it wrong?"

She screeched to another halt. This time I had to walk into a lamppost. The other kneecap took the impact.

"Omba! Omba!" she imitated.

I'd done the English thing of not pronouncing my French "re". You really have to clear your throat when you're doing it.

"My name is Amb-re," she said, giving the second syllable its full French throatiness.

"I'm sorry," I said. "It's an English mouth problem. I need to drink at least a litre of water before I can pronounce the French 're'. And I can't do your vowels either. It's like the town called Caen and the insult 'con' – I say them both the same, n'est-ce pas?"

"Yes," she confirmed, with the tiniest glimmer of a smile. Of pity, but it was better than nothing.

"And sometimes I want to say, 'merci beaucoup' but I tell someone, 'merci beau cul'." (Which means thank you, beautiful arse.) "So I'm in big trouble if ever I want to make a speech saying thanks very much to the citizens of Caen."

Her smile was microscopically warmer. Only enough to make an ice cube sweat, but there was hope.

"It's like, some French people call me poule," I said, which means chicken. "So you see, I really am sorry if I pronounced your name wrongly. It was an innocent mistake."

"What *wasn't* an innocent mistake was banging on my door at two in the morning," she said. The smile had frozen again.

"No, you're right, that was just stupid."

In reply, she shot out an arm as if to punch me. It would have been totally justified, but I ducked out the way all the same.

When I lifted my head again, she was standing almost in the middle of the street as a taxi drew up, the green light on its roof turning to red. She'd been hailing it.

"I don't have time to take the Métro," she said. "Are you on your way to the incubator?"

"No." Best to get out while the going was more or less good, I thought. Apology apparently accepted, so shut up.

I leapt into the road to open the car door for her. She handed me the solar panel, got in the taxi and then held out her arms towards me as if she wanted to grab me in an embrace. Unlikely.

I returned the panel to her, and once she was buckled in with her precious cargo on her lap, the taxi pulled away. I stood and waved goodbye, before diving for the pavement to avoid a bus that had materialized behind me.

Parisian buses have two levels of "get out the way" signal. The less urgent of the two is a dinging bell that warns, "watch out, I'm coming your way but no need to panic." The more strident is a furious hooter so loud that it could lift a family-size car off its wheels. This bus driver had opted to go straight to level two, so I was quivering with terror as I landed back on the pavement. Not only that, my hangover headache had started playing bongos on my skull again. Not forgetting my kneecaps, both of which felt as though they were smashed.

But on the positive side, the "you bastard!" enzyme had subsided, and the relief felt wonderful.

"Amb-re," I said to myself, making sure I nailed that second syllable. "Amb-re, Amb-re, merci beaucoup."

OK, I might have mispronounced that last word, but she wasn't nearby to hear me.

I felt almost sprightly as I walked to the *Métro* station. After surviving an Olympian ordeal of diplomacy, I was well primed for a trip into the suburbs of Paris. These were places best known to international TV audiences for getting torched by rioting mobs, but which were soon going to be home to the Olympic Village.

11

I'd seen a computer-generated film of the *Village Olympique* showing a cool, modernistic garden suburb with as many trees as buildings, and with pavements that were much wider than its roads. A sunlit heaven peopled by pedestrians and cyclists who moved with balletic grace along avenues lined with cafés and shops whose staff gave all their customers blissful smiles.

In the video, the new sports venues gleamed like recently landed UFOs from an ultra-civilized galaxy. Crowds emerged from trams, trains and shuttle buses and strolled towards the wide-open entrances of the new stadiums. Everyone had a ticket in their hand or on their phone.

On pitches, courts and tracks, athletes were running, jumping and playing without breaking into a sweat. The movie soundtrack was applause and inspiring music.

I wished I could be in that virtual paradise instead of having to barge my way into a *Métro* carriage as the whining beep signal sounded to warn me that the doors were going to close and leave me stranded on the platform.

Line 13 of the *Métro* was recently voted by Parisians as the "most anxiety-inducing" in the network. It was overcrowded, unreliable, unsafe. They called it "*la ligne de l'enfer*". The subway to hell.

And yet line 13 was, so far, the most direct public transport route out of the city centre to the Olympic Village and its nearest venues. For the moment, Paris's proposed new underground and tram lines were all just holes in the ground and promises – promises that, to judge by what I'd read on the internet, were receding into the distant future.

It was well after morning commuter time, but the aging carriage was pretty full, so when I finally got on the 13 at Place de Clichy, a major *Métro* hub, I was forced to edge buttocks-first into the crowd and stand by the door as other passengers discreetly elbowed me in the kidneys and grunted down my neck.

I didn't want to hold on to the metal bar beside the door – someone once told me that this was the equivalent of shaking hands with 200 people who had not washed their hands after going to the toilet – so I clenched my cheeks and used all my surfing muscles to stay upright as the train clunked and jolted its way north towards the poor suburbs and the Olympics.

Of course, Paris was never going to knock down the Louvre to provide temporary accommodation for a bunch of athletes, but it went to the other extreme and decided to build its Olympic Village more than ten kilometres outside of town.

An equivalent distance north from the Tower of London might take you to a pleasant low-rise suburb with pubs full of hipsters who have relocated to find better schools for their toddlers. But the north of Paris has been developed differently. Back in the 1960s and 1970s, French planners' recipe for suburban living seems to have been: find an architect with no artistic taste, no social conscience and a sadistic streak, and tell him or her to base their designs on the most run-down housing estates in Soviet Russia. Cheap concrete, no playgrounds, no shops, and crap transport. That will teach its future residents to be underprivileged.

Admittedly, when you take the Eurostar these days, you see some nicely refurbished areas near the Stade de France, with repaved canal paths, glass-fronted low-rise apartment blocks, and multicoloured kiddies' playgrounds. But even those neighbourhoods are still pretty poor, so that it would be pure provocation to go walking there after dark with an Olympic gold medal around your neck. Even a bronze could get you into trouble.

Originally, *banlieue* was just the French word for suburb, but these days, in many minds, it carries an undertone of crime and poverty as well as inaccessible distance. Most Parisians believe that civilization ends at the *périphérique* ring road which circles the city around seven kilometres from its epicentre at Notre Dame cathedral. Some snooty Parisians even think that anywhere outside Saint-Germain-des-Prés is as sophisticated as a truckers' toilet in the Australian Outback.

And now the city authorities had chosen to build the "Paris" Olympic Village way out in the northern suburbs. All those naïve athletes were going to think: "Hey, as the pigeon flies, it's only an hour's jog to the Eiffel Tower, let's go." They were in for a shock.

It wasn't only the physical crush of passengers on line 13 that was hard to bear. It was a warm day, so the air temperature in the *Métro* trains was hovering around volcanic. And the human lava was emitting volcanic vapours – several different brands of sweat, clouds of baked-on perfume – as well as a haze of pure steam.

Every time we arrived in a station and the double doors opened, there was a scrum that had me dancing on the spot to avoid roaming hands and shoving groins. These people weren't doing anything sexual – they were just trying to get off and on the train.

Of course the athletes wouldn't be taking the *Métro*. I guessed that the organizers of the Games were intending to lay on shuttle buses, but they must have known that driving north out of the city at any time other than 4am on a winter Sunday was semi-gridlock at best. During the Olympics, with thousands of athletes and spectators on the road, it would be quicker to walk across the roofs of the gridlocked vehicles.

Eventually the train arrived at the station I wanted, Carrefour Pleyel, and I fought to get off, a salmon trying to leap up a waterfall. Fortunately, I was an old hand at the game, and, chanting "Pardon, pardon!" like an apologetic Buddhist monk, I barged and thrust my way to freedom.

Checking my pockets to make sure I still owned wallet, phone and testicles, I made for the outside world, and emerged at the foot of the tallest building site I've ever seen. It was a skyscraper that was being renovated from a skeleton of rusty iron into a gleaming tower of glass.

I googled it: a future luxury hotel, salvaged from the remains of an old asbestos-ridden office block. With its 40th floor panoramic swimming pool (warning: don't swim too near the edge), the building was due for "delivery" just before the Games. I hoped the delivery men didn't have too far to carry it.

The area around the base of the tower seemed to be getting a full re-landscaping, and I made a mental note to put it on my list of potential *pétanque* venues.

My route towards the Olympic Village took me along a wide road that could have been almost anywhere in the capitalist world. It featured chic but anonymous office buildings, an international brand of hotel, a pizzeria. I hoped the Games people would be hiring students to walk around wearing berets and carrying baguettes under their arms, just to remind athletes which Olympics they were attending.

I walked on, regretting that I hadn't brought a litre bottle of Célestins with me. The sun and that *Métro* ride had dehydrated my brain.

Soon I caught sight of hope on the horizon – cranes. I changed course towards them, but a couple of hundred metres further on, my oasis turned back into desert. On an anonymous street corner, opposite faceless office blocks, was a building-site fence, a low but impenetrable barrier of wire. Behind it, people in hard hats and fluorescent jackets were busy working on the Olympic dream. They were perched on scaffolding, crouching in the cabs of diggers and carriers, shouting up at distant crane drivers, or just standing about in heavy boots.

Fans of machines and builders' outfits would have been mesmerized, but all I could think was, is it going to be finished in time? In a matter of months, it all had to be ready and cleaned up. You couldn't risk a world-champion high jumper tripping over an abandoned breeze block or force them to climb up a ladder to their room. Or jump up, of course.

Right now, every square centimetre of unconstructed space was a potential *pétanque* pitch. It was gravel and sand as far as the eye could see.

I walked away, wondering whether the choice of new Olympic sports wasn't the last thing on the organizers' minds. Everyone in the team ought to be panicking: "Oh merde, the buildings are never going to be ready on time, we're going to have to hold the Paris Olympics in London. Those Anglais are going to be smugger than ever."

To avoid the subway to hell, I decided to walk further east, past several more building sites (France seemed to have a glut of concrete and glass that it had to get rid of) towards the train station at the Stade de France.

That stadium, of course, has long been finished, and it reminded me that I ought not to be too concerned about the Olympic Village being ready. The French have always been good at building things on or ahead of schedule.

I remember reading about the bridge on the west coast of France between La Rochelle and the Île de Ré. Despite ferocious opposition from ecologists, the bridge was up and open even before full building permission had been obtained.

I should add that many of those "ecologists" were in fact rich Parisians with holiday homes on the island who didn't want the place flooded with carloads of plebs. The full-time islanders were said to be all in favour of a bridge, because previously anyone in need of urgent surgery had to pray that a helicopter ambulance was available.

Then there was the Stade de France itself, which was built for the 1998 World Cup. The nation decided it needed a brand-new football stadium, and the whole job took around two years from the arrival of the first bulldozer to the kick-off of the inaugural match. Compare this to London's Wembley Stadium which took seven years, went vastly over budget, suffered roof cave-ins, collapsed sewers and countless lawsuits, and forced the

English national team to play some of its matches in Wales, where everyone hates the English.

When in doubt, do it the French way, I say.

Soon the Stade de France was looming up ahead of me like a huge white frisbee. Its perimeter fence was decorated with billboards advertising a pre-Olympics athletics meeting, and the prospect of all that physical exertion made me think that I ought to visit a sports shop on my way home.

Sports superstores with equipment for every kind of sport, whatever the season, are another French speciality. And I had decided to buy one particular piece of gear. Nothing to do with *pétanque* or the Olympics.

This was a piece of sporting equipment that just might help me to win a very special prize.

12

"Maybe you should suggest a big pétanque tournament, right here by the canal?" I told Marjorie. "All you need is the permission from the Paris committee to use their logo, maybe not to make pétanque an official Olympic sport, but more as a sort of ...?" As so often, my French was exhausted.

"No," she said.

Oh well, I'd tried.

We were standing next to one of Paris's trademark straight-backed green benches. It was early evening, not yet dusk, and on this weekday, most of the people around us on the canal bank were dogwalkers, joggers or dog-walking joggers. (I would call that last group doggers, but I think that means something else.)

Marjorie and I met up early so that we could claim this bench as our picnic HQ. She had already covered it with a bright-red blanket and laid out a couple of cool boxes and several bottles of red wine.

"No," she repeated. "We can't have a tournament here. In summer, this whole zone along the canal is always Paris Plages."

Paris Plages is the annual event for which long stretches of the River Seine and both sides of the Bassin de la Villette are turned into beach-themed playgrounds, with trampolines, ping-pong tables, wooden dance floors, temporary swimming pools (one of them actually using canal water), even a few *pétanque* lanes. There are also plenty of pop-up cafés and deckchairs. It's not all about exercise.

"Paris Plages does not accept competition," Marjorie said. "They expel all the restaurant boats and theatre boats that are usually moored here. It's Paris Plages or nothing."

"OK," I conceded, "but if you want pétanque at the Olympics, I think it has to be in Paris itself. You can't force people to go out to the banlieues. What about the Tuileries?"

Surely, I thought, all those wide gravel alleys in the gardens were perfect for a spot of *boules*. Louis XVI and Marie-Antoinette must have played there of an evening, before they came a poor second in the Revolution.

"Yes, interesting idea," Marjorie said. "You're really taking this pétanque campaign seriously, aren't you? I'm flattered." I could have sworn she let her eyelashes flutter at me.

"It's a good cause," I blustered.

She laughed, clamping a hand on my bicep as if to stop herself falling over at the hilarity of it. Her fingers stayed there a bit longer than was necessary to prevent an accident, and I couldn't help being reminded of Jake's advice about playing the hand you've been dealt. If I played my poker cards right, I thought, I might be in with a sporting chance. And Marjorie was very attractive in a slightly scary way. This evening she had put on jeans and a light cotton shirt, and she was wearing Converse sneakers – the French person's casual uniform. To me it looked as if she'd made a conscious attempt to dress down, like an army general wearing civvies.

Her fellow club members turned up soon afterwards. Three men, three women, all in their late twenties or early thirties, and a typical Parisian mix of origins. Marjorie told me they'd met at business school.

She began filming interviews while two separate *pétanque* games were started, so that we could stake a claim on as much gravel as possible before other groups arrived. It was all very territorial – military almost. Napoleon must have been a keen *bouliste*. He was heavily into gaining territory via cannonballs.

I found myself scanning the horizon hoping that Ambre might turn up, even just on her way home from the incubator. I hadn't repeated the invitation to join me beside the canal, but a symptom of old-school wooing seems to be that you constantly hope that the object of your woo will pop up out of the blue.

Shut up, I told myself. When your thoughts start to rhyme, it's brain-burnout time.

To take my mind off solar panels, I joined in a game. Marjorie had brought a spare set of *boules* for me.

"You know how to play?" The guy asking me was very tall and very blond with flouncy hair. His shirt bore an expensive logo and he had the kind of valuable watch that no one would risk wearing while playing *pétanque* unless they had a couple more of the same at home. I took an instant dislike to him.

He had addressed me in almost accent-free English, but I replied in French.

"Explique-moi. Si la pétanque n'est pas trop compliquée pour un Anglais." I'd asked him to explain – using the familiar "tu" form – if it's not too complicated for an Englishman to understand. Yes, I was using passive-aggressive irony, a very Parisian tactic.

His three game partners laughed. They were markedly less arrogant-looking than him, but just as well groomed. They made me think Marjorie's business school published a catalogue of casual wear for plebian locations.

The tall blond guy explained that you had to throw your first *boule* of two as close to the *cochonnet* as possible. Then someone from the other team has a go, and if their *boule* doesn't land closer than yours, they and their team have to keep throwing until it does.

"Simple enough even for an Anglais," I said. "But there are five of us. Don't you need teams of two?"

"Why don't you go on the team with the two girls?" blond guy said. "That should make things equal."

The two women jeered at him and promised retribution. And when we started to play, my team did get off to a dominant start. I was actually pretty good at the game, I found. The gravel was flat, the *boules* hardly bounced or rolled after impact, so you just had to judge distance. I even managed to cannonball one of the blond guy's potentially winning *boules* out of the game. Highly satisfying.

"Who needs a drink?" he asked. His *boule* had been catapulted towards the bench.

"I brought a good bottle of Chardonnay," his male chum said. "I put it in the biggest cool box."

"No wine for me, merci, just water," I called out.

"No wine, Englishman?" This was one of my women teammates. She was small, lively and friendly. She had high-fived me when I slammed the blond guy's *boule*.

It always sounds stupid to say, "I got really drunk last night." As stupid as someone in a rainy tourist resort who says, "You should have been here yesterday, it was lovely."

So I just replied, "Not this evening." Better to be a man of mystery.

"What is he saying?" the blond guy said. He was walking back towards us, Chardonnay bottle in one hand, wine glasses expertly fanned in the fingers of the other hand, while my water bottle warmed in his armpit. "The Englishman doesn't drink wine?"

If there's one thing I hate, it's being talked about as if I wasn't there. It reminds me of when my mum and grandmother used to do it – "Paul hasn't eaten *all* that cake, has he?"

So I took some petty revenge.

"I often drink wine," I said, extracting my bottle of Vichy Célestins from under said armpit. "But this evening I've decided to drink only collaboration water."

I called it *eau de collabo*, using the common French slang abbreviation for a wartime collaborator. It sounded quite poetic, rhyming like that, but to an upper-class Frenchman like this blond guy, it was an English *pétanque* ball aimed right between the eyes.

"Oh, you English," he said, making a show of being unconcerned as he uncorked the bottle. "It's very easy for you to sneer at France about collaboration, you weren't invaded."

A raw nerve, I thought. Did his *grand-père* work for an Oberleutnant during the Occupation? Or did his *grand-mère* exchange sex for sausage? The Nazi Occupation is never far from the surface of the French mind, just as Dunkirk pops out of British mouths whenever there's a crisis.

"Do you mean we English had it easy?" I asked. "My grandparents didn't think it was easy when the bombs were falling on their street. My great-uncle didn't think it was easy when he landed in Normandy to liberate France." Somehow my French grammar and vocabulary managed to stay in tight military formation, and the attack hit home.

"England wasn't occupied," blond guy said, tugging viciously on his cork. "So you weren't faced with the complex moral choices that we had to make."

I unscrewed my water with a satisfying puff of gas.

"No, because Churchill made a simple moral choice in 1940," I said. "We will fight them in the streets, on the beaches, in the trees ..." My memory and French vocabulary ran out. "De Gaulle was in London," I went on, "and he told the French soldiers to come and join his army. But they just surrendered."

I'd read this in a book that Jake had lent me. Something about a thousand ways of annoying the French[2].

Well, this particular way of annoying one particular Frenchman worked very well. Abandoning his attempt to uncork the Chardonnay, the blond guy rose to his full height and glowered down at me.

"What were our men supposed to do in 1940? Abandon their families? Leave them at the mercy of the Nazis?"

"All the men in my family did that," I said. "Except my grandad. He was only five. The others joined the army. A lot of the women were in uniform too. All I'm saying is that *some* French people collaborated. For complex moral reasons, maybe." I took a long slug of Célestins.

"It's true." The small energetic woman waded in. "Simone de Beauvoir worked for Vichy radio. Jean-Paul Sartre took a teaching job that was free because a Jew had been fired."

"My great-grandfather was a grand Résistant," the other male chum said.

I've lost count of the number of times a French person has

---

[2] Paul is probably referring to *1000 Years of Annoying the French*.

told me that they had a "great resister" in the family. It's surprising the Nazis managed to stay in France for more than two weeks, let alone four years.

"Your great-grandfather was a good man," I said, raising a toast of my Vichy water. "I know there were lots of grands Résistants and grandes Résistantes," I added, giving the feminine form. "It's just a pity there weren't more."

It was another low blow, and it hit home.

"You'd never have won anything without the Americans," blondie growled. "It's easy when you've got a big brother."

That old chestnut. Well, of course, like an actual chestnut in its pricky casing, it does sting a bit. I was still wondering whether to accuse him of watching too many Hollywood films – snooty French people hate being accused of watching Hollywood films – when Marjorie parachuted in to save me. She must have heard the raised voices.

"Come and film an interview, Hervé," she ordered blondie.

"Do you have some red wine?" he asked her. "I'm really not in the mood for white."

"Yes, an excellent Brouilly," she said.

"Well thank you for saving me," he said. He gave the Chardonnay bottle to one of the other guys, and went off with Marjorie, his honour apparently saved.

The rest of the evening was far less warlike. The *pétanque* was competitive but friendly, and only once did a ball plop into a camouflaged dog poop. Even then, these Parisian neo-*boulistes* had wet wipes at hand, so the game was barely held up.

Meanwhile Marjorie filmed all her interviews and kept Hervé away from me. She couldn't keep him away from herself, though, and later on in the evening, I saw him getting over-persistent with the physical contact. When she brushed him off, he stalked away along the canal bank carrying an open bottle of wine and two glasses, as if announcing to everyone that he was perfectly capable of landing himself some receptive company.

When we'd all had enough of *pétanque*, the others bade more convivial farewells, and then Marjorie and I were alone with a collection of unbroken glasses, two empty cool boxes and a clutch of empties.

"I'll edit the interviews and we can send them to Switzerland," she said. She was looking ever so slightly drunk. She was smiling much more than is usually necessary when speaking about Switzerland.

"Can you subtitle the interviews in English?" she asked me.

"Of course," I agreed.

"Maybe you want to download the films now, on to your computer?"

"Now?" I asked. "Tonight?"

"Yes, you live near here, don't you?"

"Yes, not far from here," I confessed.

She raised her eyebrows at me, as if to say, "Is that all you're going to say? Only an idiot would fail to understand what I'm suggesting. And are *you* an idiot?"

"But I live in a students' residence," I said. "We're not allowed to have visitors."

"What? Impossible! May sixty-eight was all about that." She was referring to the student riots of 1968, one of France's many revolutions.

"I thought it was about throwing stones at policemen?"

"Yes, but it all started because the university authorities wouldn't allow men and women to live in the same buildings." Suddenly she shook her head and looked much more sober. "But OK, no problem, I'll send you the films tomorrow," she said.

She had seen through my obvious lie about visitors and taken the hint with cool efficiency.

"It was a good idea to have this game," I said. "And I hope I didn't annoy your friend too much."

"Hervé? C'est un gros con, mais c'est un ami." He's a major twat but he's a friend. I respected that. We all have at least one friend like that. Jake, for example.

I walked back home, steering away from the canal bank, where alcohol had now taken hold of the remaining picknickers.

There was laughter, breaking glass and then a body-sized splash followed by an outburst of cheering.

My mind was clear, and I wondered if I'd handled the situation with Marjorie well.

Jake was going to tell me I was an idiot, but my attentions were firmly focussed elsewhere. Even now, as I walked along the empty street that ran parallel to the canal, I was thinking about Ambre, weighing pros and cons.

I was almost certain that she would be in her room right now. And even though it was diplomatic suicide to go and knock on her door, I really wanted to do it.

"No! Don't do it!" the common-sensical side of my brain was pleading.

"Fuck off! I want to do it!" the rest of my neurones were yelling, hoping to drown out the common sense.

"She'll get mad and never want to talk to you again."

"Fuck off!"

When I arrived outside the students' residence, and looked up at Ambre's window, I saw a light behind her curtain.

Heroically, I resisted the temptation to go and say "bonsoir". I went into my room and ordered myself to lie down and go to sleep instead of disturbing her. It was time to put this stupid idea to bed, literally. Wait until daylight if you want to see her, I urged myself. Don't, whatever you do, remind her of the previous night when you banged uninvited on her door. That would be cretinous beyond belief.

Two minutes later I was in bed and counting French sheep. Or trying to – as the French language differentiates between masculine and feminine nouns, I thought I should decide if the sheep were ewes or rams. So should I start counting with *un* or *une*?

No, of course I wasn't doing that. I was standing outside Ambre's door with my fist raised, wondering how to knock. One swift rap with all the fingers? A couple of taps with one knuckle? A paradiddle of fingernails?

In the end, indecision tensed my muscles so much that my

neck twitched and I gave the door a headbutt. From inside it must have sounded as though a bull was trying to barge into a china shop.

"Kyess?" she asked, a short, irritable form of "Qui est-ce?" Who is it?

"Sorry, it's Paul," I said, not the first time in my life I've had to apologize for being me.

"What?" She didn't sound at all pleased.

An unpleasant "told you so" voice began to whine in my head.

"I've got something for you," I told Ambre.

"What is it?" She still didn't sound as though she wanted to open the door.

"Sorry, no, forget it, I'll show you tomorrow." Good sense had finally won me over.

For some reason, though, this last argument convinced her to open up. I heard a lock being undone and then, poking into the corridor, there was her head, her locks tied back, her dark eyes aimed suspiciously at me.

"I just wanted to give you this," I said. "It's too big for the mailbox. And maybe you can use it tomorrow morning. Alors voilà."

I held out the piece of sporting equipment I had bought that afternoon.

It was a boogie board cover, like a large, flat rucksack with adjustable straps.

"It's for carrying your panneau solaire," I said.

It had occurred to me that a boogie board cover would be just the right size, and I'd bought the most robust model, which ought to take the weight of her panel.

"Oh," she said. She touched it, feeling the thickness of the black nylon fabric. "Merci beaucoup."

"Je t'en prie," I said, as she'd taught me to say.

"That's very kind."

"Sometimes I do kind things, juste comme ça. Like when I feed the sparrows."

93

"The ones that you don't want to fatten up and eat?"

"Exactly," I said. "And I don't want to eat you, either."

I swore silently at myself. Eat her? Why the hell would I come out with that?

"Sorry," I mumbled. "That sounded really stupid."

"Yes, really stupid," she said, "I think you should stop talking."

"I'll just say goodnight and go."

"Yes. Goodnight. And merci beaucoup."

The door closed, much more gently than it had opened.

One thing was for sure – the two halves of my brain were going to be yelling at each other all night long.

13

Marjorie worked fast. By the end of the next morning, she had sent over her edited canalside interviews.

I decided to go into the incubator to subtitle them. For a start, it would be good publicity to be seen sitting there, headphones on, subtitling video footage. People can never resist peeking at your screen as they walk by, and these were cool films, featuring good-looking talking heads. Obviously, if I'd been subtitling a documentary about nasal hair removal, I would have done it at home.

Plus, of course, at the incubator there was also the possibility of bumping into Ambre.

I'd prepared in my mind a short dialogue that would take place next time I saw her in the students' residence or at the incubator, or anywhere in between. It consisted of me asking how things were going in general, and whether the boogie board cover was proving useful.

That was it. Nothing more. Definitely no unscripted lines in reply to whatever she might say.

The only chink in my conversational armour was what I would say if the boogie board cover straps had broken and sent her solar panel crashing to the ground. If that happened, my plan was to run away and change my address.

Subtitling Marjorie's film was easy because all the people she had interviewed were saying basically the same thing: "I'm French and I play pétanque." Anyway, her most important message wasn't in the words, it was in the pictures. The players were all young, they were of different origins, and one of them

(I hadn't noticed this on the night) was wearing a rainbow badge. The message was clear: *pétanque* is diversity with added *boules*.

Marjorie's editing was slick, with some nice cutaway shots of people playing, in one of which, if you looked carefully, you caught a very brief glimpse of Hervé ranting at me. Luckily his voice wasn't audible, or I might have had to tweak the subtitles.

After a quick, typically nouveau-Parisian lunchtime snack – a Mediterranean vegetable wrap, or as the French pronounce it, a "vrap" and a kidney-cleansing green smoothie, pronounced "smooty", I re-read what I'd written, corrected a few bloopers, then sent the film back to Marjorie.

I was surprised to get an instant reply, inviting me to meet her at the École Militaire.

"You can count the hours," she said, so I knew it was work. But why meet at Napoleon's military academy, which still provides France with its highest-ranking officers?

Before leaving the incubator, I wandered casually to the meeting rooms and back, hoping for a chance encounter with, maybe, a solar panel developer or two. Then, accepting failure, I took the *Métro* across town. It was early afternoon, so the journey was much less of an endurance test than my trip out to the Olympic Village.

Marjorie was waiting for me on the terrace of a large brasserie by the *Métro* exit at École Militaire station.

I like these big cafés. They have the old-school charm that Paris conjures up when it's not trying too hard to be Paris. The waiters were all wearing starched white aprons, and they were accustomed to serving military officers or the civil servants from the nearby ministries, so they possessed the same mixture of strategic subservience and withering self-assurance that the best English butlers probably used to have.

As soon as I sat down with Marjorie, an apron materialized at my elbow. I mentioned that I'd like an espresso, and mere seconds later the cup was there, with a glass of water, a couple of sugars and a small square of chocolate, the bill neatly tucked under the saucer. No doubt it was going to cost a fortune, but then it had just been served by one of the world's top waiters. And besides, I wasn't paying.

Marjorie was looking her usual business self, like a well-designed attaché case.

I asked her why we were here.

"My papa works at the École Militaire."

"He's a soldier?"

"He was, but now he works in the képi service."

This, she told me, was a department at the school that specialised in producing the complicated headwear that French officers don for official occasions. We've all seen the cylindrical French gendarme's hat, like a bean tin with a peak. Well, French officers wear different versions of this basic *képi*, in various regimental colours, and decorated with an amount of gold braid proportionate to their rank. Their whole military ID gets sewn on to their *képi*. Marjorie explained that her dad measured heads and ordered designs.

"Are we going to order a special képi for Alain?" I asked. "Our pétanque general?"

Luckily she thought I was joking.

"My father will show us something interesting *inside* the school," was all she would reveal. I guessed it was Bonaparte's very own *boules*, preserved in a glass cabinet.

I finished my coffee and wanted another. There's nothing more moreish that an excellent espresso and a dark chocolate with one edge slightly melted where it was touching your cup. But we had no time for treats, so I accompanied Marjorie along the wide avenue to the École Militaire.

The Eiffel Tower loomed on our right, looking surprisingly khaki in daylight, as if it was a clumsily camouflaged annex of the military academy.

The soldiers at the entrance to the École were armed for a commando raid, and infinitely more security-conscious than the civilian guards I'd seen at the nationality office. My phone and computer stayed so long in the X-Ray machine that I was sure they were downloading or erasing all my photos.

Before going through the metal detector portal, I had to dig
into the hidden folds of my pockets to make sure no metal filings
had rubbed off my coins. Even then I beeped, and the soldier
who frisked me only just stopped short of a colonoscopy.

My passport was scanned, and I'm pretty sure they phoned
the French ambassadors in every country I've ever visited to find
out whether I'd misbehaved on holiday. I can only assume the
security guys decided to disregard the time some friends and I
mooned at a busload of German football fans in Berlin. Or
maybe, as French soldiers, they approved.

When I was finally let out into the empty corridor beyond, I
felt as though I'd just been through a kind of dry waterboarding.

Marjorie seemed unconcerned by it all. She had passed
through security much faster than me. Maybe, as the daughter
of the *képi* designer, she had a loyalty card.

She led me across a small courtyard towards a slightly run-
down building with a loose-hanging grey door that bulged as
though it had been repainted every year since 1800.

Inside, it was like stepping back at least a century in time. We
were in a musty old shop with a long wooden counter and walls
covered floor to ceiling in shelves that held nothing but hats.
Most of them were wrapped in plastic or brown paper, but you
could see the *képi* shapes inside their packaging.

Everything in sight was a shade of grey or brown except a
few unwrapped *képis* that were probably waiting to be picked up
that day. These were light-blue, white, black-and-gold, all with
intricate embroidery on the sides and peaks. It was the most
uncool and yet exclusive shop I'd ever been in, ten times more
intimidating than those places in London that cater for dukes
who have worn the same style of yellow corduroy trousers for
ten generations.

Marjorie rang a bell on the counter and a middle-aged man
in an anaemic beige uniform appeared from a doorway at the
back of the shop. He was tall, thin and fast-moving, as if he'd
recently retired from a career dodging bullets.

"Bonjour, ma chérie," he said, and came around the counter

to kiss Marjorie on the cheeks. It was, I guessed, her dad.

She introduced me and I shook his bony hand while his eyes subjected me to another X-raying, which is the prerogative of any parent who meets someone he or she suspects might be shagging their daughter.

"Paul is a colleague on the pétanque project," Marjorie explained, as though to warn him off. But he completed his analysis anyway, before letting go of my hand and storing my DNA for future reference.

"Ah oui, la campagne Olympique," he said, and told us he only had a few minutes to show us what we wanted to see, because a colonel was due to come and collect his new headgear.

So I followed father and daughter as they marched side-by-side along the edge of a parade ground that was devoid of paraders, then through a short tunnel that bore gouges along its walls, as though tank drivers had sped through it while drunk, and finally into a wide open area of sports fields.

Over to our right, a tennis match was in progress, a hard-hitting mixed doubles.

Beside what looked like small football goals – a handball or hockey pitch, I guessed – a group of men and women in tracksuits were limbering up, stretching muscles. And right in front of us was the biggest sandpit I've ever seen. It was at least half the size of a football pitch.

"Do they use the sand to practise desert combat? Or beach landings?" I asked.

"C'est pour l'équitation," Marjorie said. Horse-riding. So the French still had cavalry? I'd thought they were more technologically advanced than that. "Dressage," she added. Not an integral part of modern warfare, I thought, unless you're using it to confuse the enemy.

"More often to train horses for military parades and riot control," her father said. "And it's not sand, it's fine gravel."

"I'm going to suggest to Alain that we ask permission to turn this area into a pétanque stadium," Marjorie told me. "Several members of FUCPET are retired military officers."

"But what about all the security?" I asked. Those *pétanque* balls were going to set the metal detectors beeping loud enough to topple the Eiffel Tower.

"People wouldn't come through the main building," she said. "There's a street entrance at the back. It's blocked usually."

"Seen enough?" her dad asked. He was getting impatient.

"Can I take some photos, papa?" she asked him.

"No."

And he led us back the way we came.

"Did Napoleon himself ride his horse there?" I asked, trying to make conversation.

"Probably. As did the Duke of Wellington, I imagine," he added, giving me a glare as if I personally had been holding the invading Englishman's reins.

Once we were back in the civilian world, Marjorie led me across the street into the Champ de Mars – the "Martial Field" – where, in the 18th and 19th centuries, troops used to practise manoeuvres like Napoleon's favourite tactic of lining up expendable men and waiting for them to be mown down by enemy musket fire and cannon balls.

Soon the field would be the scene of more picturesque exercises, Marjorie explained. Here, in the evening shadow of the Eiffel Tower was where Paris was going to build a temporary beach volleyball stadium.

"My boyfriend was a volleyball player," she added, almost wistfully.

"Was?" I asked.

"I separated from him during the first lockdown."

"Oh. Why was that?"

She laughed. "Strangely enough, I got fixated with his feet – he walked around with no shoes or socks, and I realized that his feet were really ugly. I was forced to look at them every day. Also he had long Zoom meetings from home. I heard some of them and he was a real twat." She seemed to enjoy using that French word *con*. "I never knew he could be so aggressive. In fact, the problem was that during lockdown I got to know him *really well*. I think lots of couples don't actually know each other at all."

"That's true," I said, thinking, is it really? I bloody hope not.

"As soon as lockdown ended, I asked him to go and live with his parents. He was really furious and aggressive, but it turned out OK."

"He calmed down?"

"Yes, he remembered that I do taekwondo and he doesn't."

"Taekwondo?" Now that she mentioned it, she had shrugged off that Hervé guy almost effortlessly when he started pestering her by the canal.

"This is where the entrance to the beach volley stadium will be," she said.

We were in a formal garden area, where the lines of trees and shrubs already formed a kind of arena. It was a spectacular setting, with the Eiffel Tower filling the sky as if it was preparing to peek over the roof of the stadium at all those beach volleyball swimsuits.

"And just by the Tower, in the Seine, will be the swimming for the triathlon," Marjorie said, pointing towards the river.

"In the river?" I had to grimace as I asked.

"Yes. Eurk." This is another of the French words for "yuk".

We shared a few seconds of silent erking. I didn't even want to think about swimming in there. As every Parisian knows, rainwater runoff from the city streets goes straight into the Seine after minimal filtering, which, added to the sheer number of bargees flushing their bilges every day, makes the river a kind of *eau de merde*.

In addition, there's a nuclear power station about 100 kilometres upriver. It's 40 years old, so I guess that like a middle-aged man it is bound to suffer leakage.

All this made me very glad that I'm not an Olympic triathlete.

"This whole neighbourhood will be at the heart of the Olympics," Marjorie said. "Even the Champs-Elysées will be taken over. And almost every possible location for sports in the city has already been reserved. So having a pétanque stadium in the École Militaire would be fantastic."

I could see her reasoning. Back up your request for a new Olympic sport with the offer of an ideal venue in the heart of

Paris and you had a much stronger case.

"And this is where you can help me," she added. "I want you to do a bit of espionage."

"You want me to spy on the École Militaire?" I hoped not. I was scared of the French military's metal detector, let alone any of its actual weapons.

"No. I want you to pose as an English journalist and try to find out for sure if absolutely *all* the Olympic venues have been announced. Is the Olympic committee planning to announce a few more? Maybe they are even hoping to use the École Militaire's horse training ground for some practice? It's a fair question for a journalist to ask, and they might be more open to you if you're foreign. The French are paranoid about questions from other French people."

"OK." It didn't sound too risky. "Who am I going to ask?"

"I need you to contact at least one of these people." She showed me a list of names and photos on her phone. "They are in charge of all the Olympic buildings. The village, the training grounds and all the venues."

She handed me the phone and I scrolled down, before being confronted by a familiar face.

"What is it?" Marjorie asked me. "Is there a problem? Are you OK, Paul?"

14

The reason for my sudden mental meltdown was the joyful smile on a face I knew much too intimately for comfort.

Imagine you're a zebra on its way to a waterhole in the baking savannah. You're just about to take a refreshing drink when you catch sight of a crocodile in the water. But it's a crocodile you know. You may even, in a past moment of weakness, have slept with the crocodile. And since then, you have annoyed the crocodile on several occasions, most recently when you caused it to lose its job.

This is why you're uncertain where you stand – will the crocodile let you drink in peace for old time's sake? Or will it come and sink its fangs into your throat as vengeance for past grievances?

That was how it stood between Elodie and myself.

Elodie was the scheming daughter of my former boss Jean-Marie Martin. She had most recently hired and then fired me as one of her parliamentary assistants in Brussels, where she had got herself elected as an MEP purely to further her family's business interests and, as a bit of fun on the side, sabotage the EU from within.[3]

I had conspired with one of her other assistants to whistleblow on some shady dealings, so that Elodie had been voted out at the next EU election. This had vexed her somewhat because of the EU's generous policy of giving huge life pensions to anyone who serves two mandates as an MEP. Partly thanks to me, she had served only one.

---

[3] In the novel *Merde in Europe*.

All in all, Elodie was probably not a happy crocodile.

"I know one of these people in charge of the Olympic buildings," I told Marjorie.

"That's excellent, no?"

"Not necessarily." I gave Marjorie a brief rundown of my long history as an English maggot in Elodie's very French apple.

"No problem," Marjorie declared. "In martial arts, you have to exploit your opponent's aggression. Sometimes the best thing is to be attacked. The worst adversary can be an unaggressive one."

"Really? I'd have thought the best opponent was the one who said, 'why don't we go for a beer instead of hitting each other?'."

Marjorie was firm. "I think you should go and talk to this Elodie. You might be surprised."

Yes, as surprised as the zebra who is just enjoying a quick drink when a crocodile rips his nose off.

I don't do martial arts, so I decided that the best form of self-defence is cowardice. I promised Marjorie I'd get in touch with Elodie, but secretly vowed to postpone the call until the next morning at the earliest.

Meanwhile, I had agreed to go to a comedy club with Jake, to watch Cécile perform.

"You'll love this club," he told me. "It's in a cave."

Knowing my luck, it would probably be squatted by bears.

A Parisian *cave* is, as French speakers know, a cellar. A *cave à vin* is a wine cellar, for example. In fact, when French archaeologists talk about their stone-age ancestors living in "caves", I suspect that they are referring to highly civilized prehistoric cellars where meats, cheeses and wines were kept at controlled temperatures. I'm sure French "cavemen" invented complex methods of food storage long before they got around to more workaday stuff like iron, the wheel and language.

Jake's "cave" was beneath a bar near Père Lachaise cemetery, and to judge by its tiny stone staircase and lack of fire exit, the bar's customers were in imminent danger of ending up alongside Jim Morrison, Oscar Wilde and the other famous residents of Paris's most famous boneyard.

"Best to sit near the sortie," Jake said, meaning the exit.

We perched on a low wooden bench, one of a dozen or so that were rapidly filling up with eager comedy fans.

Just like at my students' residence, I was several years older than almost everyone else. The punters here were mostly in their early twenties, and were chatting excitedly as if this was their first visit to a below-ground health hazard.

I've been to the Edinburgh Fringe a couple of times, so I'm not unfamiliar with near-death experiences in the pursuit of laughter. Here, just as in an Edinburgh comedy dungeon, the lights on the ceiling were positioned to collect every drop of dampness dripping from the toilets above, and speaker cables meandered through small puddles of water. On top of this, I sensed that it wouldn't be long before all the oxygen ran out.

The performance area, approximately the size of Ambre's solar panel, was against one wall, with the benches forming a semi-circle around it. The stage was empty except for a lone microphone stand and a backcloth announcing "All You Need Is Laugh!". Like I said, there is probably a law obliging French naming committees to use ungrammatical English puns.

In such a confined space the combination of chat and mood music was deafening, so Jake had to lean in close to yell in my ear.

"I wrote some new poésie," he shouted, meaning poetry.

That is the last thing you want to hear when your ears are already hurting, but I nodded to show interest.

"On the Nolympiques," he yelled. "Listen."

I had little choice given that his lips were almost kissing my eardrum.

"The Olympics come around every four years," he began.

"Time for you to save up your tears,
And then with every sport and game,
The superheroes put you to shame.
They can jump and run and ride and swim,

And perform aerobatics in the gym.
They've been training and dieting every day,
While you eat and drink your life away.
They're young and slim and their movements flow,
They make you feel gross and clumsy, and so,
Nolympics are the way to go,
And fuck them if they dare say no."

His mouth unglued itself from my earlobe. The poem seemed to be over.

"What do you think?" he asked.

It was my turn to nuzzle against his nearest cheek.

"Yes," I said, "it's much less obscene than your usual stuff. And it's effective. Maybe because it's all English. No French words at all."

Jake nodded. "Cécile traducted it into French and she also helped me traduct it into pure English. Merde man, how do you keep your languages separate?"

"I have no idée," I said.

"Cécile writes really formidably," Jake said. "You know, she invents all that stuff she tells her clients about the viticulteurs. Like, this wine is made in the Pyrenées by a woman with green hair and a hamster called Charles de Gaulle."

"She makes it all up?"

"Yeah, you should hear her doing it late at night, when her clients are drunk. 'Oh, this vin naturel is made by Jérôme, he gives every grape an individual name. His Côtes du Rhône contains only grapes called Marcel.' She is formidable."

"Well, I'm disappointed," I confessed. I'd really bought into the idea that Parisian hipster cafés were turning their back on big producers and buying from the little man or woman. I loved imagining that my wine had been delivered to Paris by a hippie on a bike.

"We're inhabiting the Facebook world, mon ami," Jake went on. "Everyone thinks they know everyone, so Cécile gives it to them. She makes it so you really know the viticulteur as a friend. And you also know his dog or his hamster."

As if on cue, Cécile appeared at Jake's side. She was dressed in a white catsuit and she had punked up her hair with gel. She looked like a giant asparagus. She greeted us with a nervous smile and handed Jake a ukulele.

"Merde," Jake said, and I repeated it. This is what the French tell anyone who is about to go on stage. It comes from the days when piles of horse's droppings outside a theatre were a promising sign because they meant that carriages were delivering a large audience.

"Je prends," Cécile said – I'll take it. Performers don't reply "*merci*" to "*merde*". Then she ducked back into the dressing room, which was a storage cupboard under the stairs.

Before I could ask why Jake had been left holding the ukulele, the background music cut out and an invisible Frenchman started shouting at us through the PA system. He sounded very keen to know whether we were in the mood for comedy. Fortunately for him, the general feeling seemed to be that we were.

Reassured, he made his appearance. He was a short balding guy who informed us that he was the owner of the club. This, I assumed, explained his presence on stage. He certainly hadn't passed any auditions. His attempts at banter with the audience fell flat, especially given that whenever he asked someone where they'd come from tonight, the answer was "Paris".

Even so, the small crowd lapped it up. I assumed it was because they were too young to drink more than one glass of alcohol without giggling.

After a couple of painful minutes, the MC called up the first comedian, a young guy whose act consisted largely of him telling us how he had got stoned and then … pause for effect … felt really *hungry*!

This had everyone in the audience guffawing hysterically. It couldn't just be the alcohol, I thought. It was as if they'd never heard someone try to be funny in public before.

Next up was a tall, chic-looking guy who spent five minutes imitating my *pétanque* buddy Alain's southern accent and saying that people from Marseille were stupid. I think the idea was that he was satirizing Parisian snobs. But I wished Alain had been there to heckle him with a set of *boules*.

Cécile came on, and I began to pray that she would be good.

"Salut!" she yelled, and everyone laughed.

Oh *merde*, I thought, they even think "hello" is funny.

"I'm not very developed physically," she said. It was true. Her white catsuit was almost contourless. "In fact, I've hardly changed since I was conceived. I'm a twenty-year-old sperm."

The crowd howled. She did look the part.

"And talking of old sperm, I've brought my two grandfathers with me."

She gestured down towards Jake and me, the oldest people in the room. The audience howled some more.

"One of them has put on his grandad shoes. Stand up and show us your shoes, papi."

She pointed at me. I obeyed, lifting a foot to show everyone a finely polished piece of English leather. For some reason, this was hilarious. Were my best shoes really that old-fashioned?

"He has to polish them that much so he can see where he's putting his feet. He can't see a thing, poor old man."

I did my best to look amused rather than confused.

"Now, my other grandad, do you remember what I told you to do?"

Cécile gazed down at Jake like a geriatric nurse asking a pensioner if he remembers how to use a spoon. Jake pretended he didn't know what she meant.

"The ukulele?"

Jake got up and handed it to her.

"That's right! Well done, grandad!"

I had to admit that Cécile knew how to work the audience. She was nerveless, in control, a real stage persona. The other acts had just been ordinary people holding a microphone.

"Now, I'm going to sing you a song, a really serious song," she announced. "It's about all the advantages of being in a stable, loving relationship."

She strummed a chord on the ukulele, opened her mouth, and stood silent. She held the mute pose for a full ten seconds, and laughter began to grow. Finally she shrugged.

"There are *zero* advantages, right? Who wants a guy or girl who's there *all* the time, being nice to you, saying they love you? What if I don't want to be nice? What if I don't love you? What if I want to fuck someone else?"

The audience whooped. Jake was cheering the loudest. She was describing his ideal woman.

"Hey, grandad, how long have you and grandma been married? Two hundred years?"

She was pointing at me.

"I'm not married," was all I could think of to say.

"But you're in love, grandad, I can tell. Aah, look at his in-love face." If being in love meant looking horrified, that was me. "What's her name, grandad?"

I didn't answer.

"Come on, don't be shy."

"Ambre." Jake had shouted it out, the bastard.

"Ambre, nice name, very warm. What does she do?"

"She sells panneaux solaires," Jake told her.

"So she's Ambre solaire? At least she's protected when she's up on the roof fitting her panneaux."

This earned Cécile her biggest laugh so far. I thanked the sun god that Ambre was too busy to come out with me of an evening.

"Now I'm going to sing you a song about *my* love life. And this one has words."

Cécile launched into a lightning-fast ditty which was a list of names, male and female, and all the things she'd done with these people. If even half of it was true, she led a hyperactive life. What she did with Blaise, one afternoon in Père Lachaise, probably contravened all the cemetery's regulations.

I didn't concentrate much after that. I was too busy kicking myself with my grandad shoes. I'd never thought of the connection between Ambre's name and her job, and now I had to use pain therapy to force myself to forget Cécile's pun about "Ambre solaire". Knowing me, I'd let it slip out and kill my chances with her as dead as that Blaise surely was after what

Cécile did to him or her in Père Lachaise.

After the show, Jake and I waited outside in the street while Cécile hung around downstairs to get her share of the hat money. She had to wait, she said, because the bar owner was known to be bad at counting cash when no one was looking.

Several of the departing punters called out "Bonsoir, les grand-pères!" as they passed. Jake didn't notice. He was too busy lecturing me about love, or his version of it.

"You've got to be like Cécile, mon ami. Direct. You tell Ambre, OK, ma chérie, maybe you have no time for lunch or dinner, but everyone has time to fuck. I mean, bees and ants work all the time, but they find time to fuck, n'est-ce pas?"

"You want me to tell Ambre she's like an insect? Brilliant idea. Besides, I don't think bees or ants fuck, do they? They just fertilize the queen's eggs."

"You have no sense of poésie, Paul."

"Les grand-pères!" It was Cécile, leaping out of the club, a grinning asparagus, or sperm maybe, armed with a ukulele. "Make room for me." She squeezed in between us, wriggling wildly. She was still high after coming off stage. "Why don't we all go to my apartment, all three of us?" she said, and her eyes made it clear what the purpose of our visit would be.

"Wow," Jake said. She'd even managed to shock him.

"Merci, mais non merci," I replied quickly.

Cécile wriggled some more. "Come on, after performing, I need sex."

Jake was right about her. She could be rather direct.

"I'm sure Jake will be prepared to help," I said. "I'm just going to go home."

"Home?" She couldn't believe it.

I managed to nod and shrug at the same time.

"You really are a grand-père, aren't you?" Cécile gurgled an adrenaline-fuelled laugh and tapped me on the head with her ukulele.

And so yet another evening in Paris ended up with me walking away from a woman. Something had to change.

15

Next morning, I was woken up by the concierge Madalena bringing me a letter. It was an official envelope, stamped with the tricolour and the head of Marianne, the symbolic heroine of 1789. Maybe, I thought, the French government was announcing a new revolution, and, as a prospective citizen, I was being invited to an audition to see if I was any good at carrying heads on spikes.

"Votre nationalité?" Madalena asked, breathing tobacco vapour into my room, something I was forbidden to do myself by the house rules.

"Let's see," I said, and opened the envelope to find a single sheet of administrative notepaper. I scanned it quickly for any hints that it might be welcoming me to the *République* club.

It was an invitation of sorts, but not to a swearing-in ceremony.

"We have received your application," the anonymous writer informed me. "Please under no circumstances try to contact us while it is being considered."

So it was a case of "don't call us, we'll call you."

"Votre nationalité?" Madalena asked again.

"Pas encore," I told her.

"Let us pray," she said, and wandered back towards the lift, crossing herself with vape incense.

The sunlight wasn't hurting my head this morning. Neither was anything else. The previous night, Ambre's light had been off, so there had been no temptation to go and bash on her door to make a stupid remark.

It was a good thing my head was clear, because now I had to face up to the task of contacting Elodie, which is not something I would willingly have done unless fortified by at least three amphetamines and a bulletproof vest.

Her number was still in my contacts list, but as it rang, I was praying I'd hear the "no longer in service" message.

No such luck.

"Paul? What do you need? Money? A job? An apartment? Sex?"

Fair questions, I suppose, because in the past she had supplied me with all of those.

"Hi Elodie, how are you? Divorced yet?"

"If that's an offer of marriage, Paul, you'll have to ask papa if you're eligible."

She always spoke to me in English, in the slightly American accent that the most expensive French business schools teach. We could have carried on sniping at each other for ever, but one of us had to get serious, and I guessed it was up to me.

"Actually, Elodie, I'm just looking for some information. It's to do with your new job."

"Which new job?" Of course, in her circles, jobs are like cars. You must have at least two, and they have to be very shiny.

"The Olympics." I took a quick glance at her job description on the Paris 2024 website. "You're in charge of what they're calling 'Héritage', right? Deciding what happens to all the Olympic buildings after the Games?"

"Ye-es." She sounded suspicious, as if I was going to ask for the loan of a stadium.

"Well, I'm working as the interpreter for an English journalist who's doing a story on all the Olympic sites in Paris, so I was looking for some information on them."

Elodie had a quick think about this. I heard her tapping a pen or a fingernail, though knowing her, it might have been a dagger.

"If your journalist is English, tell him to call me," she said. "I'll tell him direct."

"It's a she, actually," I said, seizing the chance to get the moral high ground on Elodie. Not that that was ever difficult.

"What's her name? Where is she published? Maybe I've seen her articles."

Shit. I hadn't thought it through that far.

"She's called Sue," I said, for some reason.

"Sue who?"

Now she'd got me. What was a good journalist's name?

"Writer," I said.

"Writer?"

"Yes."

"A journalist called writer?"

It did sound pretty coincidental.

"No," I said. "Not writer. Rider. With a D. Like horse rider. It's a very common English name."

"Sue Rider? Never heard of her. But why don't you tell her to call me?"

This was a very good question. Why didn't I?

"What, and do myself out of a paying job?" I improvised. "Thanks very much."

"Oh yes, Paul, I always forget you're poor. How is your English tearoom doing? Since you stole it from my father, I mean?"

"Stole it? He sold me his share, which he had tricked me into selling to him in the first place, as you very well know."

She laughed.

"I'm only joking with you, Paul. You're so easy to provoke. OK, why don't you come and see me? It will be fun to meet up again."

As the crocodile said to the zebra.

She sent me the address. It wasn't the one given on the Paris 2024 website as the HQ for her department. That was out in the *banlieue* of Saint Denis, near the Stade de France. Not as far outside the city as the Olympic Village, of course. The Games' organizers weren't masochistic. No, their offices were just a baguette's throw beyond the *périphérique*, in what looked on Google Street View like a tastefully restored area of old industrial warehouses. It had been turned into a sort of Silicon

Valley campus with a laid-back restaurant at its heart. The building where Elodie ought to have been working looked like a six-storey log cabin. Trust the Games organizers to choose a hip location for themselves while sending the athletes into the furthest depths of the *banlieue*.

Elodie wasn't working in the log cabin, however attractive it might look. The address she sent me was in the Latin Quarter, the heart of old Paris.

The *Métro* ride from my place to Elodie's in-town office was direct but long. Line 7 seems to have been traced by someone who was trying to fill in all the bits of Paris missed out by the other lines. It meanders across the city like a river in no hurry to get to the ocean.

I could have changed lines a couple of times and got there within half an hour, but no one in their right mind takes the shortest route to meet Elodie.

I exited the *Métro* near the rue Mouffetard, where tourists come to buy expensive cheese and wine in what they imagine to be a typical Parisian market street, and walked up the hill along a road that still bore the traces of the Latin Quarter's intellectual past.

There was a publisher's office with a shop window displaying (now literal) dust jackets, and a bookshop that had been turned into a *crêperie*.

Nowadays, the nearest you get to hearing Latin scholars in Paris's old university district is when someone orders a pizza.

In a street of fairly ordinary 19th-century apartment buildings, I punched Elodie's door code into a keypad, and a tall green gate swung slowly open to reveal a cobbled alley that was wide enough for a car but rutted as though it was still used by horse carriages.

Elodie's message had said "*au fond de la cour*" – at the end of the courtyard – but I couldn't see an end to the alley, so I set off up a gentle slope between the high walls of the neighbouring buildings. As the automatic gate clanged shut behind me, the street noise disappeared and I could hear only the tap of my shoes on the rectangular cobble stones, the kind that the students lobbed at the police not far from here in 1968. Clearly the rioters hadn't found this hidden passageway.

The *cour*, when it finally turned up, was wide and square, ringed by apartment buildings that were completely hidden from the street. Mature trees provided shade, and birds were flitting about as if this was a village square.

I'd heard about these vast hidden courtyards behind Paris's anonymous façades, but I'd never seen one as big as this. It was like being transported back to the 18th century. Perhaps, I thought, that's what Elodie likes about it – she feels like Marie-Antoinette before the Revolution, and she can play at being queen.

In the far corner of the courtyard, I found her family name, Martin, on a head-high fence. When I rang the buzzer, a section of fence swung open. Now I was in an actual garden, with a lawn bordered by rose bushes that bloomed pink, red and yellow. At the end of the lawn was what could almost be described as a cottage, a two-storey house built of what they call "Parisian stone", misshapen hunks of beige, lava-like rock.

It felt as if I'd got to the end of a magically short tunnel to the Normandy countryside.

Hansel and Gretel came to mind, so I watched out for witches as I walked along a stone pathway to a terrace with white-painted iron garden furniture – a round table and four chairs. From here, appropriately French windows opened into a wooden-floored lounge.

I peeped in. The room was empty except for a three-piece suite in cream leather and some oil paintings of rustic scenes that, knowing Elodie's family, were either fake or stolen Monets.

"Come upstairs, Paul. Take off your shoes."

It was Elodie's voice coming from an intercom. I assumed that she'd watched my arrival on CCTV or via satellite.

Despite the feeling that I was being asked to leave my most reliable weapons at the door, I unlaced my leather brogues and stood them on the terrace.

After sock-skating across the shiny parquet floor of the

lounge into an equally polished hallway, I climbed some mercifully carpeted stairs to a landing with four or five doors leading off it.

"In here, Paul. Don't worry, I'm dressed."

Dressed to kill, I thought. I found her sitting at a desk in one of the rooms that overlooked the gardens. Her view was of leaves and branches. A bit like my own room, really, except that her trees were about a hundred years older, and the interior was infinitely more elegant than my student's cupboard.

Elodie's desk was French presidential – varnished wood with curvy legs and gold-painted trimmings, no doubt in the style of Louis something-or-other. Her own legs were in full view because her bare feet were propped up on the desk. She was lounging in a high-backed office chair with a screen on her lap.

She was in much too regal a mood to stand up, so I was forced to bend down and kiss her on the cheeks. Her expensively simple pink skirt and white blouse were accessorized with pearls and various large chunks of gold, one of which was ticking. The Martin family had never been interested in hiding its wealth. Even her skin looked expensive, as though it had recently been treated to a week in the Caribbean.

"What is this place?" I asked her.

"My house, of course. You forget, my husband works for a private bank and my papa is rich. Beautiful, isn't it?"

"Yes, it is. I can see why you prefer to work here instead of Saint-Denis."

"The advantages of télétravail," she said. This is the French word for working from home. "So much less stressful."

"Well, it certainly agrees with you. You're looking annoyingly wonderful." It's always best to butter Elodie up with compliments. She believes them all.

"Thank you, Paul. I wish I could say the same for you. You're looking poor."

"Unlike you. Have you been melting down the gold medals you're meant to be giving to athletes?"

I nodded towards her left hand, which bore almost as many rings as the Olympic logo.

"Engagement, wedding, papa, boyfriend," she said, counting them off.

"Husband *and* boyfriend?"

"Of course, what do you expect me to do with all this holiday time they give us in France?"

"I thought you had more than one job?"

"Yes, so two lots of holiday." She took her feet off the desk and sat up straight. She didn't seem to like where the conversation might be going. "I'm also doing some work for papa."

I didn't dare ask what that was, for fear of being called as a witness at the inevitable trial.

"Your husband's not around?"

"No, you have me all to yourself, Paul. What do you want to do with me?"

It sounded seductive, but below her bantering surface Elodie was as cold and calculating as a deep-frozen cobra.

I sat down opposite her, in a leather armchair that probably cost more than the whole contents of my apartment, including all my shoes.

"I need some info about the Olympic venues that are actually in Paris. In the city itself, I mean."

"Not the village?" She looked almost relieved for some reason. "We have a list of the venues, and there's a new film." She scrolled around on her screen. "Yes, here it is."

She handed her tablet over to me, and I watched a short movie in which a very enthusiastic French actress whose face I knew, but whose name I didn't, introduced a dozen or so venues, some of them conversions of existing buildings like the Grand Palais, others temporary constructions like the beach volleyball stadium at the Champs de Mars and the triathlon set-up on the riverbank. Most of the images were computer simulations of how things would look during the actual Games.

As I watched, I felt that there was something about the venues that bothered me, something wrong. I wished I could put my finger on what it was. It might give me some leverage.

I handed the screen back to Elodie, who was idly consulting her phone messages.

"What do you want to know?" she asked me.

"Are these *all* the Parisian venues?" I asked. "Will any more be added?"

"Why? Do you want to rent out your bed as a venue for trampolining?" She laughed happily at her own joke.

"No. Just asking if there are any plans to build other venues in Paris."

"No. Is that all your journalist wants to know? What's her name again? Sue?"

"Yes," I said, trying to remember if that was what I'd told her.

"Didn't this Sue give you a list of other questions? You came all this way for a yes or no answer?"

"Well …"

"Presumably that's why she didn't tell you to record the interview?"

"Er …"

Elodie laughed again, even more mockingly this time.

"Come on, Paul, I've done hundreds of interviews in my time, and this is bullshit. What do you *really* want? Did you come to bribe me so that your tearoom will get a catering contract? If so, the answer is no. We can't serve those pathetic little English sausages at the Paris Olympics. Or are you looking for a job? We're still recruiting. Is there anything you're actually good at?"

Having finished her demolition job on my honesty, nationality and limited skill set, she sat back in her throne with her arms folded and looked at me like a headmistress who has just proved to a pupil that he copied his essay word-for-word off Wikipedia.

Her smugness annoyed me so intensely that I decided to tell her the truth, or part of it, anyway. It's never wise to tell Elodie *everything*.

"If you must know, I've started working with some people who want to get pétanque accepted as an Olympic sport."

She stared at me for a second or two, then almost screamed with laughter.

"That's very funny, Paul. If you ever decide to tell me the *real* truth, get back in touch."

"But that *is* the truth."

She ignored me.

"You can be straight with me, Paul. You know that in my family, we always work out a deal for our friends."

Yes, I thought, like when her dad tried to sell me a country cottage on the site of a future nuclear power station[4].

Thinking about her father gave me an idea. Maybe Jean-Marie could be of use.

"I promise you it's true," I said. "And I'd tell you the name of the pétanque federation I'm working for, but it would only make you laugh even more. They are campaigning to get 'les boules' adopted as an exhibition event in Paris."

Elodie was shaking her head, no longer laughing, but still grinning in semi-disbelief.

"But it's a sport for ploucs!" This is a French word for hick that describes every level of snobbery victim, from someone who doesn't know the best years for Mouton-Rothschild to people who tuck their pullovers into their trousers and have never been to Paris. "They have no chance!" she went on. "Paris 2024 is all about being hip and young and – to be frank – American. Which, frankly, disgusts me. I mean, breakdancing? Is that a sport now?"

She was sounding like my friend Alain.

"Exactly," I said. "Pétanque would add some Frenchness to the Paris Games. Your father would be all in favour of that."

Elodie's family has always erred on the more rabid side of French nationalism. Her father was an MP for a party voted for by the crustiest *ploucs* in rural France, the same party that Elodie had represented in Brussels. I was surprised that their manifesto didn't include obligatory *pétanque* for all schoolkids.

Not that the Martin family in any way empathized with the *ploucs* who got them elected, of course. It was all about opportunism. Jean-Marie wanted to control the French beef market, so he had to pretend that he liked farmers. And Elodie

---

[4] In the novel *A Year in the Merde*.

had been sent to Brussels to defend the family cause at the EU.

"Surely it would help your father if he campaigned in favour of pétanque and against this Americanization of the Paris Olympics? At the very least it would get him on TV."

"That is true." Elodie was nodding slowly, apparently stirring ideas in that witch's cauldron she called a brain. "Pétanque is Provençal, which is a shame because papa represents a region in the north," she said, "but you're right, there is the anti-American angle. Don't tell anyone –" she leaned across her desk, within stabbing distance of me – "but he is already planning a campaign against the use of English at the Games."

I'd heard this one before. The French are furious that the world prefers to speak English rather than *français*, a much purer, more noble language. The French see the world domination of English as a kind of perpetually repeated slap in the face to remind France that Napoleon lost control of Europe, leaving the way open for English-speakers to conquer the planet. And the French maintain that they invented the modern Olympics, so they're mad at the way English has become the Games' first language.

"How can he stop them using English?" I asked. "It's an international event."

"At Paris 2024, he wants all the signs and notices to be in French first, of course, then Chinese, then Spanish or maybe Arabic, I can't remember the exact order. Anyway, he wants English to be at the bottom."

"But that's absurd."

"Well, yes, but it's symbolic. English will be only the *second* language of most people there, not the first." I could see that she'd studied her father's propaganda. "Anyway, anyway –" she waved her arms in the air to dispel any rational argument from the atmosphere. "Maybe you and he could get together on this."

"No, no." This was my instinct talking. There was no way I was going to get embroiled in any kind of deal with Jean-Marie. I wouldn't go halves with him on a baguette to give to a hungry old lady. He'd get the lady to testify that I tried to pick her pocket while she was busy chewing bread.

"OK, maybe you and papa working together is not a good idea. But how's this – your pétanque people talk to the central Olympic committee in Switzerland about elevating the role of the French language in all future Olympics, starting with Paris, and I can maybe put some pressure on people here in Paris in favour of pétanque?"

I examined this. It sounded suspiciously devoid of complications.

"OK," I said. "I'll put it to the pétanque people."

"Good. And tell me, what is their funny federation called?"

"You really don't want to know."

"But I'll have to tell papa."

"OK, but you're going to laugh."

"Just tell me, Paul."

"FUCPET."

She didn't laugh. She looked as if she was going to choke.

16

I put my shoes back on and waved goodbye to Elodie's house. She returned the wave from her first-floor window. She was smiling as though we were bosom buddies.

All this chumminess made me even more suspicious of her motives. It felt like there was something very *poisson*-y going on.

With anyone else I would have decided I was being paranoid, but not with Elodie. Nothing about her is ever straightforward. If she drew a straight line on a piece of paper, when you viewed it under a microscope it would be as twisted as her family's DNA.

Maybe that was why I'd also felt uneasy watching her film of those Parisian venues. What was it about them that bothered me? I couldn't pin it down.

Nevertheless, I had some good news for Marjorie. As I trekked across the courtyard towards the streets of Paris, I called to tell her that there was apparently no new venue planned at the École Militaire. Though even as I said it, I couldn't help looking over my shoulder in case Elodie was listening in.

Arriving back in the street, I saw that I'd received a message. It was from Ambre. Something in my chest gave a jolt.

It was an invitation to a presentation she was giving that same afternoon at the incubator. She needed spectators, she said, to fill out the audience. Not exactly an intimate dinner at her place. It was even addressed *"Bonjour à toutes et à tous"* – hello everyone (be they feminine or masculine) – so it was a group message. But I decided to go along, even if she had sent it to her whole contacts list. After all, it's always interesting to meet a woman's hairdresser, parents, schoolmates and ex-boyfriends.

Ambre and her business partner Lara had reserved the biggest meeting room, a rectangular aquarium that looked out over the mass of railway lines leading to the Gare du Nord. The double glazing was very efficient, judging by the silent way an old suburban RER train was shaking up its passengers cocktail-style as it lumbered north.

I sat halfway back in the meeting room, in about the tenth row of brand-new plywood seats. There was a large screen at one end of the room, on to which a headline was projected: "*Le Futur Solaire*". Ironically, the title was faint because of the sun beaming in through the glass outer wall.

Ten minutes later, the room was half full. Several of the attendees were people I'd seen hanging out at the incubator, but there were others in business suits who looked as though they might actually be bringing finance or experience into the room.

Dead on time – a Parisian rarity – Ambre and Lara strode in, and the lighting changed. The blinds were drawn shut and electric lights came to life. The slogan on the screen was sharply visible at last.

Ambre and Lara both arrived with boogie board covers on their backs, and I had to congratulate myself because they looked very cool indeed. Greeting everyone with a cheery "Bonjour!", both women laid their board covers on the table in front of the screen, unzipped them and revealed the sleek solar panels within. Still synchronized, they lifted their creations and stood before the audience holding what looked like a double TV screen. The "*Futur Solaire*" headline was projected across the two panels. After a few seconds to let the message sink in, they laid the panels carefully down and began to pitch.

It was very technical, so I didn't follow all of it. And I have to admit that I spent an inappropriate amount of time admiring Ambre's moves rather than concentrating on her message.

Both women were pitching hard and flicking smoothly from one visual to the next. Electrical diagrams, pricing, energy-saving projections, it was all there, and at the end of half an hour the whole audience was applauding even louder than Cécile's hysterical crowd down in the comedy cave.

The two pitchers fielded questions, including a brief interrogation about the cost of raw materials from a guy in a banker's suit and tie, and when I followed the plebs filing out of the room, I saw Ambre deep in conversation with him.

I was sitting in my favourite armchair next to the coffee machine, skimming through some bumph that Marjorie had sent me in preparation for our Swiss meeting, when a finger prodded a nerve in my shoulder and made me jump.

It was Ambre, wearing her boogie board on her back, as if she was off to the beach after a day at the office. She was grinning down at me, looking as high on adrenaline as Cécile had been when she came off stage.

"I just wanted to say thanks," she told me, in French.

"Je t'en prie," I replied, as usual. "What for?" I added.

"For this carrying bag, it's cool. When you turn up to a presentation looking like this, people really pay attention. So merci beaucoup."

"Je t'en prie beaucoup." I wasn't sure if I pronounced the *beaucoup* exactly right, but what the hell.

"Thanks for coming to the presentation, too. And please don't say 'je t'en prie' again."

"OK. Merci pour le merci," I improvised. "It was a great pitch."

"Ah!" This loud exclamation came from yet another woman carrying a boogie board. It was Lara, a smaller, more Mediterranean version of Ambre. They looked a bit like half-sisters. "Judging from the accent, this is the Anglais you have been talking about?" she said to Ambre.

While Ambre did an embarrassed "Er ...", Lara looked me up and down, smiling.

"Je suis Anglais," I confirmed. "Paul." I shook Lara's hand and congratulated her on the presentation.

She said that it had been really promising. They'd had some serious interest and made some excellent contacts that they were going to explore. It sounded as if she was still in pitching mode.

"You're still looking for financing?" I asked.

"Yes," Lara said. "As you probably heard in there, we need a big injection of funding to take it all a stage further."

"Either that or a major contract," Ambre said.

"Yes, and that's another thing," Lara said. She used the slang word "*truc*", as if the "thing" wasn't really that serious. "Sol Mineur. We might have to change it to Sol Majeur, or something else."

"Yes. Sol Mineur sounds too ... minor," Ambre said. "Two different people said we needed something more dynamic, more positive."

"Ambre Solaire," I said, and even as I spoke, I was simultaneously kicking myself and biting my tongue. Why the holy hell had I said that? My mouth was apparently like Jake – on a permanent mission to annoy women.

"What?" Ambre said, her eyes sending out slivers of ice.

But Lara laughed, and prodded Ambre in the ribs.

"So this definitely *is* the Anglais you've been telling me about," she said.

"L'idiot anglais," I confirmed.

Ambre looked as though she wanted to leave, but Lara held on to her arm.

"You would not believe the stupid suggestions we've had for company names," Lara continued, still clinging to Ambre's arm. "Someone told us that we should call ourselves 'Yes We Panneau'. You know, like Obama, 'Yes we can'?"

"Just say pan no," I said. "I'm sorry," I told Ambre. "It was a friend who suggested Ambre Solaire."

"When you told him all about Ambre?" Lara gave Ambre another of her meaningful nudges.

Now it was my turn to do an embarrassed "Er ...".

Lara smiled at me, and I smiled back. It felt good to get the approval of The Best Friend. I felt certain she would argue my case with Ambre, even after I'd committed an awful gaffe. I really needed that kind of back-up.

"I'll stop suggesting stupid French names for you," I

promised. "But you have to admit that you French come out with some incredibly bad English puns."

"Maybe it's something about the English language that produces stupid puns," Ambre said.

"No, it's something very French," I said. "You say that French is the most beautiful language in the world, but you love playing around with English. You think it's more fun than French. You think *we're* fun. You think we're all Mister Bean."

"Block up your ears, he's going to start singing 'God Save the Queen,'" Lara said.

"King, you mean," I corrected her.

"Oh, yes, sorry your Majesty!" Lara bowed, and then she and Ambre poked fun at the English for a minute or two, concentrating mainly on our slavish allegiance to people who wear crowns.

I took it all on the chin and made a note to send Lara a bouquet of flowers as a thank-you for getting me out of trouble with Ambre. Or maybe not. Flowers might be misconstrued.

"I'll go and write the bilan," Lara said, meaning the debrief of their presentation. "Au revoir, Pol. I hope," she added, raising an eyebrow at Ambre, exactly like a woman telling her friend that it was OK to dance with the guy who was inviting her to tango. Wow, I thought, Lara deserves a bouquet *and* a year's supply of chocolates.

"If you're going back to the foyer, we could share a taxi," I suggested as soon as Ambre and I were alone. It sounded a lot more enticing than "maybe we could share a crowded Métro carriage."

"OK, why not, yes," Ambre said.

"I promise I won't offer to carry your panel," I told her.

"That's a shame, I'm feeling suddenly exhausted."

Naturally Sir Paul stepped up to bear the damsel's burden. He even offered her a healing elixir from the nearby elixir machine.

But all she wanted was to get back to the students' residence – for a quick nap, she said, because she hadn't slept much the night before.

"And this time it wasn't even my fault you didn't sleep," I said. "Oh, sorry, did that sound weird?"

"No more than usual," she said.

We found a taxi at the nearest rank and placed the panel across both our knees like a stiff blanket.

"Are you going surfing?" the driver asked, wittily.

"Yes, in the canal," I answered, and we all had a chat about why it wasn't a good idea to swim in that murky water. He lived nearby, so he knew the murkiness well.

Sitting so close to Ambre, almost thigh to thigh, it was horribly tempting to put my hand on hers. Perhaps Ambre felt this, and wanted to avoid it, because as soon as the conversation with the driver ebbed away, she began talking quickly to me, as if silence between us might lead somewhere too compromising.

"Was there ever a time in your life when you wanted to focus everything, all your energy, all your time, all your thoughts on one thing?" she asked me.

Like any red-blooded bloke, I could think of one thing, yes. But before I had time to reply, she went on. It had obviously been one of those famous French rhetorical questions.

"A time," she said, "when you felt that this is your big chance, this is something that will change your whole life if you can just get it right, if you can really make it work. Have you ever felt that?"

She turned to look me in the eyes. Now was apparently my time to answer.

"What kind of thing?" I asked, just to make sure.

"A project, an idea, for which you have to be one hundred per cent focussed."

So it was work, then. I ought to have known.

"When I was starting my tearoom," I said. "I spent a month living in the building site, eating dust, sleeping in dust, just to get it finished."

Suddenly I saw where all this was leading. It was her "too busy for blokes" refrain. I wasn't sure I could agree with her. Thinking back to that building site of mine, I remembered that even at the worst times, when I was screaming down the phone at the architect while hanging on to the builders' tool belts to stop them disappearing to another job, I still found time to enjoy the company, as it were, of my girlfriend.

But then maybe that was why I was now too old to be living in a student room whereas Ambre, still a genuine student, had her sights set on a villa with solar-heated pool in Provence or California. She had the true drive and ambition that it takes to succeed big-time.

"I see what you mean," I conceded.

"If Lara and I can just get investment for our project," Ambre said, "it will change my life totally and get me going where I want to go. Which is why I'm afraid I don't have time for lunch or a drink, or anything else."

At last she'd got to the point. But in a twisted way it felt encouraging. If she was saying no to my various invitations, it might mean she'd been thinking about saying yes.

Sadly, she'd taken so long to get to the crux of the matter that we'd already crossed the canal and were only a few minutes away from the end of our most intimate ever conversation.

"Is it OK if I carry on inviting you?" I asked.

"If you want to. It's flattering. Or it would be, if you didn't keep finding ways to insult me, or terrify me at two o'clock in the morning." She smiled as she said it, though.

Oh well, I thought, in for a centime in for a kilo.

"There's one invitation that would take only a second or two if you said yes," I said.

"What's that?"

"A kiss," I said, almost applauding myself because I had remembered to say *"un baiser"* with the *"un"*, instead of just *"baiser"*, the verb to fuck. French is a minefield for the foreigner trying to sweet-talk a local.

I saw the taxi driver's eyes in his rear-view mirror. Maybe he hadn't heard the *"un"*.

"Un baiser?" Ambre repeated. Probably making sure she'd heard both words.

"Yes. It would take just two seconds."

She stared at me as if this might be a trick. But not a wholly unpleasant one.

"Just two seconds?" she asked.

"Or even three, if you have time."

"Three seconds? It's a deal."

"Excellent, where do I sign the contract?"

"Just shut up and kiss me, you English idiot," she said, and it seemed impolite to refuse.

I didn't count the seconds, but I was sure I spent more than three of them tasting those curvaceous lips. And even – kiss and tell – the tip of her tongue.

I felt the taxi swerve, so the driver must have been enjoying the show in his mirror.

"Merci," I said once it was over.

"Merci à toi," Ambre replied. "But I'm sorry, I really don't have time for more than that. You understand, n'est-ce pas?"

"I understand," I said, though understanding didn't make it any less painful.

17

Back in my room, I took my mind off the idea that Ambre was lying upstairs in bed – OK, maybe I didn't take my mind off it very successfully – by looking at a link that Marjorie had sent me.

In the accompanying message she warned me that "as an Englishman trying to influence the Olympics" I needed to be "very prudent. You're not the first Englishman to get entangled in French sport."

I wondered what that meant.

The link was to a news site. It was footage of a French TV show from 2005, headlined "*Les Français pètent les plombs à l'annonce de Londres 2012*". I knew roughly what this meant. *Péter les plombs* could be translated literally as something like "to fart lead", which sounds very volcanic and dangerous, but it also refers to blowing a metaphorical fuse. So it was a news item about France's fury when London was given the 2012 Olympics.

I watched a film showing how badly the French had taken the announcement in 2005 that Paris was not going to host the 2012 Games. It was from the midday news on one of France's big national channels, France 2. The anchorwoman told viewers that an announcement by the international Olympic committee was imminent, and in the studio with her to give their live reaction were a French sports journalist, a former French minister of sport and an English writer – the latter because London was a co-contender for the big prize.

The sports journalist was a middle-aged guy who looked as though he had never played anything more active than whist. I thought there was something familiar about the politician – yes, unless I was mistaken, it was the smooth French playboy who more recently had been running rings around British negotiators over the Brexit deals. The English writer looked just like a writer – glasses, cropped grey hair, anonymous face, un-ironed shirt.

The anchorwoman said we were going live to Singapore, and they cut to a crowded auditorium. A man was standing at a lectern on stage. He opened an envelope and said something like, "And the winner of the 2012 Olympic Games is ..."

As soon as he uttered the word "London", we saw famous British sporting faces in the Singapore auditorium erupt into delirium, and then French TV cut back live to the Paris studio, where the two Frenchmen were already grinding down the enamel on their molars. They were both livid.

The sports journalist declared outright that the British had cheated. The Queen had been sent to Singapore to lobby committee members, he said, which was plainly unfair. Britain had a Prime Minister, the then-glamorous Tony Blair, as well as a Queen, while France had sent only a President, Jacques Chirac, who had gone to bed the previous evening, whereas apparently Blair had stayed up all night lobbying.

The English writer interrupted this tirade to point out, in very good French, that lobbying is a marathon not a sprint, and that if France had acted differently in 1789, it could have had its own monarch to lobby for the 2012 Olympics.

In reply, the sports journalist looked as though he was about to fart molten lead.

The ex-minister for sport started complaining that London's campaign had been about advertising rather than sport, that it was style over content, the opposite of Paris's more "serious", less commercialized, bid. London, he said, was an unworthy winner.

The English writer interrupted yet again to say that the journalist and the minister seemed to be forgetting the Olympic spirit: "After all, Paris didn't *lose* this contest to host the Games. You won the silver medal, and London got the gold."

The ex-minister growled at him, "You English think you're funny, but you're not."

Suddenly I understood why this same Frenchman had been so keen on humiliating Britain during the Brexit talks.

Maybe it was something in the barely suppressed fury amongst the French that made me click on a "related news" link further down the page. The headline was "*Trop de violence aux Jeux Olympiques*", and it was an item about a pressure group that was currently trying to ban violent sports from the Games. Their key argument seemed to be that you shouldn't win an Olympic medal for hitting, kicking or trying to throttle someone. Boxing, this group said, should be withdrawn from the list of Olympic events, along with wrestling, judo and all the other combat sports. The group was also against the shooting events and even javelin, which was, they pointed out, just an ancient way of killing people in battle. "If you keep the javelin, why not have machine-gunning or missile-firing?" a spokeswoman asked.

Here, I thought, were some allies for Jake's mob. The most violent sport the Nolympians were promoting was swallowing a hotdog.

I sent him the link.

Though I just hoped these anti-violence protesters wouldn't make the connection between *pétanque* and cannonballs.

After this bout of online productivity, I gave into temptation and fired off a quick message to Ambre. I thanked her for three of the best seconds I had experienced in a long time, and said that if she had even one millisecond free in the near future, I would make sure I was free for that same millisecond. Or words to that effect. It was one of the longest French sentences I had ever written.

Her reply was much shorter.

"Le plus léger des baisers peut être lourd de conséquences," she wrote. The lightest kiss can have heavy consequences.

"Merde," I said, but only to myself.

I suggested to Alain and Marjorie that we hold our side of the Zoom meeting with the Swiss at my incubator. Of course, I was hoping to run into Ambre and another of her merciless yet enticing snubs.

Marjorie and Alain came along to the incubator about half an hour before we were due to go live. Alain had obviously never been anywhere like this before, and the feeling was mutual. He was stared at as much as he stared. And not all the stares were hostile or mocking. Looking like he did, a hairy-faced peasant in a loud yellow shirt that fit his pot belly as snugly as a burst cushion, some of the start-up kids probably thought he was a billionaire. He certainly attracted a few cordial *bonjours* from people who hardly ever glanced in my direction.

We took some coffees into a small meeting room and set up three chairs side by side. Marjorie said we'd each have a screen so that we could appear individually in the meeting. Alain had brought along his own computer in a supermarket shopping bag. His laptop was as thick as a baguette sandwich and looked as though it had been manufactured somewhere around the turn of the 19th century. He'd also brought along a grime-covered mains lead that seemed to have been employed to pick up crumbs, dog hairs and gobbets of discarded sausage from his kitchen floor. It was a miracle that Marjorie managed to get Zoom to work on his screen.

We sat Alain in the middle, with Marjorie to his left, myself to his right. She set us all up with the same backdrop for the meeting – a blue-sky photo of the Eiffel Tower poking above the Paris rooftops.

Now all we had to do was wait until check-in time, in ten minutes or so. We sat in a line gazing out the window at the silently passing trains.

"The Swiss will have seen our film," Marjorie said, in French.

"A very good film," Alain said. "It was formidable to see so many young people having fun, drinking, playing pétanque." He then added, "Où sont les waters?"

Marjorie stifled a scream. *Les waters*, pronounced "what-air", are toilets in old-school French. I expect the term dates back to the days when the Brits introduced the sit-down flushable "water closet" into France. Some French people – the sort

Elodie would never frequent – still call loos *les WC*, which they pronounce "vay-say", like the French letters "VC". Pretty disrespectful to the Viet Cong, venture capitalists and the Victoria Cross, as well as being what Elodie would call very *plouc*.

Still, the plouciness of French words for toilet wasn't what was bothering Marjorie. We were mere minutes away from our meeting time and Alain wanted to head off for a pee?

"I'll show you where it is," I offered, grabbing Alain's nearest shirt sleeve and hauling him into the corridor. "Allons-y vite."

I jogged him towards the loos in the entrance hall, listening to his complaints about how inconvenient it was that males had to possess prostates.

I knew that if he failed to pee within the next eight minutes or so, Marjorie would make sure he didn't possess a prostate for much longer. So, after a brief discussion about which toilet he was willing to use – they were all marked with the symbols for both male and female, and he was adamant that he didn't want to go *chez les femmes* – I shoved him through the nearest door and urged him to be "vite, vite!"

It took him almost seven minutes according to my watch, and he was still trying to zip up his trousers when he emerged from *les waters*. I grabbed his shirtsleeve again, and off we jogged. He protested as he wrestled with his zip, but we had no time to hang about.

Kidnapping an old man who was begging to be allowed to do up his fly, while tugging on his shirt so that it untucked to expose the hairiest navel outside the trophy room of Alain's local boar-hunting club, was not how I wanted Ambre to picture me, but this was the image that now confronted her as she came out of a meeting room. She was with Lara, and they stood aside to let us pass, Ambre open-mouthed, Lara shaking her head as though I was just being typically English again.

There was no time for an explanation, so I blew Ambre a kiss and told her "One millisecond, please!" I didn't have time to see how she reacted.

When Alain and I made it back into the meeting room, Marjorie had all three screens logged on to the Zoom session and she was confirming in English, "Yes, I ear you."

I sat down quickly and saw my head appear in the Zoom mosaic on screen.

Alain swore loudly – "Putain!" – and zipped up before he sat down, so that the first sight the Olympic dignitaries got of him was his straining trousers. Zoom being sensitive to loud voices, it decided to place his crotch full screen.

"Allo," Marjorie said, forcefully enough to make herself appear. "Per'aps we all present us?"

It always surprises me when someone French who is well educated and modern-looking speaks really bad English. Arch snobbery on my part, I know, and plenty of French people have made fun of my mutilation of their grammar and pronunciation. But hearing Marjorie abusing English again, I felt the need to step in.

"I'm Paul West, and I'll be interpreting for the French team today, if they need me."

"Good day," a middle-aged woman said in a clipped Germanic accent. She had a muscular face, with busy eyes like a boxer or security guard. "I am Monika Birgit. I am co-director of the development team." The only thing she looked keen on developing with us was a fight.

"Hello." A male head took over. He was younger, with a fleshy face and thick neck. A retired shot-putter, perhaps, so a potential supporter of our cause? "My name is Karl James, I'm on the Events Evaluation Committee." He sounded American. I suspected that he might be on the breakdancing/skateboarding wing of the development team.

I saw Marjorie nudge Alain, who coughed loudly, then flinched as he saw himself take centre stage.

"Alang Fyong," he said. "Fuck pet." Both faces in Geneva raised their eyebrows.

"Monsieur Fillon is the president of the French federation of pétanque clubs, acronym F-U-C-P-E-T," I explained quickly.

"Vous avez vu nos films?" Alain demanded. I was about to translate but the Olympians had understood.

"Yes, your films are impressive," Monika said. "You argue a

strong case. Young people, a diverse population, popular participation, inclusive."

"Qu'est-ce qu'elle dit?" Alain asked me, leaning over so that the main part of our screens suddenly showed nothing except his ear.

I translated for him as best I could.

Marjorie asked the Swiss pair, "So you av seen that we correspond to your craters?"

I thought it best to translate this too: "Do you agree that pétanque meets the *criteria* for the selection of new Olympic events?"

"Well ..." Karl looked pained. "You know this is really a Parisian decision. They chose their guest events, which the IOC approved. If you can't convince Paris, I don't see what we can do."

I whispered a summary to Alain: "C'est Paris qui décide."

"Mais putain!" he exploded, and went off on a rant in a twanging southern accent so strong that I didn't get all of it. I hoped Monika and Karl didn't either. In the parts I understood, he moaned about Parisian snobbery towards the provinces, elitist prejudice against "people's sports" and the need for the International Olympic Committee to grow some *couilles* (balls) and put its foot down, otherwise what was the point of having a committee?

There were a few seconds' shocked silence before I translated: "Monsieur Fillon is wondering if this might not be a decision that *you* could take, as the governing Olympic body?" Well, maybe I paraphrased a little.

"Hmm." Karl didn't look as though he had enjoyed being ranted at. His neck was throbbing. "As you must be aware, Monsieur Fyong, pétanque isn't the only game of its type. There's tenpin bowling, for example ..."

"In Germany also, we have Kegeln," Monika pitched in.

"Skittles," Karl said. "Yes, and in the Paralympics there's boccia." I saw Marjorie grip Alain's arm, presumably to shut him up in case he had an outbreak of inappropriateness. "I don't see how we can favour one of these many bowls-type sports above another," Karl added. "As I said, Paris could decide to favour its local sport as a one-off demonstration event, just as Berlin or Munich might hold a Kegeln competition. So the ball is in your court. No pun intended."

People who say "no pun intended" always intend it, and I think it was Karl's self-satisfied expression that set Alain growling before I'd even begun whispering the gist to him.

"Mais putain!" he repeated. This time he went off on a speech about history. The International Olympic Committee ought to be more grateful to France, he said. It was a Frenchman, Pierre de Coubertin, who invented the modern Games. The first Olympics outside Athens were in Paris in 1900. In the 1924 Paris Games, one of the events had been *pelote basque* – the squash-style game played with open palms, a regional French sport. In 1924, there had also been medals awarded for art, music and architecture, to highlight Paris's identity as a cultural city. Surely, he concluded, it wasn't too much now to ask the Olympic Committee to authorize the organization of a *pétanque* event in the country that invented the sport?

He certainly knew his stuff, and this time he spoke much more clearly, as if hoped the others might understand enough French to get his drift.

The only problem was that he had been stressing his central points with a soft but resolute karate-style chop to the table in front of him. Just after the start of his speech, one of these chops hit his keyboard, so that he was suddenly sharing his screen with us. We got a close-up of a message from someone called "Fillon_Yvette", Alain's wife presumably, informing him that she was due to go into hospital for two days "because of my veins".

To his credit, Alain was not put off by all this. He carried on talking while Marjorie leaned across and made the email disappear.

He also kept talking when, a few seconds later during his point about *pelote basque*, he hit his keyboard again, this time changing his backdrop so that a pair of grinning dolphins suddenly appeared behind him.

Marjorie cured this problem too, but it was not surprising that the effect of his rousing speech was slightly dampened.

"As we have said," Monika replied, shaking her head. "Only Paris can give the decision on this."

"And we hope your wife's veins will recover quickly," Karl added, the bastard.

"We 'ave other kestion," Marjorie cut in. "On the French language." She was undeterred by Alain's mishaps and Karl's sense of humour. "We are sure that Paris will listen more to our demand for the pétanque if you can agree wiz them for the priorité of the French in the Games."

All this left our Swiss correspondents frowning in silent confusion, so I dashed to the linguistic rescue.

"Paris has hinted that it might accept pétanque as a demonstration sport," I said, "if the IOC lets them use French as the undisputed first language of the 2024 Games."

"It's the *Paris* Olympics," Karl said. "Of *course* French will be the first language." There was just a hint of "duh" in this.

"That's not all," I said. "They want all the signs, public announcements and instructions to be printed in order of linguistic priority. So, first French, *of course*, followed by, say Chinese, Spanish and whatever comes next. They're going to do a statistical study of the genuine linguistic needs of the visitors and athletes."

"Really?" Monika asked, looking surprised and almost impressed.

"Qu'est-ce qu'il dit?" Alain asked Marjorie, but she didn't answer. She looked across at me, urging me to go on.

Most of what I'd just said was bullshit, obviously. Paris was not saying this at all. I was just elaborating on Elodie's propaganda.

"Paris also says," I continued, "that if you sanction their study of language priorities and support its results, even if English is relegated to a much lower position, then there is a real possibility that pétanque will be accepted as a demonstration event. Only for the Paris 2024 Games, of course."

"Qu'est-ce qu'il dit?" Alain demanded again, showing us all

a close-up of his right ear.

Marjorie began to whisper an answer.

"But if you follow that principle," Monika said, appearing full screen, "French will lose its high status at future Games. The 2028 Olympics are going to be held in Los Angeles. Who speaks French there?"

Marjorie whispered this in Alain's ear, and I was expecting another "Putain!", but he began nodding.

"Zis no prob-lemm," he said. "You say French numéro one in Paree, we say, thank you, and Los Angeles, on s'en bat les couilles." He turned to me. "Tell zem."

His last French phrase meant literally, "We bash our balls at the issue." It's an idiom I've never really understood, because I personally would never be tempted to bash mine, whatever the problem. But it's the strongest expression of French indifference, so I translated it: "Los Angeles is not Monsieur Fillon's immediate concern."

"Anyway, French is only still in there for historical reasons," Karl said. "Precisely because of Monsieur Coubertin and the 1900 Games. But globally it's on the way down."

"That's precisely what Monsieur Fillon is saying," I replied. "Perhaps Paris 2024 is its parting shot. If you can just consider their request to give the French language supremacy over English at *these* Games, the future can take its course."

Elodie and her father would have had me guillotined for accepting the idea that the French language might one day slip from its Eiffel Tower-like position in the world, but all Alain wanted was for *pétanque* balls to get thrown around on worldwide TV in the summer of 2024. After that, as far as he was concerned, Proust and Molière and *où est la plume de ma tante?* could go and jump in the Seine.

"We will consider this compromise," Monika said. "It is interesting." She looked much less like a boxer now. She was almost a kindly judge in an American courtroom reality show.

After the meeting, we stayed on so that Marjorie and Alain could make sure they had understood everything that went on. Alain was in positive mood.

"You played a good match," he told me. "It's strange to have an Englishman in the French team, but you are a team player. Merci."

"Je vous en prie," I told him, adapting what I'd learned from Ambre to the polite "*vous*" form.

"You stayed calm," he explained. "And on top of that, you threw two or three very accurate boules." This, I presumed, was his highest compliment. I thought I might ask him to write it down and send it to the French citizenship people.

"I am impatient to meet your friend Elodie and her father," he said.

"I agree," Marjorie said.

"Are you sure?" I asked.

"Very sure," Alain replied. "They sound like people who can influence decisions."

That may be true, I wanted to warn him, but any decision they influence will only be in their own favour.

18

Alain and Marjorie went off to plot their unwitting downfall at Elodie's hands, and I decided to risk my own demise by sending a message to Ambre. I hoped she might still be somewhere in the incubator.

"I can explain why I was kidnapping a Provençal peasant," I wrote.

A message pinged back a minute or two later, but it wasn't from her.

It had a decidedly un-Ambre-like tone. It was in French and began, "Hello my English bee, from your flower."

It was from my old lockdown connection, Fleur. Which was a surprise. It had been fully two years since our last encounter.

Her message went on, "Sorry but I don't do that anymore."

I didn't understand what she meant by this, so I replied, "??"

Two question marks are polite, I think. Three is too many. Three or more says, "Are you a complete idiot???"

Fleur came back straight away with: "Merci for the invitation but non merci."

I hadn't invited her to do anything, so I quite naturally replied, "??" again (though this time I was tempted to add the third.)

She answered immediately, "Please stop saying ??"

So I said nothing for a while, and wondered about our brief conversation. Why would Fleur think I was asking her to meet up?

I asked her.

She replied, "??".

Then, after her little joke, she sent a screen shot of an

invitation to her sent via the dating app – by me.

Which was very weird, because I wasn't on that app anymore.

Except that I was. When I checked, there was my profile, with my name and my photo. And when I tried to open my profile to delete it (again), I couldn't get in. My password didn't work. I was locked out of myself.

I made a gulping noise that meant "?????".

The go-to man in all matters moral and amoral had to be Jake. His advice was often terrible, so at least he might help me decide what *not* to do.

Like the true friend he is, he said he'd meet me at my place as soon as he finished what he called "an English stage", meaning a training course. I pitied his students more than I did myself.

Identity theft has always freaked me out, so I made a dash for the incubator exit. I even bypassed the coffee machine in my hurry to get back to my room.

It was unfortunate that Ambre and Lara saw me running down the corridor again, this time peasant-less, but looking just as hurried as before. They were in a meeting room with a man in a suit, and both goggled at me through the window as I bounced past. I remembered to blow a kiss at Ambre, but I must have looked as though I was dashing to catch the last Eurostar before the tunnel was cemented up.

I needn't have rushed. Jake arrived at my place a couple of hours later, puffing on a parsnip-sized joint. I told him that smoking was forbidden in the *foyer*, so he stuck his head out of my window, and addressed his advice to the sparrows.

"Fuck it, man!" he shouted at the startled birds. There were probably hatchlings out there who had never heard such language. "It's evident! When I forget my mot de passe and can't create a new one, I just open another profile." He exhaled enough smoke out the window to intoxicate an ostrich.

"But I don't want another profile. I don't want *any* dating profile," I told him.

He inhaled and took in this insane concept.

"What?" he spluttered. "You're totally quitting the apps? You're paddling in the Ocean Arctic without a canoe? You're leaving the battlefield before the légumes are ripe?" (As a poet on weed, he was free to mix nonsensical metaphors). "Come on Paul, what will you do if you get lonely on a Samedi night? Or Sunday? Or Monday?"

I stopped him before he recited the whole calendar at me.

"I suppose I'll just feel lonely," I said. "It doesn't do any harm now and again."

"Oh Paul! You're so out of touch with la vie moderne. No one feels lonely these days. Everyone just hooks up with the nearest available person. Life today is the contraire of feeling lonely. It's about cancelling the people you don't want. And dating the rest."

"Well, I want to cancel myself. From these apps anyway."

"Ah, I have peejed!" Jake suddenly shouted out the window. He was using the French word *piger*, to understand. He turned round to laugh at me, and took another long toke on the joint. "You have commenced to sleep with this Ambre!" He grinned, and my whole room was suddenly a cloud of vegetable smoke.

I didn't answer at first because I was trying to think how I was going to fumigate, or rather de-fumigate, my room after his gaseous onslaught. Jake took my silence as a yes.

"Now I see your problem, Paul." He was nodding sympathetically. "You want to stay, how do we say, fidèle?"

"Faithful." Hardly surprising that the word had slipped his mind.

"You want to fuck only with Ambre." His eyes boggled at this wild idea.

It seemed simpler to agree with him. The concept of simply not wanting to hook up with someone else was beyond Jake's comprehension.

"Right," I said.

Jake finished his joint and then stood chewing on the stub, staring hard at me. He appeared to be taking my feelings on board. But it was only an appearance.

"You want me to go and see this Fleur?" he asked out.

"No thanks, Jake. Not on my behalf."

"She sounds beaucoup fun."

"Fleur's not the issue here. The issue is I've been hijacked, and she's getting messages from some impostor."

Jake blinked at me. Maybe "impostor" was too complex a word for him to deal with right now.

"I might go and see her anyway," he said. "You have her numéro, right?"

"I'm not giving you her number."

"Why not?"

That short phrase was Jake's whole attitude to life.

"If you want to see her, Jake, use the app. Then she can decide if she wants to see *you*."

"Hey! C'est vrai!" Jake applauded my brilliant scheme. "Wow. Did you hear that? 'Hey ... c'est vrai.' It rhymed. I'm on fire."

Burnt out, more like, I thought, as he slumped into a seated heap under my window.

19

After ejecting Jake, I spent an uncomfortable evening lying on my bed, trying to watch a movie while simultaneously keeping an eye open for incoming messages.

I'd chosen a classic French film recommended to me by my most highly cultured ex-girlfriend, Alexa. She once told me that every human being had to see this film or die a philistine, that cinemas in every town ought to be streaming it non-stop to educate the people, and all that ultra-French intellectual guff.

As a result, she'd scared me off watching it in case I wasn't intelligent enough, which seems to be the idea behind a lot of French culture – "Don't even try to understand, you're too stupid." But now I decided to give it a go. I hoped it would engross me so much that I would forget the Fleur/dating app situation for a couple of hours at least.

In the event, though, what it did was convince me that 1960s male French film directors were incredibly seedy. All they did was convince their girlfriends to take their bras off on screen, and for this they were funded by producers who let them get away with murder because it was "art", and presumably because French boobs were so saleable on the world market.

Personally, I would have told every single character in the film, including the semi-naked girlfriend, that they were a bunch of self-obsessed, unconvincingly dialogued, pretentious Parisian farts, and gone for a game of *pétanque* with some real people.

So in the end I spent the evening clicking endlessly about on social media in between occasional bouts of staring at a topless French 1960s starlet whose voice I had mercifully muted.

Ambre got in touch, saying that she would indeed be

interested to know what I had done with the poor old man I had abducted, because when she last saw me it was obvious I was running away from a murder scene.

It was a nice, jokey message, tarnished only by an extra bit at the end begging me not to come and bash on her door. Explanations could wait, she said, until we next saw each other at the incubator. She and Lara were still *très occupées* chasing deals.

It occurred to me that if Ambre thought I was still active on the on-line dating scene, she would be *très occupée* telling me to get lost.

Next morning, there was still no reply from the dating app, and my impostor's profile was still up. I'd already written to their contacts address complaining about identity hijacking, and now I fired off an impatient reminder.

While I waited for a reply, I had a bit of admin to catch up on, and decided to do it in bed.

I was staring dozily at an invoice when there was a loud thump on my door.

Madalena, I thought, coming to complain about finding a mound of cannabis ash under my window.

But it was Jake, who looked – if that was possible – even more bedraggled than usual. He was wearing sunglasses and seemed to be buckling slightly at the knees.

"Café?" was all he said before crashing out where I had been lying.

I made him a high-octane brew while he displayed his talent for groaning.

A few gulps of coffee got his brain working enough to mumble, "I saw Fleur, *putain*." I wondered whether this last word was just the typical French expletive of surprise, regret, frustration, etc, or Jake's insulting description of Fleur.

"I thought she didn't do that anymore?" was all I could think of to say.

"I offered her weed," he said. "She sure does *that*."

"And what happened?"

In reply, he grimaced, either at the memory of what had

happened or the strength of my coffee.

"Putain, I don't know. I was so stoned even before I went there. I'm smoking some shit that Nolympics kid sold me. You know, the garçon who fell asleep in the meeting? No wonder he was asleep. Putain."

Satisfied with his report of the night's activities, Jake took off his sunglasses and rubbed his eyes.

"Did you tell Fleur it really wasn't me who was hassling her?" I asked.

Jake squinted blearily into the past.

"I don't know. I remember I told her I'm a friend of Paul. She was, like, oh comment tu t'appelles? So I'm like, je suis Jake. And she's like, Jacques? And I'm like, non, je suis Jake. And she's like –"

We were clearly in for a frame-by-frame rerun of the last twelve hours.

"Forget it, Jake. I'm dealing with it my way. The app will take down my profile, I'm sure." I crossed my fingers anyway. "I just wish the bastards would hurry up about it."

I went to the window to get some fresh air. The sparrows were leaping merrily from shrub to shrub as if the planet was still spinning on its normal axis rather than careering off into the unknown.

"Hey, good news, though," said a croaky voice behind me.

"Oh?" Had he remembered something?

"Yeah, man, Fleur just messaged me. She wants to see me again next week."

I wondered what the sparrowese was for "kill the American!"

At last, later that afternoon, I got a call from the app. A guy asked me my security questions (this being France, I'd chosen my favourite goat's cheese and the name of the greatest French philosopher – Eric Cantona) and agreed to remove my profile.

"Merci beaucoup, beaucoup," I told him. Never in the field of human dating had a man sounded so relieved at the prospect of sleeping alone.

My life now felt more or less back on track.

At the end of the day I had a gig attending a meeting between some American software creators and the Human Resources team at their French subsidiary. It wasn't interpreting in the language sense, because the French team all spoke great English. My job was to convince the Americans that they were hearing right.

I backed up the French team when they insisted that French people don't want to work as many hours as Americans, especially in summer. Of course, some French people will want to work overtime, but others will prefer to stick to 35 hours a week and spend long weekends with their families, pets and barbecues.

However, I said, this did not mean that the project would drop behind schedule, because France has one of the best person/hour efficiency rates in Europe.

The Americans weren't entirely convinced, but that wasn't my problem.

Besides, after an hour or so of this clash of cultures, I was only half-listening. I was thinking, just my luck that Ambre was one of those rare French people who were keen to do overtime. I wanted to see her. Why couldn't she be a stereotypical Gallic slacker who saw work as no more than an occasional intrusion into her leisure time?

I did see her a couple of times, but only by chance.

Once when she was heading out of the students' residence, solar panel on her back, and I was heading in. We had a quick chat, and I explained who Alain was and why he had needed to be transported at top speed from toilet to meeting room. That was all we had time for before she dashed away.

The next time I saw her was at the incubator's coffee machine. I asked her how things were going, and she looked slightly glum. She said the financiers had cold feet because so far, the only paying customers for the solar panels were Ambre's parents who were heating all the water in their seaside cottage. That wasn't enough to unlock the big funding. She needed one sizeable corporate client, and then the money would come gushing in, like the hot water into her parents' bath.

I tried to think up something witty about not getting her fingers burnt, but by then she'd jogged off on her way to another meeting.

Jake, too, was pretty absent, apart from telling me that his Nolympics team had been in touch with some French gamers who were pushing for the creation of a videogame Olympics. These were apparently to be called the Electrolympics.

Soon, I thought, the real Olympics will be a sideshow for the tiny minority of people who still want to watch real athletes doing real things. Given modern attention spans, sprinters will always be popular, but the marathon will become a thing of the past, and in most other sports, spectacular fails will get more clicks than gold-medal winning performances.

To stay popular, the real Olympics will probably have to introduce a challenge to find a magical ring. Or they'll need to introduce zombies. Who wouldn't run a hundred metres in under nine seconds when chased by a flesh-eating mutant?

One morning I got a call from Elodie. She sounded suspiciously chirpy. She told me that she'd talked to Marjorie and Alain, and that their upcoming meeting with the Paris 2024 committee was bound to go well.

"I'm going to talk to my colleagues today," she said, "and make sure they fully understand the importance of the deal being offered: *pétanque* in Paris in exchange for the supremacy of French at the Paris Olympics. I just wanted to reassure you. I'm on your side."

"Thanks, Elodie. That's very reassuring."

"Je t'en prie. Oh, and Paul, congratulations."

"What for?"

"Not bad for an Englishman, beating all those Parisian playboys."

"What are you talking about?"

Elodie laughed joyously, which never bodes well.

20

Elodie told me where to look.

It was a famous French dating app called Meet-ologie, a typical French pun based on the fact that they pronounce their word for myth – *mythe* – as "meet". Though from its reputation as a sure-fire pickup service, it could have been called "Meat-ologie". Anyway, I had never signed up to it. But there was my photo, above my first name, headlining a "news" item on the app's home page describing how its most active profile of the month was, well, guess *qui*.

"Shocking!" it declared – this is one of France's favourite English words – that an *Anglais* was enjoying so much more success than any of *les French lovers* – another favourite Franglais term – amongst its subscribers. This Englishman Paul had ten dates in a single week! *Quelle énergie!*

In a daze, I skimmed through the rest of the blurb, stopping at the final line, which announced that I had given permission for my name and photo to be published.

"What," I asked Elodie, "the fuck?"

Her only reply was a gurgling laugh.

"This isn't me," I told her. "I've been hacked." I didn't add "again". No point revealing my Fleur problem to Elodie. She thrived on other people's signs of weakness.

"It's not you? I'm disappointed, Paul. I thought you had suddenly blossomed into a true Parisian. Unless, of course, you're lying and this really is you. Paul, the ruthless but modest seducer." She gurgled again.

"No it bloody isn't me and I shall be writing to inform them immediately."

"You want your fifteen minutes of fame to end so soon?"

"Yes. And I trust you won't share this with anyone else, Elodie?"

"It's public, so people can see it anyway."

"But you won't help them find it?"

"Would I do that?"

The true answer was yes of course she bloody would if she thought it might be fun and/or useful.

"No, Paul, of course not!" she replied. "You and I are working together again. You're on my team, helping me get the French language back on top of the world."

Strange, I thought, that someone campaigning for the supremacy of French should always speak to me in English. But maybe this time she was doing it to be sure that her message got across: if she felt like it, she could take a screenshot of my fake profile on Meet-ologie and publish it on every social media platform on the planet.

Like I said, a crocodile can't change its spots.

"I'm glad to hear that, Elodie. Thanks for letting me know so I can nip it in the bud."

"You're welcome, Paul," she said, with what sounded like a tinge of regret, as though she wished she'd shared the joke with everyone on her contacts list before telling me.

I found a phone number for Meet-ologie's offices and hunted down their marketing department. Weirdly, a guy told me that "this Anglais isn't a real person."

"He is," I assured him, "c'est moi." And I sent a photo to prove it.

"Merde," the guy replied, the sure sign that a French person is taking something seriously. He told me he would "occupy himself with it".

"Immédiatement?" I asked.

"Immédiatement."

An hour later, I realized that "immediately" doesn't mean the same thing in French.

I called Jake – the only other person (I hoped) who knew

about my app worries. His reaction was predictable.

"Assume, Paul." This was French for "live with it."

"But I would prefer to live without it."

"It's every man's dream. You come to France and turn into Paris's sexiest playboy. You're sexing your solar power friend Ambre" – again I didn't deny it – "but you're too hot for just one femme. Assume your ass. Hey, that's très bien. Assume your ass. Assonance using ass. Genius!" He seemed to have forgotten my problem already. "You know, I'm writing a new poème about sex," he went on.

"You? A poem about sex? You surprise me."

As usual when discussing his art, he ignored my leaden sarcasm.

"It's in français, too. Cécile's aiding me, but we have a dilemma."

"Whether to bother or not?"

"No, listen, Paul."

"Do I have to?"

But there was no stopping him when he was in poetry drive.

"You know the French saying 'pierre qui roule n'amasse pas mousse'?"

"It sounds like 'a rolling stone gathers no moss'."

"Right, yes. Well, my posy starts with an adaptation of that. 'Boules – plural – qui roulent ramassent les poules.' You see? The rolling balls gather the chicks. Good rhyme, no?"

"Pure genius, Jake."

"But Cécile says change poules to moules. You get it?"

"Yes." I did, unfortunately. It was gross. *Moule*, or mussel, is an obscene word for the vagina.

"Boules qui roulent ramassent les moules. Cécile says it's more comic, more shocking. You know, she's really into provocation."

"Unlike you, Jake." He ignored the jibe.

"But I'm thinking, is it less poétique?"

"What would I know about poetry, Jake? I'm just a playboy."

He laughed smokily. "That's it, man, live the dream."

I managed to extricate myself from Jake's phone call without further exposure to his poetry, and was left alone with my own dilemma.

The big question was: should I panic about this new theft of my online ID, or not?

My gut reaction was, yes, definitely start panicking. First someone had hacked into my old profile and re-activated it. And now someone – the same hacker, maybe? – had given my name and photo to Meet-ologie to be used in a commercial, whilst telling them that I didn't really exist. I was being well and truly trolled.

Who, I wondered, would do such a thing? It was pranking taken to a level of sick unfunniness, like tipping red wine down a wedding dress just outside the church.

My main worry, though, wasn't whodunnit. It was that if Ambre saw the Meet-ologie ad about my dating prowess, it would look really bad, even if I denied it. How many millions of guys have denied that they are on dating sites when all the evidence points to the contrary? It's the oldest lie in the online world.

Then again, maybe I should just come clean and tell her that I had been hacked – twice now. Surely she would see that I was an innocent victim of some malign repeat offender?

Ambre and I weren't in a relationship, so I didn't really have to tell her anything. Sharing all this with her could even be considered as an intrusion into her life. But on the other hand, a pre-emptive confession might prevent misunderstandings between us in the future. And I for one was hoping there would be a future.

So should I find a way to tell her, or not?

I pondered a while before deciding that, until I got my French nationality, I would carry on doing things the good old English way: when faced by a serious dilemma, especially of a sexual nature, it was best to ignore the whole problem and hope that it would disappear.

Even so, I blasted off a quick voicemail to the marketing guy at Meet-ologie, reminding him that he was supposed to take down the ad *immédiatement* and demanding to know who'd given him my photo.

Then I got a message from Ambre.

Fearing the worst, I opened it.

"Apparently you know a lot about how Anglo-Saxons should seduce the French," it began, and I feared even worse than the worst.

But it went on much more innocuously. Ambre and Lara were due to pitch to some financiers in English and wanted my help with the language. This was the only "seduction" she was talking about. She obviously hadn't seen Meet-ologie. I almost wept with relief.

"I know you're an expert at gaffes," she went on, "so maybe you can help us avoid them." She'd even added a little smiley at the end.

That same afternoon I went over to the incubator so that Ambre and Lara could pitch at me in English.

They were good. Very good. French people might claim to be rubbish at English, but they usually underestimate themselves. When a Brit says he or she can't speak French, it's no lie. It means we can only just manage *"café au lait"*, "Galeries Lafayette" and *"je t'aime"*. But what the young generation of French people mean is something more like, "I might mispronounce Worcestershire."

My two pitchers made some of the classic French mistakes – they thought "information" had a plural and mistook "benefits" for profits because the French call them *"bénéfices"* – but the rest was smooth and understandable. If, that is, you knew anything about solar power. The technical details flew far over my head in English, just as they had done in French, but the bits in between were almost perfect.

I was as pleased as they were. This was a great way to spend time with Ambre. Didn't most love stories start in the workplace?

After the pitching session, we went out to the coffee machine, and Lara began teasing me about how much I charged for my services. Was I so expensive because an Englishman who can give reliable advice on seduction is so rare, she asked.

I decided to zap the seduction metaphor and told her that if they needed me to help out in any way – attend their English-language meetings, for example – it would all be on the house.

"Sometimes I do good things for nothing," I said, with a nod to Ambre.

"You are too kind for your own good," Ambre said, "but you're right that we don't have much money. Do you give credit? As soon as we get finance, you'll get paid, how's that?"

"I'm your man," I told her, trying not to sound too creepy. I was re-assured to see Lara nudge Ambre in the ribs, as if to say, "He wishes he was." Ambre grinned at her. It was all getting very flirty.

Tragically, it was at this moment that Jake appeared, trailing smoke and disapproving stares behind him.

"Ah oui, Paul, c'est l'homme!" he called out.

For a second, all three of us were in silent shock at the sudden arrival of this grinning, joint-smoking apparition, and Jake leapt into the breach.

He slapped me on the back and continued in loud French. "It's formidable that he says this to you," he told Ambre. "Usually Paul only wants to *eat* with women. But now he declares his love in public? Fantastique! I am happy to hear that you two are screwing at last." His use of the verb *baiser* drew even more stares from the people around us, though this time they were curious rather than disapproving. "So what if it took a long time," Jake panzered on, "you made the right decision, Ambre."

I was stunned. It was as though someone had marched up to me in the street and headbutted me on the nose.

I looked across at Ambre, who seemed to have received the same blow.

"But how could you resist the body of mon ami Paul?" Jake continued, still oblivious to the effect he was having. "He is a champion of pétanque and you know what they say: les boules qui roulent ramassent les moules."

Ambre broke free of her trance, shot a furious glower at me and stormed out of the building, with Lara at her heels.

By the time I had followed them, calling out that Jake's nonsense was exactly that, they were in a taxi and away.

Still in a daze, I went back to Jake, who was watching the departing car, shaking his head.

"Sorry, man," he said, "but didn't I predict it? Moules are less poetic than poules."

21

I couldn't explain to Jake exactly how he'd just screwed up my life. His excuse would have been that he honestly thought I had slept with Ambre. And he would say that it was all my fault for *not* sleeping with her.

So all I could do for the time being was ask him what the hell he was doing at the incubator. Not that he was going to be there for much longer. Over by the front entrance, a woman was pointing him out to the security guy, probably saying that he should have stopped this smoker entering in the first place.

"I was coming back from buying some shit in Saint-Denis," Jake said, "and when the train arrived at Gare du Nord, I thought, I'll go and see mon ami le playboy anglais. You have free café here, n'est-ce pas?"

I was still standing by the coffee machine, so I poured an americano for him.

The coffee only added to the mounting confusion in his brain. He stared at it, then at his joint, clearly wondering in which order to consume them.

"Let's get some fresh air," I said, gesturing to the approaching security guy that there was no need for his intervention.

The bright sunlight hurt Jake's eyes and my head. It was ironic: perfect solar power weather, and I'd just lost my briefly-held role in that industry.

"You've got to like it," Jake said, incoherently.

"Like what?"

"Our show."

"Which show?"

157

He stared at his hands again, and this time decided that the coffee might boost his thinking power more than the joint. He took a long draught, then gasped and poked his tongue out to cool it down.

"Cécile et moi," he said as soon as he'd stopped gagging. "We're doing a show in favour of the Nolympiques. Songs, comedy, posy."

"When?" I asked.

Jake shook his head. He had no idea.

"Where?" I asked, more tentatively.

"I can't remember when or where or any shit like that," he said. "But you have to like it."

"I'm sure I will," I lied.

"No, I mean, like the teaser online. You know, like, press 'like'. Cécile says we need *followeurs* qui *like*."

The French have adopted both these English words, no doubt infuriating the language boffins at the *Académie Française* who will be debating on how to translate them into "real" French, with a decision due sometime in 2045.

I was still mad at Jake for his insurgency into my love life – or lack of it – but being angry at him is generally as pointless as yelling at a hailstone for denting your car, so as we walked towards the canal, I found the teaser for his show.

It was due to take place a couple of nights later, on a theatre boat moored on the Seine. The show was called *Paris Nolympique*, and the event was illustrated with a picture of Cécile puncturing a volleyball with a model of the Eiffel Tower.

I hit "like".

True to his Nolympic cause, Jake gave up walking as soon as we reached the canal and slumped down on a bench. He said he needed a rest before giving an "English course" nearby, at République. Once again, I pitied his poor students.

I left him there and walked along the bank towards my students' residence a couple of kilometres away. The misshapen cobbles along the old towpath massaged my feet and activated my brain.

A refreshing breeze was blowing along the canal from the northeast (if you follow the canal's course into the connecting river network, you will end up at the mouth of the Rhine), and it cooled my bubbling thoughts enough for me to compose a message to Ambre in my head.

Once I was back in my room, I typed it into Google translate, simplifying everything so that there were no possible ambiguities.

Writing to a woman in French is a dangerous business. The colloquial words for friend – *copain* (male) and *copine* (female) – can also mean boyfriend and girlfriend. *Aimer* can mean like or love. *Excuse* can be an excuse or a simple apology, and in my experience, a woman can sometimes forgive me after receiving an apology, but throw a total wobbly if I try to offer her an excuse.

In this case, I needed both an apology and an excuse, so infinite subtlety was going to be needed. And subtlety is not usually my thing.

I honed my text in English, hoping that it successfully mingled abject apology with believable excuses, then carefully copied and pasted the *français* translation into a message.

Here's the original English:

"Dear Ambre, sorry about what Jake said. He is a cretin. So am I, as you already know. That is why he and I are friends. We are both cretins. I lied to him that you and I had made love. It was the idea of a cretin, because I am a cretin. But I lied to him for a very good reason. I don't want to write this reason in this message because, even though it is a very good reason, it is also the reason of a cretin. I would prefer to explain it in person, to be sure that you have understood. If you will permit me to explain this reason to you, I am almost sure that you will laugh and tell me 'Paul, you are a cretin'. And I will say, 'Not only that, I am an *English* cretin, and we are the worst.' I hope to see you soon, whenever you are free, Paul."

OK, so I had erred on the side of abjectness. And I'd simplified the language so much that my cretinousness was way too convincing.

Even so, after reading the French translation through ten or fifteen times, back-translating it into English to make sure the message had come across, and realizing that translating a translation back into its original language is almost entirely pointless, I clenched my eyes shut and hit "send".

A short while later, I received some good news. Or rather an absence of news, which was, as is the custom, good. Checking Meet-ologie for the millionth time (my phone was going to think I was the most indecisive seducer on Earth), I saw that I had finally been deleted.

Cue long puff of relief.

Then the marketing guy messaged me that my name and photo had originally been given to them by an advertising agency. He gave me their contact details, along with an offer to enjoy a month's free access to *le lounge VIP* (yet another French adoption of English) that guaranteed Meet-ologie members access to the best-looking profiles in the gender(s) of their choice.

I told him "Non merci."

Then I phoned the advertising agency, demanding to know where, why, who etc., and was assured that my inquiry would be looked into *immédiatement*. That meaningless word again.

Meanwhile Elodie was providing me with plenty of distractions. She called me up.

"So, Paul, you think being a French lover actually makes you French?"

"What?" was the wittiest retort I could manage.

"Well you seem to think that you have some talent that entitles you to French nationality."

"How do you know about my application?" I asked.

"Oh, it helps to have a father with contacts."

"He has access to nationality applications?"

"He has access to just about every database in France, Paul, except the list of my lovers. I hope. But what made you suddenly want to be French? Do you really love pétanque that much?"

"No," I said, "it was Brexit."

"Ah, yes, my dear Brexit." She had been one of the French MEPs trying to force Britain out of the EU, before we took the decision ourselves. Like most French politicians at the time, she thought that the Brits had it too good: access to the free market without the burden of the euro, free movement without being in Schengen, as well as massive rebates obtained by the arch French-basher Margaret Thatcher. As ex-president Sarkozy once said, the Brits in the EU were like husbands at a swingers' party who refused to share their wives. (Some French presidents seem to move in unconventional circles.)

"I never thought I'd ever become French," I told her, "but now I have to."

"OK, well, I just wanted you to know that my papa is on your side."

That sounded ominous, a bit like hearing that a Mafia boss loves your newly-opened restaurant.

"What do you mean, Elodie?"

"Let's just say that your route to French nationality should resemble a quick Eurostar through the tunnel instead of a cross-Channel swim."

"I'm not sure I need Jean-Marie's help," I said.

I wanted my future passport to be real, not fake. And I didn't want it cited in a future trial about a rogue politician's cronyism.

"Don't forget that he's also giving his support to your pétanque campaign."

"Just promise me one thing, Elodie: he's not going to be at the meeting with the Paris Olympic people."

"Not necessary," she said. "I've decided to be there myself."

She giggled and rang off.

22

My one consolation was that I wouldn't be at that Paris meeting myself. Marjorie and Alain were planning to deal with the 2024 team on their own.

But then Marjorie called me.

"Elodie wants you," she said, sending a flash of panic down my spine, "to be at the meeting. She says she also wants us to discuss something Anglophone, so you must be there."

"What Anglophone thing?"

"I don't know. I asked her, but she didn't really answer."

"How did it go between you and her?" I asked.

Marjorie hesitated a moment before replying.

"I think we're on the same track. Potentially."

It sounded as though Elodie was trying to rope Alain's federation into one of her semi-legal political schemes. Which was precisely why I didn't want to be at the meeting.

"OK, I'll be there," I said.

"Good. It's lunch at the Jules Verne restaurant."

"We're meeting Elodie up the Eiffel Tower? I'll bring a parachute."

I arranged to meet Marjorie and Alain the following morning at half past eleven, at the usual brasserie near the École Militaire. I got there to find Alain haggling with a waiter about whether he would be allowed to sit where he wanted. This is not a given in a Parisian café, especially around mealtimes. All the free tables on the terrace were set for lunch, with tablecloths, cutlery, glasses and napkins. There was no way a waiter was going to let a mere drinker sit there.

"But there are plenty of free tables," Alain was saying.

"Free for *lunch*," the waiter replied.

If pure bulk had been the deciding factor in the argument, Alain would have crushed the opposition. It was the wine barrel against the carafe. Alain, his sack-like belly barely held in check by a burgundy shirt that was tucked, but only just, into a straining pair of khaki cargo pants with bulging thigh pockets, was up against a white-aproned waiter so thin he was leaning backwards to counterbalance the weight of his empty tray.

"I want to sit outside," Alain said.

"Would you like to have lunch?" the waiter replied, as if it was a personal invitation.

"It's too early for lunch," Alain argued.

"If you just want a drink, monsieur, I invite you to consult my colleagues indoors," the waiter said, smiling helpfully.

I stepped in to save Alain.

"I think I saw Marjorie inside the café," I told him.

"Oh, really?" Alain regained his composure. "I have a meeting with a charming young lady," he informed the waiter.

"Très bien, monsieur," the waiter said, with a mixture of warm approval and crushing indifference.

Alain and I went inside, to a corner where a few tables were still free of cutlery. This was the drinkers' corner.

The nearest waiter, a tall old guy, nodded his permission for us to sit.

"Oh, it wasn't Marjorie after all," I said, nodding towards a woman about forty years older and with completely different-coloured hair.

The real Marjorie arrived a couple of minutes later. She and I ordered coffee, but Alain decided that it was aperitif time.

"Vous avez du Ricard?" he asked our waiter, enunciating the brand name as if it was a herb known only to Provençal wizards.

The waiter didn't bother to reply. He turned away and went to the bar. He returned a couple of minutes later with a tall, branded Ricard glass, a carafe of water and a bowl of ice cubes on a small metal tray.

"What are we going to tell these Parisians?" Alain said,

mixing his drink with a yellow plastic Ricard stirrer.

"What we agreed with Madame Martin," Marjorie reminded him.

"And what exactly did Elodie propose?" I asked.

"She will support our claim that pétanque is part of a necessary patriotic ingredient that must be introduced into the Paris Olympics," Marjorie recited, as if it was straight out of a political manifesto. Which is almost certainly was – Jean-Marie's.

"And have you found out this Anglophone thing that she wants to discuss?" I asked.

"Olives," Alain said.

This, it turned out, was not a reply to my question. It had just occurred to him that something was missing from our crowded tabletop.

"Vous avez des olives?" he asked the waiter, who did his usual thing of apparently ignoring the question.

"We'll see," Marjorie said, apparently answering both Alain and me.

"I am a bit hungry," Alain said. He pulled half a baguette from one of his thigh pockets. "I saved this from breakfast."

He offered it to Marjorie and me, as if holding out a cigar case. We both refused, so he tore off a chunk for himself and returned the partial baguette to his pocket. He began chewing like a man who relishes meals between meals.

The olives, when they came, were small and shrivelled, bathing in a bowl of gold-green olive oil that was speckled with stalks of thyme or some similar herb. Half a dozen cocktail sticks were standing in the oil amongst the olives.

Alain tried his best to deal with these intricacies, but his stocky fingers were clearly more used to grabbing heftier objects. He prodded at an olive, impaled it on the fourth attempt, chewed it for a second or two, then spat the stone into his hand.

"Parisian olives?" he said. "Less flesh on these than on Edith Piaf. And she's been dead for 60 years."

Satisfied with his putdown of Paris's whole cultural heritage, he paid with a hundred-euro note that even our blasé waiter treated with respect, and we left for our meeting.

The Eiffel Tower is one of those places, like the private beaches on the Côte d'Azur, that proves France is not really a country of *égalité*.

While the tourist masses queue up to get frisked and buy tickets, people with a reservation at the Jules Verne restaurant can walk unhindered to a private lift in the south leg of the tower.

I love going up the Eiffel Tower, which is less a building than a giant pile of girders. It always reminds me of the tall matchstick structures I used to make as a kid. The Eiffel Tower looks as though you could pull out one stick of metal and the whole thing would come toppling down. But this is its beauty. It's very rare that a tall building can actually look delicate.

The hostess at the door to the lift was acting as the Tower's protector. She looked us up and down, and seemed highly satisfied with Marjorie's suit and my brightly polished shoes, but less so with Alain's trousers. There is a "no casual wear" dress code at the Jules Verne, and those cargo pants were so casual they were almost falling down.

"In what name is your reservation?" she asked, making it sound as though only De Gaulle or Napoleon would be enough.

"Elodie Martin," Marjorie replied, and got the same reaction as if she'd name-dropped an emperor. The Martin dynasty were clearly regulars here.

Mollified, the hostess allowed us access to the hallowed door.

The lift took off almost sideways, which didn't bother me, as I've been up in plenty of English seaside funiculars, but it got Alain reaching out to steady himself against the wall.

He looked even more nervous as we rose into the body of the Tower, all of us gazing out through the lift windows at the apparently flimsy criss-cross of beams that were holding everything upright. It was as if we were seeing the Tower's strands of DNA.

Alain didn't seem to be very reassured when we stepped out into the restaurant itself. He tested the floor for solidity before putting both feet forward.

Another hostess interrogated us briefly, and then we were led across an almost-empty dining room to a large circular table by the window, overlooking the Champs de Mars and the École Militaire, which did, I had to admit, seem to be a very long way down. I let Marjorie and Alain take the seats nearest the edge.

A female cloakroom attendant came over and asked Marjorie if she would like to hang up her jacket.

"Non, merci."

The attendant turned to Alain.

"Monsieur, would you like me to take your ...?" She hesitated, and I thought she was going to say "baguette" but in the end she decided he had nothing that she wanted to take off him, and left.

We had arrived exactly on time, so naturally we were the only ones at the table. We had time to look around the restaurant.

"Très chic," Alain said, half-disapprovingly, as if his income tax was paying for the place. Which in the case of this meal, it probably was. Elodie was hosting the lunch, and I guessed it was coming out of France's Olympic purse. She never uses her own money if someone else's is within reach.

Aptly, the white plaster ceiling was moulded with what looked like Olympic rings, though there were seven instead of five. A good omen, maybe, pointing to the possibility of extra events.

On our table, the napkins were as thick and stiff as rolls of parchment, and the glasses were enormous, as if a half pint of wine was the smallest measure.

A young waiter in what looked like a silk jacket shimmered over and asked if we would like an aperitif.

"Non, merci," Marjorie answered, but I thought what the hell, I used to pay French taxes when I was earning more.

"Une coupe de champagne, s'il vous plaît," I said. Although French bubbly always comes in a tall flute, I love their way of ordering it that suggests it might be served in a "cup". It sounds so medieval.

"Champagne?" Alain was impressed.

"Yes, Elodie won't mind."

I remembered the last time I'd come to this place, which was also the first. I'd been with Elodie's father, Jean-Marie. I'd just joined his company's marketing department as his star international signing, and he brought me here to show me his clout. We'd had lobster and champagne, all on the company card, and had chatted away like best chums. This was before he fired me on a rigged-up charge, had me evicted from my apartment and tried to get me deported. The loyalty of the Martin family was even flimsier than the Eiffel Tower's girders. This was why my motto was, if the Martins offer you champagne, take it, because things are bound to go belly up later on. As the Romans probably said, *carpe bubbliem.*

Alain and Marjorie decided to join me with *une coupe,* and we were all sipping champagne and enjoying fat, easy-to-skewer olives when we were joined at our table by two slightly-rushed people who introduced themselves as Louis Something and Héloïse Something-Else. I'm not very good at remembering French surnames unless I see them written down.

Louis, a tall forty-something with a balding head and, like almost all balding forty-something Parisian guys, a stubbly grey beard, was wearing an electric-blue suit that was almost as bright as the sky outside.

When he said his first name, he pronounced it weirdly, adding an extra syllable: "Loui-sha."

Héloïse was a few years younger but almost as tall and slim, with metal-rimmed glasses and short dyed-reddish hair held back by a headband. She wore a Breton T-shirt as if she was about to go sailing. She looked at our champagne glasses and I could almost hear her thinking "chancers", or whatever the Breton equivalent was.

Louis-sha and Héloïse explained that they were both on the *Calendrier des Compétitions* team – which had to be something to do with deciding what happened during the Paris Games. An excellent start.

The only off-putting thing about all this was the way Louis talked. He added whistling syllables to any word that ended in the "ee" or "ay" sound, of which there are lots in French. So Paris was "Paree-sha" and *calendrier* was "calendri-ay-sha". It sounded as though he was trying to be refined but ended up merely prissy.

Héloïse was far from prissy.

"Why exactly are we meeting here?" she asked Marjorie. "This place is exorbitant."

"Madame Martin thought it would give us a good view of the future Olympic emplacements," Marjorie said.

"She's not here yet?" Héloïse asked needlessly, making a point about punctuality. "But then, what is her role in this meeting? Aren't we just having another discussion about pétanque, after your conversation with Geneva?"

Marjorie avoided answering by taking a diplomatic gulp of champagne.

"And you, Monsieur?" Héloïse turned her gaze on me. "What is your role here?"

"To consume free champagne and order the second most expensive thing on the menu," I wanted to say. Most expensive would look greedy.

"I understand from Madame Martin that there is an Anglophone element to the discussion," I said, proud of my technical-sounding French.

"Really?" Héloïse didn't seem to think I was any kind of element.

Elodie turned up a few minutes later, unhurried, unapologetic, the lateness proving her importance. She shook everyone's hand, greeting her two Olympic colleagues as though she knew them without actually enjoying their company. She smiled pityingly at Alain, probably the least sexy man she had ever allowed herself to touch, and scrutinized Marjorie, whom she'd only ever seen on Zoom. Elodie seemed to recognize that she and Marjorie were two similar products of expensive French business schools, although Elodie was richer and wielded more power, so that it was like a hyena eying a golden retriever.

"Champagne, excellent idea," Elodie said, half to us, half to the waiter who rushed off immediately to execute her order. Héloïse shook her head, but didn't refuse to join in.

As soon as the extra glasses of bubbly arrived, Elodie raised her flute to the Olympics – I had just enough left in my glass to sip a toast – and said we needed to get down to business quickly because she had a meeting with *le Ministre*. She didn't specify which one, as if we ought to know.

"Tell us, how did it go with the Swiss?" Héloïse asked.

Alain opened his mouth to speak but Marjorie got there first and said that the International Olympic Committee understood France's desire both to increase the importance of the French language at the Paris Games, and to include a traditional French sport like *pétanque*.

Louis tried to reply, but Elodie cut him off.

"Geneva has acknowledged that with your breakdancing, skateboarding and BMX cycling, you're turning the Paris Olympics into an American circus." She scowled at Héloïse and Louis as if this brutal crime was all their fault. "I'm sure the food stands in the stadiums will all be selling nothing but wraps and smoothies." With arch snobbery, she pronounced these words in proper English rather than "vrap" and "smooty".

Héloïse gave Elodie a withering look, which merely bounced off the latter's Louis Vuitton hide.

"As we have repeated before," Louis said, cha-cha-ing through the syllables, "our demonstration events, reflecting the philosophy of the whole Paris Games, will be youth-oriented and inclusive, attractive to both spectators and the media."

"Like curling?" Alain said.

The jibe hit home.

"Curling is a very popular Olympic event on television," Louis said.

"And it is played right across the planet," Héloïse added.

"As is pétanque," Alain said.

"And to be fair, no one plays curling in Africa," Marjorie added.

There was an awkward silence. Suddenly Héloïse and Louis seemed to be very interested in the tablecloth and the ceiling. The Parisians clearly didn't want to budge.

"If I may contribute an Anglo-Saxon view," I said.

I have no idea if my ancestors were Anglo-Saxon, Norman, Celt, Viking or Neanderthal, but the French describe all English-speakers as members of this one tribe dating back before the Norman Conquest. They feel comfortable with the notion of Anglo-Saxonism, so it's useful to wheel it out occasionally.

Héloïse squinted sceptically at me, but didn't tell me to keep my nose out of their French business.

"If I have understood correctly from your Paris Olympics website," I said, "the central problem is that every new event means an old event must disappear?"

"Oui-sha," Louis conceded. "The fifty-kilometre walk has been abolished, for example."

"I didn't even know it existed," I replied, "and I'm probably not the only one. But if the new events are all younger and more inclusive, soon the Olympics will be *all* kitesurfing, paddle boarding, skateboarding, breakdancing and parkour."

"Exactement," Alain added. Pronounced "exacta-mang".

"Maybe 2024 is a final opportunity," I went on. "Before everything becomes American, Paris can give a traditional French sport, pétanque, its last chance to be Olympic."

"Exacta-mang!"

"Well said," Elodie chipped in, giving me a rare approving look. She seemed to think I was merely paying lip service to her crusade, but I meant it. I enjoy watching breakdancers swivel on their heads as much as the next man, but surely *pétanque* had as much right as breakdancing to a place in the Paris Olympics?

"That doesn't sound like an Anglo-Saxon view to me," Louis said.

"It's like an Anglo-Saxon confession," I replied.

"Yes, and the Anglo-Saxons have a lot to confess." Elodie took charge again. "As you probably know, our government is strongly behind the campaign to make the Paris Games more French overall."

"The government? Or just certain politicians?" Héloïse aimed the question at Elodie like a fencer's thrust at the torso.

But Elodie was fully-trained in verbal combat and simply side-stepped the attack.

"You have seen the film of young people playing pétanque in Paris by the canal?" she asked.

"Oui-sha," Louis said.

"You must admit it is strong argument," Elodie said. "It is young, inclusive and *French*. Now, our Anglo-Saxon ally Paul has already subtitled the film in English, so what I'm hoping is that you will agree to making it an official part of the Paris 2024 publicity. We can broadcast it in support of the campaign to include pétanque in the 2024 Games. The world will love the idea of France becoming even more French. Foreigners idealize us. They will support this campaign to impose our French identity on our French Olympics. You can edit in some of your own material about the Games in general, and I'm sure the new film could be ready, say, next week, if Monsieur West is ready and willing to subtitle the extra material?"

Given this sudden outbreak of politeness, and the offer of some more paid work, I could only nod in agreement.

"It is much too early," Héloïse said, sounding harassed. "We can't declare public support for pétanque just like that."

"Yes, the full committee has not decided," Louis added. *Décidé*-sha.

"I think the time is right," Elodie said. "And I know the people will agree with me." From anyone else, this would have sounded absurdly pompous, but Elodie was at her most Napoleonic. "Quite frankly, chers collègues, with the Swiss on our side, I am beginning to think the decision is out of your hands." This was where Napoleon's musket-bearing guards would have marched in and escorted Héloïse and Louis out to the firing squad.

They were struck dumb. Héloïse stared at Elodie as if she was deranged. Louis gave her the full "who the hell do you think you are?" eyebrows.

Alain, meanwhile, was gaping over his moustache at Elodie, clearly in love.

"Well, I'm sorry but I must leave you," Elodie announced. "We have an appointment to say exactly the same thing to the minister." This time, we were clearly meant to know the identity not only of the minister, but also of the "we". I was guessing Elodie and her father. "Enjoy your lunch, as my guests," she said, "and we will speak again soon."

She wafted out, leaving behind an almost-full glass of champagne. I've never seen anyone abandon an almost-full glass of bubbly before, unless of course they've already drunk five or six. It was killer touch, a show of sublime indifference to budgets or any other bureaucratic obstacle to her goals.

"Alors là," Héloïse said when Elodie had left, a French way of saying "well, what do you know?" or "what the hell just happened?".

Alain was grinning as though he'd just won a gold medal, but Marjorie was waiting anxiously to see how things played out.

"Was Elizabeth like that, the Queen of England?" Louis asked me. *Angleterre*-sha.

"Less regal," I said.

He laughed.

"You know, I am starting to think that this decision is out of *all* of our hands," Héloïse said. "Yours too."

"What do you mean?" Alain was concerned.

"Well, in the strictest confidence," Héloïse went on, "we have heard that Madame Elodie has her eyes on the post of director of the whole Paris 2024 committee. And once she has ousted the current director from his office, she will certainly change the faces in the team around her."

"A purge of the committee," Louis said. *Comité*-sha.

"Yes, and if she controls the committee, she will do what she wants, with exhibition sports, venues, languages, everything," Héloïse said. "Promises about pétanque will be forgotten, and we will be told to clear our desks. Of course, firing us won't be easy. We all have work contracts. We will sue."

"But that won't bother her, I don't think," Louis said. "Because by the time we are re-instated, the Games will be finished." *Fini*-sha.

"You may think that today's meeting was a victory for you and for pétanque," Héloïse said, turning to Alain. "But you are nothing to her, you are just one pawn in the game. One boule, if you prefer."

Alain appeared to think this over, as if he was analysing the game so far, wondering where to throw next.

"In a pétanque team," he finally said, "you need players who can point," a word meaning to throw with pinpoint accuracy, "and players who can shoot," that is, knock the opponent's ball out by force. "Madame Martin's ambitions don't bother me. I think she just shot, and the rest – the pointing – is up to us. She has opened the way for our team to win the game."

He turned to Marjorie, who nodded as though she agreed. But then, as long as the game was on, so was her job.

"My team will continue playing," Alain said, nodding towards both Marjorie and me, "and I think we can win."

I felt sure that Alain was being over-optimistic. I knew from past experience that once Elodie started shooting, there was a strong possibility that everyone except her would end up with bullet holes. But then again, if *pétanque*'s interests coincided with hers, which they seemed to do for the moment, for whatever reason, there was hope.

"Madame Martin said she is paying for lunch, n'est-ce pas?" Alain asked, running his finger down the menu, apparently counting up all the dishes he was planning to eat.

"Yes," Héloïse said. "Just try to forget who is *ultimately* paying, or it might spoil your appetite."

23

I don't know what it says about me, but I prefer cheap Paris restaurants to very chic ones, even if I'm not paying.

Whenever Parisian restaurants try hard to impress, they go too far. Whereas if they feign indifference, they can be excellent, like Cécile's place on the canal. There, the chefs and waiting staff seemed to take great care to give the impression they didn't give a *merde*, and the results were unpretentiously delicious.

I mused on this as I walked, or rather dragged my overstuffed stomach, away from the Eiffel Tower.

The food had been wonderful, creative, perfectly cooked, but – for me – too complicated. I mean, if you've got a sumptuously flash-grilled slice of red tuna, do you really need a hunk of hot *foie gras* draped across it like a greasy blanket?

Also, why top off a piece of yummily über-rich chocolate cake with a frozen globule of raspberry coulis *in the shape of a banana*?

And who, under any circumstances, needs a diamond-shaped plate?

I had decided to walk a couple of *Métro* stops to help my digestion along, and as I strolled the wide boulevard pavements, I wondered whether my work on *pétanque* wasn't almost complete, despite what Alain had said about his team carrying on with the game. I might need to start looking for new jobs.

From what I had seen and heard, Alain was like one of those infantry soldiers you see in war films, cautiously advancing towards the enemy behind a massive tank. The tank in this case being Elodie, who was storming ahead with her patriotic cannon blazing.

I would subtitle those extra bits of film for her, and then it would all be over. Either she would dump *pétanque* as a side issue in her family's political manoeuvrings, or it would all come to a happy conclusion and we'd be looking forward to seeing Alain in a bikini playing beach *boules* in 2024.

The idea of imminent unemployment made me think of someone who was currently overworking – Ambre. There was still no reply to my message of abject apology.

Now I hate it when things go wrong between me and a woman, which has happened quite frequently in the past, and not always through my fault. And I hate it even more when it's because of a misunderstanding.

So when I arrived back at the students' residence and saw that Ambre's window was open, I decided to be Elodie-like and charge in like a tank.

I didn't even go to my room first, to give myself time to chicken out. I was running on champagne and semi-raw tuna, both of them high-energy fuels, so I jabbed at the figure four in the lift and a mere minute later I was outside number 42, the Meaning of Life suite.

There was silence inside the room.

I knocked twice on the door, firmly but not threateningly.

After a couple of seconds there came a predictable but impatient "Kyess?" – Qui est-ce?

"It's the cretin," I said.

"I'm working."

"I know." Wasn't she always?

After a few more seconds, during which I was afraid Ambre might be powering up a Taser, the door opened. As a famous writer once said, she didn't quite look disgruntled, but she was far from gruntled.

"Nice lipstick," she said, which wasn't what I was expecting.

"Pardon?"

"Is it fashionable for Englishmen to wear lipstick on one side of their mouth?" She pulled out her phone and showed me a camera shot of my face.

"Oh, that must be raspberry coulis from the frozen banana."

175

"If you just came here to confuse me, you've achieved your mission." At least she was half-smiling now.

"No," I said, licking my lips in what I hope looked nothing at all like lasciviousness. "I have come to explain."

"I read your message, and there is nothing to explain," she said. "Men boast and lie about their conquests. It is a fact of life. You should be relieved that your masculine psychological profile is so normal. You are a completely predictable male."

"I lied," I said, "but I didn't boast. Well, yes, I did boast. But for one simple reason, and I just want to explain."

"I don't have time, Paul. I'm preparing a bid for a contract."

"Just take a one-minute break. I'm sure you do that sometimes. To do a pipi, for example."

"Pardon?"

Seeing the expression on her face, and the door beginning to close, I realized that the conversation was going in the wrong direction, almost literally down the toilet.

"I lied to Jake because he would not have believed the truth," I blurted, letting the words rush out.

The door stopped closing.

"Is that a good reason for lying to someone?" she asked.

"When it's Jake, yes. There are concepts that he cannot believe, like, for example, *not* making love to a woman as soon as you meet her."

"He is *that* successful with women?" She was clearly as incredulous as I was about it.

"I know. Amazing, isn't it?"

"Yes, but I don't have time to debate that kind of paradox, so –"

"The reason I told him I had made love to you was because I was trying to tell him I didn't want to make love to *another* woman." Again, I blurted it out. But to be honest, it was a sentence I'd been preparing for quite a while.

"What? Who?"

"Oh, a woman I used to know, who re-appeared. Nobody important. I wanted Jake's advice about how to, what do you say, pff?" I swatted Fleur like an imaginary fly.

"Hit her with a tennis racket?" This was said with another half-smile.

"No, you know, tell her *fous le camp!*" This is a French phrase meaning bugger off. It literally means "fuck the camp" Why, I have no idea. Something to do with the seductive shape of French tents, probably. "Jake said to me, go to see this woman, and I said no, and I invented a reason that he would understand. I told him I did not ever want to see this woman again, because I was with someone else – you."

"Oh." She seemed to have got it. And not been repelled by it.

"Which, to me, would be a very good reason. I mean, if it was true."

"Oh." She even looked mildly – very mildly – flattered.

That was when I should have left her to get on with her work and gone back downstairs. She would have thought, OK, so he's not just a stereotypical macho boaster after all, and he fancies me. That would have been an excellent position for me to be in. Maybe I might even have got another quick kiss.

So what made me drop the strategic *pétanque* ball on my own big toe by continuing to talk?

"Normally, I would never ask Jake for advice about a woman," I said, "but this was an extreme case." Something told me the ball of lead was now hovering over my foot, but I did nothing to avoid it. "You see, the other day this woman got an invitation from me via a dating app – or at least, she thought she did."

Ambre was staring at me as I'd seen her do before. It was an expression that said, "Why am I listening to this freak?"

I began to panic.

"It was my profile, except it wasn't," I gabbled. "The invitation came from me, but it didn't."

Help.

"So are you on this dating app or not?" Ambre asked.

"No! But I was on it during lockdown."

She shook her head.

"Well, thanks for this entertaining interlude," she said, "but

I really must get back to work."

"I haven't finished explaining."

"I think you have." She got hold of the door, ready to close it.

"No, you see, I was hacked. Someone sent a message in my name."

"Listen, Paul." Now she was just plain impatient to escape. "I *really* have to work."

The *pétanque* ball had squashed my toes and I finally realized it was time to duck out of the game.

"OK, sorry, Ambre. Remember, if you need any help with English –"

She held her hand up like a traffic cop enforcing a red light.

"Paul, do you know what French men used to say to French women?"

"Je t'aime? Voulez-vous coucher avec moi?"

She held her hand up again.

"Sois belle et tais-toi," she said. Be beautiful and shut up. "It was the old sexist way of keeping us in our place. Times have changed, happily, but I'm still fighting against that old attitude. And what I and my project need right now is peace of mind, silence, time to think. So please, Paul, sois beau et tais-toi."

She gave me the briefest hint of a goodbye smile and closed the door.

Staring at the number 42, I took silent stock of what had just happened.

Yes, overall, it had been a total disaster. She had told me to bugger off and leave her in peace.

But hadn't she just implied that I might be good-looking?

I walked away from the disaster smiling. Yes, once a perfectly predictable male, always a perfectly predictable male.

I'd only just got back to my room when Marjorie called me. There was the roar of traffic in the background, and voices. She was in the street.

"I've just left Héloïse," she said. "We went for a promenade along the Seine, and she revealed everything to me."

Very romantic, I thought, but why tell me?

"We discovered that we were at the same business school. She was there twenty years before me, but our school has what you in English call an ancients' network." Alumni, presumably. "And at our school, the ancients share secrets if it can help other ancients. So during our promenade, she explained everything about your friend Elodie and her father."

"What does she know about them?" I doubted that anyone knew *everything*.

"Well, it seems that part of the Olympic Village in Saint-Denis is being constructed on the site of a former abattoir that belonged to Jean-Marie Martin. And he insisted on getting the contract to build the buildings on that site himself."

"That sounds almost legal." Positively ethical by Jean-Marie's standards.

"Yes, but according to his contract, he'll also keep the ownership of the new buildings, so that he'll be able to sell them to the town of Saint-Denis after the Games. This is why he managed to place his daughter in the heritage department, in charge of what happens to all the buildings post-Olympics."

"Typical Martin strategy." But still semi-legal, by the sound of it.

"There is more. According to a rumour amongst the Paris 2024 committee, his new buildings will not respect minimum building standards. They won't be dangerous, but they will be built cheaply." Marjorie held the phone nearer her mouth and spoke confidentially. "The buildings will need extra work after the Games to pass the strict inspection before they can be used as social housing by Saint-Denis. And Monsieur Martin has a contract whereby the authorities will pay *him* for this work, and then lease the buildings from *him*. You see? He gets part of his construction paid for by Saint-Denis?"

"Even more typical Jean-Marie." And, annoyingly, even that was probably legal.

"But there's even more." With the Martins, there always was. "To ensure that this problem will not be specific to the Martin buildings, which might be considered suspect, Elodie is making sure that *all* the new Olympic buildings are not quite up to standard for other usage after the Games. So it will be a general problem, and no one will accuse the Martins of mis-using public money."

"Wow." Defrauding the entire Olympics and the French state was ambitious, even for Jean-Marie.

I heard a car horn, and Marjorie gasped. I half-expected to hear her phone clatter to the ground as a Martin-owned limousine silenced her forever.

But she carried on walking and talking, apparently unscathed.

"That is why Elodie and her father are trying to get their allies into key positions in the Paris Olympic organization, to stop any opposition to their plan."

"But why does no one, how do you say –" I tried to think of the French for "blow the whistle" but could only puff into the phone. "You know, like a football referee when there's a penalty?"

"That's the clever thing. The Martins know that the scandal would be too damaging for France. This is the Paris Olympics. It has to be clean. And anyway, France is a country of secrets. What happens in France stays in France. The meeting with the minister that Elodie was talking about, it is with the minister for *housing*. Something big is happening right up at government level. Héloïse doesn't know exactly what."

I tried to take all this in.

"Do you and Alain *really* want to do business with Elodie?" I asked.

"Oh, Alain doesn't care. As he says, 'la pétanque, c'est la pétanque'." She imitated his accent: pétank-a. "As for me, if the customer is happy, I'm happy. Even so, send me an invoice, and send it today. Let's get our money now in case everything turns to shit."

By the sound of it, there was a good chance that the *pétanque* balls would be hitting the fan very soon.

Later that afternoon, I had just woken up from a digestive siesta when I received a call from a *numéro inconnu*, an unknown number. I'm usually wary of scammers, but I answered.

"Monsieur Wess?" a female voice inquired.

"Oui," I confessed, "mais …"

Before I could tell her that I didn't want to change my energy provider or reveal my PIN code, she barged on. She was calling, she said, from the legal department of Publi-Feel, or some such name, an advertising agency, and she had been told that I was alleging that my image had been used for commercial purposes without my permission.

"Oui," I just had time to say.

"And you demanded to know who, if anyone, had provided the agency with your name and photograph."

"Oui."

"Well, you must understand that we cannot reveal our sources." She made it sound as if she were a Pulitzer-winning undercover reporter rather than a kind of pimp for advertisers.

"Mais," I managed to say.

"If you want to pursue your demand, I advise you to contact a lawyer."

"Mais!"

"Bonne soirée, monsieur," she wished me a good evening and then she was gone, presumably to plan her own *soirée*.

Contact a lawyer, I thought. Why is it that people only tell you that when they know you can't afford a lawyer?

24

Things started happening at Olympic speed. I had the impression that a shot putter was limbering up in front of me, getting ready to launch a huge lump of lead at my face. And that shot putter was Elodie's father, Jean-Marie.

Waking up one morning, I began surfing around on social media from my bed and was suddenly joined on my pillow by Jean-Marie himself. A film of him, that is.

He was looking, as usual, as sincere and trustworthy as only a true con man can. His perma-tanned face, set above a shirt collar apparently made of the finest Sèvres porcelain and a tie like liquid mercury, was oozing seductive French at me.

France, he was saying, would soon be the focus of all the world's media, and not, for once, because of riots.

He, as leader of the France Party (his political group changed its name about once a month, as French political parties tend to do, and now he seemed to have run out of creative ideas), was leading the campaign to make sure that the nation seized this great opportunity.

The camera pulled back, and suddenly he was standing in front of what I knew to be a fake backcloth. The film made it look as though he'd been at Marjorie's *pétanque* evening by the canal. This was laughable. Jean-Marie had probably never been to the 19th *arrondissement* in his life, except on his way to the airport.

France, he went on, pronouncing the name with ever-deeper affection, was refusing to feature *pétanque*, its very own sport, at the Paris Games. "C'est un scandale national!"

As we watched one of Marjorie's friends celebrate a well-thrown *boule* in the background, Jean-Marie put on a pained expression similar to the one Joan of Arc must have pulled when the flames reached her feet.

At the most recent Olympics in Tokyo, he said, French was the sixth language to be heard in official announcements. Yes, the *sixth* (and the fire was now nibbling at Joan of Arc's knees). And if France let the Paris Olympic Committee have their way, this *scandale* would be perpetrated again. English would be first, French last. In Paris itself! And to this outrage, this humiliation, Jean-Marie, in the name of all true French citizens, said "Non!".

The camera pulled in for a close-up. Instinctively, I recoiled because Jean-Marie was suddenly wearing his caring father face, the one he'd used on me before explaining that he was firing me for my own good.

It was "profoundly worrying", he confided, that the threat to the French language was coming from *within France itself*. It was 1940 all over again.

His rage boiled over. "Non!" he trumpeted. "Traditions must be protected. And this is especially true of all French traditions!"

All of them, I thought, really? Baguettes and long holidays *oui*, guillotines and certain French singers, *non*.

"La France d'abord, le français d'abord. La France," Jean-Marie concluded, his eyes as steely as a Parisian determined to get the last free lounger on a Saint-Tropez beach. France first, French first, France. Not much doubt about where his allegiance lay.

And the worst thing was that the link sending me to Jean-Marie's YouTube video had been in a message from Elodie asking me, "Can you subtitle this, Paul? Today?"

I felt like a posh French waiter who was being asked to clean the toilets.

I'd only just showered when there was what sounded like a scuffle outside my door, followed by brusque knocking.

Naked except for a hastily-wrapped towel that I was holding around my waist with one hand, I opened up to find the concierge Madalena wrestling with a young guy in a blue and yellow nylon vest. He was wearing other clothes, of course, but that was what caught my eye – the vest with its *La Poste* logo.

"Le voilà," Madalena told the struggling postman. Here he is. "Signez," she told me.

The postman thrust a large brown envelope and a pen at me.

"C'est une aggression," he complained. This was assault.

Not sure what was going on, I signed the form taped to the envelope, and the postman gruffly tore it off.

"Voilà, merci, tu veux un café?" Madalena asked him, now smoothing his nylon vest almost affectionately.

He pulled himself free, shot me a furious look, and stalked away towards the lift.

"Look, it is from the République," Madalena told me, pointing at the engraving of the topless 18th-century rioter Marianne in one corner of the envelope. "That is why I forced him to come up and deliver it. He was going to leave one of those little papers, 'You were not at home'. So I forced him. Maybe this is your nationality?"

"It's too soon," I said. "They said I have to wait months."

With Madalena watching every move of my fingers, I opened the envelope to find a white cardboard file, decorated with another topless rioter.

Inside the file was a long-winded letter, but with one highly eye-catching sentence printed in bold capitals across the middle of the page.

This sentence told me I was invited to attend an interview, the very next day, concerning my application for French citizenship. I showed Madalena.

"But it's too soon," I repeated.

"It is God's will," Madalena said, forgetting that France is one of the few countries in the world that does not allow deities to interfere in its state business.

"It is très bizarre," I said.

"It is an answer to your prayers," she assured me. "Now pick up your towel. Nudity is not permitted in the corridors."

Less than an hour later, Elodie called me.

"Are you going to say thank you?" she said.

"What for?"

"The nationality interview, of course. Who do you think organized that for you so quickly?"

Oh *merde*, I thought.

"You?" I suggested.

"No, of course not, it was papa. I told him you are working on the pétanque campaign, and he wanted to show his gratitude."

"Oh."

"Aren't you going to say thank you?"

I was meant to be grateful for his gratitude? Where was it all going to end?

"Merci," I said. It seemed curmudgeonly not to.

"You're welcome. You know, papa is even *donating* a building to be turned into a pétanque stadium?"

"Really?"

I doubted whether "donating" was the operative word.

"Yes, near the Gare de Lyon, where the trains from Provence arrive. Convenient for all the pétanque fans when they come to Paris."

"Very kind of him." I was tempted to ask how many millions the Martin family would be making out of the deal. "But are you sure the Paris committee is going to accept pétanque as an event?"

"I've got them in hand. It's a done deal. Practically."

"Congratulations."

"Now if you're feeling grateful, Paul, I need your help."

"Subtitling your dad's film?"

"Yes, but more than that."

Here we go, I thought. Back-scratching time.

"I need you to help me write to an English film director," she said.

"What? Why?"

This was all getting too random. I opened my window and stuck my head out into the cool morning air. The shrubs were rustling in a light breeze. The sparrows were doing their carefree dance.

"I just messaged you a film, look at it."

It opened with a muscular guy, wearing nothing but a pair of shorts and dark booties, climbing up the side of a skyscraper.

The climber, who I now saw was a computer graphic rather than an insanely reckless human being, reached the top of the skyscraper, strapped on a parachute and jumped off. Sailing down, we switched to his viewpoint and saw what I recognized as the Stade de France in the distance. Then the sequence froze. Apparently it was just a snippet.

"You see?" Elodie said. "We want a fake film like you English had in London in 2012. We see the climber climb up one of papa's buildings, he jumps off, or maybe she, then glides to the opening ceremony in the Stade de France. But who will climb?"

"Well you can't ask the Queen, for obvious reasons, but Meghan might do it if the price was right."

"You are an idiot, but an intelligent one," she said. "Just as you English did in 2012, we will want people to believe the parachutist is someone very famous – the president, maybe, or a French movie star."

"If it's the president, at least half the French people will be hoping for a tragic accident," I said.

"You're right. We have time to decide exactly who will jump. But we definitely want to make the film, so I need you to help me write to the English director of the 2012 film. What was his name? Danny Cook?"

"Boyle," I corrected her. "And he's Scottish, so the last thing you should call him is English."

"Oh, you Anglo-Saxons are too sensitive. I'll send you the draft of the letter. Can you correct it today? I want to get this project moving. I'd be very grateful."

That word again.

"Sure," I said. "If you're paying."

"Of course. Well, Paris is paying." It sounded as though the Martins were taking over the whole Olympics.

I watched Elodie's climber again and, looking at the skyscraper, I was reminded of the other films I'd watched recently, showing the future Olympic Village and the beach volleyball venue near the Eiffel Tower. I felt the same nagging question at the back of my mind: something was wrong with the building. What was it?

The sparrows were chattering at me as if they knew. I went to fetch some sunflower seeds from my cupboard and scattered them into the shrubbery.

Looking out my window, across the new gardens with their freshly laid pathways bordered by buildings like my own that had been renovated or newly constructed, I thought again about sparrows dying out in Paris because of the lack of nooks and crannies in gentrified neighbourhoods.

The start-up incubator and my students' residence were just two examples of Paris's massive architectural clean-up act. People like Jean-Marie were knocking down the old buildings and putting up gleaming, dreaming towers. Soon sparrows, the scruffy, urban-coloured birds that had given Edith Piaf her name might disappear from the whole region.

Yes. That was it.

Jean-Marie's Olympic towers, like all the computer mock-ups of buildings for the Games, were too smooth. Their lines were too clean. And I wasn't just talking about sparrows' nesting sites. It was another excess of smoothness that had been bothering me.

This was something that I needed to discuss urgently with the excessively smooth Elodie. Face to face, not on the phone.

It took me less than twenty minutes to redraft her letter to the film director, and then I called her to let her know I'd finished.

"Just send it to me," she said, "or have you forgotten how email works?"

"No, I'll bring it to you. I need to see you in person."

"How flattering, Paul." She sounded suspicious.

"To save you mistaking my intentions, I prefer to meet in

public. Say, at the open-air café in the Luxembourg gardens? In an hour?"

"It all sounds intriguing, but I can't just go out for coffee whenever you want me to, Paul, I'm very busy."

"When can you make it? Preferably today."

"Oh, you're so enthusiastic. How can a poor Parisian girl resist you? Let's meet at five o'clock, Englishmen's teatime."

At five I'm usually more in the mood for a beer, but I didn't want to go against stereotype.

"OK, five o'clock in the Luxembourg gardens."

"This is all very James Bond. We need a code. I'll be wearing a red rose."

I hoped not. By the end of our conversation, she would probably feel like strangling me with its thorny stem.

25

I must confess I don't really like the Luxembourg gardens.

I know they're very popular and very picturesque. There's a former royal palace at one end, an Eden-load of flower beds, and rows of vintage metal garden chairs that are cruised by Parisian males who deal in equally vintage chat-up lines.

For me, though it's all too neat, too clean. You can even sit on the grass, which is forbidden (and frankly inadvisable) in central Paris's other urban gardens. The Luxembourg gardeners seem to know that the shoes treading on their lawns will all be brand new or have travelled here by taxi. What's more, none of those metal chairs are chained down, but nobody steals them. It's so un-Parisian.

I like the park's café, though. A modest glass-and-metal chalet set in the shade of tall chestnut trees, it's surprisingly unpretentious, as most old-school Parisian cafés are, even in the poshest neighbourhoods. They have nothing to prove so they're laid back.

I found a free table on the edge of the terrace, the perfect vantage point to watch out for Elodie as she descended from her house behind the Panthéon.

The terrace wasn't too crowded. It rarely is, except at weekends and during mid-summer. There were a couple of mums trying to feed crêpes to their just-out-of-school children, who were much more interested in the prospect of chasing pigeons. A young couple were photographing their whipped-cream hot chocolates. A family of tourists were tucking into salads, quiches and French fries and apparently wondering why no one else was eating dinner yet.

I ordered a *demi*, the standard half-pint beer size, and wondered how subtle I should be in my upcoming conversation with Elodie.

Not at all, I quickly decided. I needed to unsheathe my metaphorical dagger and lay it on the table, pointing at her and her family. Only then would she take me seriously.

She turned up twenty minutes late, of course. We kissed on the cheeks like old buddies, and she smiled breezily as she sat down, but I could tell she was wondering why I'd wanted to meet up. She asked me what I thought of her new shoes, confirming my prejudices about these gardens. Did everyone buy new footwear just to come here?

They were high heels of a famous brand, very plain but no doubt cruelly expensive. And I got the subliminal message. Yes, whatever I tried to do to her, she was rich and successful, and always would be.

"Exquisite footwear on exquisite feet, Elodie," I said, "but if you don't mind changing the subject, I asked you here to tell you that I know everything you and your father are doing with the buildings for the Paris Games."

She hardly blinked.

"I doubt that, but go on," she said.

"I know about the buildings' standards, or lack of them."

"I don't know what you're talking about, but go on." She glanced all around us, looking for witnesses. "Where's your phone, by the way? Are you recording this?"

I showed her that it wasn't recording.

"I don't want anyone to overhear us, Elodie, that's why I picked this place."

"OK. Have you brought my letter, to the director, Danny Fry or whatever?"

"Boyle," I said. "Yes."

"Good, can you order for me, please? Earl Grey with lemon. I can't stand it with milk, the way you English drink it."

Classic Elodie diversion tactics.

"As soon as the waiter comes out," I said, "but first listen to me. I've seen the computer graphics of all the buildings in your films. I've been out to the building sites in Saint-Denis. And I've noticed something."

"Oh, you've seen that they're not finished yet. Well done, Paul."

But I was determined not to let her bump me off course.

"I've noticed that none of the buildings have solar panels."

I stopped talking and she frowned.

"So?" She seemed almost disappointed, as though she had been expecting me to accuse her father of making all the fire escapes out of half-empty oil barrels.

"I want you to fit all of your buildings with solar panels."

"Why? They're not obligatory. And anyway, there's not enough sun in Paris. They wouldn't be economic."

"Some solar panels work in cloudy weather, or even in the rain."

"What are you talking about, Paul? What is this nonsense?"

"It's true. There are solar panels that can produce power even in the rain, don't ask me how. And those are the panels I want you to order, from a company whose details I'm going to give you. They're to be fitted on all the buildings in the new Olympic Village and all the permanent structures that are being built in Paris itself."

Elodie was looking bemused.

"I don't get it, Paul. What do you have to gain or lose in all this? What do I?"

Personal gain was her only reason for doing anything.

"The solar panels are made by a friend of mine."

She laughed, then began nodding as though she'd finally seen through me.

"Don't tell me, Paul – a woman? It's Marjorie, isn't it?"

"No."

"I don't believe you." She examined my face for traces of deception. "But even if it's not her, it's definitely a woman." She studied me again, extracting nuggets of truth from my reactions. "Let me guess – it's a woman you haven't slept with yet?" I didn't reply. She laughed. "Oh God, Paul, this is pathetic! Just buy this girl some flowers, tell her she's the most beautiful and fascinating human being you've ever met, et voilà le travail." She meant job done. "It's a French woman, right?" she said. "You might not even need the flowers."

"Your respect for your fellow countrywomen is admirable, Elodie. But this has nothing to do with getting a woman to sleep with me," I lied.

"In that case, you won't want me to tell her that you are the one who got the solar panel contract for her. N'est-ce pas? You definitely *don't* want her to leap into your arms and say, 'oh merci for setting up this deal, Paul, mon héros, now you can fuck me!' Your motives are pure. Right?"

She gave me her most self-satisfied smile.

"Yes, pure as the cocaine you seem to have sniffed before coming here," I said. "Don't tell her I talked to you. Say you saw one of her pitches online and that you want to order a consignment of solar panels. Just make sure you contact her today."

"I don't have time to –"

I cut her off.

"The thing is, Elodie, as I said, I know what you and your dear papa are up to, building substandard buildings, and I will tell some journalists all about it if you don't sign a contract for those solar panels. Immediately."

"You have no proof," she said, the final refuge of the guilty.

"The journalists won't have to dig deep to find it."

"The government won't want a scandal about the Olympics. It's a matter of national pride."

"As you very well know, Elodie, France has some famous magazines and newspapers that don't give a shit about national pride. Journalists who don't give a shit about anything. They've survived terrorist attacks and they'll be all too keen to shovel merde all over your dad and his French Party."

"France Party," she said.

"Ah yes, how could I forget?"

The waiter was ambling towards us, but Elodie waved him

away. Apparently, she no longer felt like taking tea with an Englishman. Her eyes narrowed at me.

"You really do not understand gratitude, do you, Paul? After everything papa has done for you. Your nationality interview is like a miracle, a gift from heaven."

This made me laugh.

"Your *papa* only gives gifts for his own benefit. I bet he makes you sign receipts for your Christmas presents."

Anger twisted her usually composed face.

"You know, Paul," she sneered at me, "I've always thought it was very comical. You English, you invented all those sports like football and rugby and rickets."

"Cricket."

"Whatever. You invented them, but now everyone beats you at them."

"Not always –"

She brushed away my attempt at national self-defence.

"But there is one sport for which you will always win the gold medal."

"What's that?" I was being used as a straight man but what the hell.

"Stabbing people in the back. Especially us, the French."

I seemed to remember a jingoistic British general, the Duke of Wellington probably, saying that you could only stab a Frenchman in the back if he was running away. But judging by Elodie's dangerous mood, it didn't seem like a good time to mention it.

"I'm not stabbing you in the back, Elodie. I'm not stabbing anyone. I'm helping you and your dad do the right thing. So just order some fucking solar panels."

Like I said, subtlety doesn't work with Elodie.

26

I arrived at the Bureau de Naturalisation with a full twenty minutes to spare before my interview. I took my ticket and sat down to wait for my number.

The ping to summon me had hardly faded before I reached the receptionist's desk.

"Bonjour, Madame, j'ai une interview à dix heures."

"Ah non, Monsieur."

This could not be happening, I thought. No way had I *boules*'d up. I'd re-read my invitation a hundred times to make sure it was the correct date, time and planet. I'd even checked that the word for interview was feminine in French – *une interview*. And now she was telling me "non, Monsieur"?

Everyone else in the waiting room seemed to be holding their breath, wondering what form the receptionist's *coup de grâce* would take.

Well, I wasn't giving up just yet.

"Mais j'ai l'invitation," I said, holding up the paper proof.

"Oui, Monsieur, mais vous n'avez pas une interview à dix heures."

She looked almost benevolent while condemning my application to oblivion. But I didn't understand why she was doing it. I could only guess that someone in the department had objected to Jean-Marie having me bumped to the front of the queue and had cancelled the appointment.

"Non?" I said.

"Non, Monsieur. Vous avez un *entretien*. Les *interviews* sont à la télé ou la radio. Vous avez un *entretien*."

So it was just another vocabulary problem. A journalistic

interview wasn't the same French word as the sort of interview I was having. I was reprieved!

This woman was a magician, I realized. She could make Englishman's tears appear at will.

She told me that someone would come and fetch me, and invited me to return to my seat. As I threaded my way between the outstretched legs of my fellow waiting-room sufferers, I received nods of approval, like someone who has just had an injection without screaming.

Ten minutes later, the sweat was still cooling along my spine when I heard a female voice calling my name, or the French version of it.

"Monsieur Wess Pol?"

Standing by the door to the inner sanctum was a pleasant-looking lady of about 40, semi-casually dressed in blouse and jeans, the kind of woman you sometimes see at the customer relations counter in large French supermarkets.

"C'est moi, Wess Pol," I confessed, and went to join the lady, receiving those same supportive looks from the other applicants around me.

The office beyond the sanctum doors was open plan, divided by low partitions, creating a sort of chessboard of workstations. There was a low buzz of conversation from other *entretiens*.

I followed the lady to her desk, and she invited me to sit in the guest chair. She didn't turn an angle-poise lamp at my eyes, which was promising.

She clicked on her computer to open up my file, and then pulled a thick paper dossier off the top of a pile. My name was written on the cover.

She began flicking through the wad of pages. Had I really photocopied that many documents?

"Alors," she said, "you want to become French? Why?"

She carried on flicking through the file, but I guessed this was a key question. Naturally, I had prepared an answer.

"I think it's my only hope of winning a World Cup medal at football," I said.

No, I didn't, of course.

"There is a real danger for the future," I said, feeling a bit like Jean-Marie Martin in one of his political broadcasts, "that because of Brexit, I will be forced to leave my home, leave Paree."

"Really?" she didn't seem to think this was likely, but then maybe she hadn't yet flicked as far as my bank statements.

"Yes, the British government has imposed a financial threshold –" I'd looked this word up, and in French it was a killer: *seuil*, which you had to pronounce a bit like a posh alcoholic saying "soy".

"A financial seuil for immigrants," I went on. "And naturally the French government might reciprocate." I'd looked that up too, *réciproquer*, an easy one. "At the moment, I am just trying to expand my new business, and I am not rich."

In my experience, French bureaucrats usually lean emotionally to the left and think they're underpaid, so admitting you're poor is like expressing solidarity with them.

"I see," she said. "So you want nationality to be able to stay in France?"

"Yes."

"Why not just apply for a residence permit?"

Good question, damn it.

"I feel Parisian more than English," I said. I tried to offer proof in the form of a double-shoulder shrug.

This seemed to satisfy her.

"Did you read the Citizen's Booklet?" she asked.

"The what?"

This was less satisfactory. She repeated the name: *Le Livret du Citoyen*. I had no idea what it was, and tried another shrug.

"The link was on the invitation to your interview," she said.

Oh, *merde*, I thought.

"Sorry," I blustered. "I was so surprised, and so happy to get the invitation that I didn't –"

She raised both her hands in surrender and produced a small booklet from a drawer. Maybe I wasn't the first applicant to skip his reading homework.

"Look at this," she said.

On the bright, tricolour-coloured front cover was the face of the usual topless female with the red bonnet. Marianne was looking young and healthy, if a bit pale.

I opened the booklet and thumbed through it. There were chapters on democracy, equality, fraternity, a timeline of French history, a mosaic of famous "French" scientists and artists who, like the applicants for citizenship, had been born abroad.

And I was supposed to have learnt all this by heart before I got here?

I quickly tried to memorize a few dates and names as I glanced through the pages. Louis XIV, 1789, 1870, Marc Chagall, Marie Curie, Françoise Giroud. Hang on, wasn't he a Breton footballer?

"Look at page five," the lady told me.

It showed a picture of an engraved marble tablet guarded by two angels, one of whom was pointing to a shining triangle in the sky.

Maybe this was a freemason test, I thought. If I give her the right handshake or codeword, I'm in?

"That is the Déclaration des droits de l'homme," she said.

"Ah oui." The revolutionary affirmation of men's rights, written at a time when women had none.

"Look at the text on the right."

I read the paragraph beside the photo of the *Déclaration*. It began with one of France's beloved rhetorical questions: Can France refuse nationality to a person who does not accept the equality of men and women?

Like all French rhetorical questions, the answer was given straight afterwards: Yes it can.

"Do you believe women are equal to men?" she asked me.

The answer was simple: no way. In real terms, women like Elodie were vastly superior to men like me because she had money and power. That's why I'd had to resort to blackmail to drag myself, temporarily, up to her level. Though I guessed that wasn't the response my interviewer was looking for.

"Of course," I said. "Completely."

I was pleased to see that my interviewer actually ticked a box on her computer screen. It was that easy to score a point.

Equality was dealt with, so presumably all I had to do from now on was say I believed in liberty and fraternity, and French nationality would be *dans le sac*.

"And what, for you, is la laïcité?" she asked.

"L'iced tea?" Not so easy after all.

She saw me floundering and told me to turn to page seven. It was all about religion, and the separation of church and state. I'd often heard people say that France was anti-religious, and that the French state had separated loads of bishops and priests from their heads during the Revolution.

"Do you agree that one citizen should be free to believe what he or she wants, and to practise any religion, or none, but should not be able to impose his or her beliefs on other citizens?"

This sounded suspiciously like another leading question.

"Yes?" I hazarded.

"That is la laïcité," she said.

"Oh, then I believe that," I said. It was true. I still bore the emotional scars of Nolwenn's dietary dictates.

"Très bien." She ticked another box. This was going brilliantly. "Now close the booklet," she said, and I thought, oh no, here comes the real test. This is where they entrap applicants in the UK with questions about the number of overs in a one-day cricket match, the date of Prince William's birthday and the ideal thickness of Marmite on a slice of toast.

"What is your favourite period of French history?" she asked me.

"Oh …" Don't mention the wars, I told myself, and leave Napoleon and Joan of Arc out of it. But shit, what else was there in French history? I needed something happy, a good time for France.

"The invention of the baguette," I said.

She laughed. But didn't tick a box. Maybe she thought I was joking.

"I mean, I think it was in the nineteenth century," I stumbled on. "A time when France invented lots of very French things.

Like, er ..." I really needed that tick. "Can-can. Les Misérables. Impressionism. French things that are famous all over the world. An important period."

Her finger hovered over the keyboard. Come on, I urged her. No one was going to turn my nonsense about baguettes and can-can into a PhD thesis, but it was history, right?

"So, the nineteenth century?" she said.

"Yes."

And there it was, the tick.

"And what are your favourite regions of France?" she asked.

I was in the home straight, surely. I reeled off a few places I'd visited, taking care to omit Cap d'Agde, the nudist resort where I went with an old girlfriend and which frankly scared the shit out of me. All those dangly bits caked in sand.

"The Île de Ré," I said, "Bandol, Arromanches."

"They're all by the sea," she said, amused rather than disapproving. And she gave me another tick. Who needed Jean-Marie? This nationality business was *enfants'* play.

"Yes, I love water," I said. "And not just Evian or Célestins. I live near the canal in the nineteenth."

"The nineteenth?" She nodded. Living in that far-flung *arrondissement* seemed to be make me somehow more French than if I'd been in the Latin Quarter. Maybe it was going to earn me a bonus tick.

"Yes, the canal is very beautiful," I said. "I often go to the Bassin de la Villette to play pétanque." My philosophy is, if you're going to be French, be really *Français*. Maybe I ought to claim that I smoked Gauloises and amputated my own frogs.

"Pétanque? That is perfect," she said. "We can use that during your language test."

Language test? The cold sweat from the waiting room returned.

French grammar is the purest form of mental torture. The only reason people like Jean-Marie want the whole world to speak French is so that they can laugh at our grammatical mistakes. I was doomed.

"For five minutes," she said, "can you explain to me the rules of pétanque and how you play the game?"

I almost burst out laughing.

Mentally thanking Alain and Marjorie for introducing me to the secret world of France's national sport, I told her everything I knew about the *boules* and the *cochonnet*, and how to *pointer* (aim accurately) and *tirer* (shoot). In a fit of generosity, I gave her the Provençal origins of the word *pétanque*. The box was ticked even before I stood up and demonstrated my own favourite angle of knee bend.

"And do you usually play with French people or English friends?" she asked.

A final thrust of trick questioning, I decided.

"Oh, French friends," I replied. "Marjorie, Alain, Ambre, Hervé." I didn't think they were going to find out that at least one of those names thought I was an English dickhead who ought to be deported as soon as possible.

"And outside of pétanque, you regularly meet other French friends?"

"Yes, of course," I said, but my mind went blank. I could only think of ex-girlfriends. "Elodie, Fleur," I said. I hoped the nationality people wouldn't check up with either of them.

"All women?" she asked, teasing slightly.

"There are men, of course. For example, Jacques." I didn't think Jake would mind being Frenchified. "And Jean-Marie."

"Jean-Marie?"

Merde. Why had I mentioned him? There weren't many Jean-Maries about, and the most famous one right now was exactly the person I shouldn't have been naming in this interview.

"Well, I suppose he's not exactly a friend. He's my ex-boss. I haven't seen him for some time. No, in fact, he's not a friend."

What was it Shakespeare said — methinks he protesteth like a guilty bastard? I just hoped my interviewer didn't read too much Elizabethan drama.

"Thank you, the interview is over. You will be contacted."

It sounded like the end of an unsuccessful audition.

"Do you know when?" I asked.

"It varies. It's like the invitation to the interview. Sometimes it's quick, sometimes it's slower."

In my case, I guessed it would be slower. After my recent interview with Elodie, Jean-Marie wasn't going to be bumping me to the front of any more queues.

27

It was the day after my nationality interview.

I was busy on some DIY with a hammer and chisel when there was a knock at my door.

Madalena, I assumed, coming to complain about the noise. Or a hitman courtesy of the Martin family.

But no, it was Ambre, looking as delectable as usual, and staring at me as if I was drunk. If I'd known it was her at the door, I would have wiped the sweat off my face and maybe even put on a shirt and some trousers.

"I just came to say thanks in person," she said.

"What for?" I asked her.

"The contract, of course. For the solar panels. It's really great for us."

So Elodie had told Ambre that I was involved, even though I asked her not to. Typical.

"Though I hope you won't be disappointed," Ambre went on.

"Disappointed?"

"That you won't get your so-called commission."

"What commission?"

I now noticed that Ambre was looking less pleased than someone normally would if they'd just received a game-changing, life-changing order for their new solar panels. She hadn't budged from the doorway, and had her arms folded defensively. Her expression was one of distrust rather than gratitude. That word again.

"What you hoped to get in return for the deal," Ambre said.

I was lost. I put on a T-shirt to give myself time to think.

Back to front, but what the hell. A pair of Bermudas too, the right way round. I framed some French sentences in my mind, and went for it.

"I don't know what Elodie said to you," I said, "but I asked her not to mention my name. I told her I had noticed that none of the Olympic buildings had solar panels. So I told her to contact you. And I said don't mention me."

Ambre thought about this.

"Really?" she said.

"Yes. I thought you would think –" but my French hit a wall of impenetrable grammar. "It was like I said with the sparrows. It was generosity, not a deal. No commission."

"Oh." She squinted deep into my eyes. "Do you promise me that's true?"

"I promise."

And her arms unfolded.

"You know what she told me?" she said.

"Something unpleasant?"

"Unpleasant if it's true, yes. She told me you were setting this up so you could sleep with me."

"No!"

Well, OK, that was partially true, but this was not the time for total honesty.

"And she said she was happy to agree, for your sake, because you were an old friend, an old lover in fact. Is that true?" Without waiting for a denial (which was fortunate for me), Ambre imitated Elodie's way of tipping her head to one side when she was being hypocritically honest, and began to speak in Elodie's posh voice. "Mon dieu, how Paul and I used to do it when we lived together! Oh, he was so excited about bais-ing the boss's daughter!"

"It was le contraire," I defended myself. "She wanted to baiser her papa's new English employee to shock her parents. It was years ago."

Ambre shrugged at that but returned to the more worrying present. She continued in an uncanny imitation of Elodie at her most silkily malicious, "You know, very recently, my ex-lover

Paul had the most active profile on Meet-ologie."

"That was fake news!"

Ignoring me, Ambre ploughed on. "And you must pay attention, Ambre, and defend yourself, because in any deal Paul does, he always has to be the winner. That's why he tries to sleep with every woman he meets."

"You don't believe that?" I protested.

"Why shouldn't I?"

"Because Elodie is just trying to –"

Ambre laughed and held up her hands as if in surrender.

"It's OK, Paul. I remember the first time I met you. You carried my solar panel up the stairs. You were the perfect gentleman. Not at all relou." This is French backslang for *lourd*, or heavy, and means anything and everything potentially bad.

It took a second for this to sink in. Ambre was saying that I hadn't gone into instant French lover mode with her, therefore I had disproved Elodie's theory. It was a case of *quod erat desperandum,* or whatever.

Ambre nodded when she saw that the penny had dropped.

"I was teasing you," she said. "I know Elodie's type. She's a real fouteuse de merde." A shit-stirrer, or more accurately shit-dumper.

"Exactly."

"And for some reason, Paul, she loves fout-ing it on you."

I nodded regretfully, the personification of innocence.

"But even so, you have signed a contract with her to sell your panels?" I asked.

"Yes. We had a lawyer look at the contract, and it was fine. I don't think Elodie wants to fout la merde on Lara and me."

"Excellent."

"Yes it is. Really excellent."

"Just make sure you see the money before you deliver the panels," I said. "You can't trust that family."

"Yes. In case Elodie turns relou with us."

"She can be very relou." I savoured the French feel of the two syllables in my mouth, the rasping "rr" and the long, round "ou".

Ambre laughed again. I guessed my pronunciation wasn't quite up to the mark yet.

But this was turning into a normal conversation.

And then Ambre actually entered my room. She looked down at my row of gravestone shoes without screaming. She inspected my clothes hangers and saw that I owned more than just a back-to-front T-shirt. She even walked past the bed without flinching at the rumpled state of the duvet.

"The money is only part of it," she said. "With a major contract from the Paris Olympics, we can attract interest from financiers. We'll get investment to build all these panels, then we'll get more contracts, I'm sure of it."

Now she was smiling at me, and I saw why Elodie thought that gratitude was such an attractive commodity.

"What were you doing with this?" She picked up the chisel from my work surface.

"Look."

Leaning out of the open window, I pointed to a hole I'd made in the masonry just below my window ledge. I'd chipped away the plaster, and there was a now a hole about as big as a plum leading into the hollow section of a breeze block.

"It's for the sparrows," I said. "They need holes." I didn't know the French word for nest. Ambre was nodding that she'd understood. "I'll go into the gardens and make some more," I told her. "I'll buy some little boxes for the sparrows, too – what do you call them?"

"Nichoirs," she said.

"Nichoirs. I'll get one for you. You can put it under your window. We have to protect the sparrows. If we don't, Edith Piaf will regret it."

Ambre laughed again.

"That's really kind," she said, and simultaneously, we both seemed to notice that we were side by side in a window frame, our shoulders touching and our faces just inches apart.

She leaned the extra few inches and kissed me. This time I didn't count the seconds.

Then the kiss was over and I was alone in the window frame.

"You're a very generous guy," Ambre said, from a full metre away. "To me and the sparrows. But ironically, your generosity means I'm going to be even busier than before. Lara and I have to seize the opportunity and make sure we meet the Olympic contract. So I have to get to work. Sorry, Paul, if I had the time, you would be someone I'd like to spend it with. But at the moment, I have no time for a copain." That double-edged word, meaning friend or boyfriend.

"No time for un petit ami?" I asked. This was a term that made it absolutely clear we were talking about boyfriends.

"No time. Sorry, Paul."

And she was out the door.

I picked up my hammer and chisel. The masonry was going to bear the full brunt of my frustration.

28

"I hope she has the sense of l'humour?" Jake said. "A girlfriend must have the sense of l'humour. She must be the opposite of a, what do we say, un chien pour les aveugles?"

"A guide dog for the blind?" I suggested.

"Yes, she must be the exact opposite. Imagine, if you can't see anything, you don't want a chien with a sense of l'humour, do you? The dog will be, like, 'Oh, sorry, I couldn't resist walking you into that lamppost. It was so funny.' With a girlfriend, it's the opposite. If she has no sense of l'humour, every time you try to say something funny, it's like walking into a lamppost, tu comprends?"

"I think so, Jake."

"That's why I love Cécile. She mocks everyone, she fucks with other guys, women too, but she has a sense of l'humour."

"You're a lucky guy."

"Chin to that." He held up his almost-empty wine glass and we clinked.

Jake and I were sitting on a party boat that was moored on the riverbank not far from Notre-Dame. The cathedral was still being renovated after the fire, but was beginning to take on its old shape. The building materials lying about in the grounds made it look as if it was hosting a medieval crafts show with demonstrations of stonecutting, woodcarving and glass-staining.

This reminded me of something I wanted to tell Jake.

"Hey, you know that at the 1924 Paris Olympics, there were arts events? They awarded medals for painting, sculpture, architecture, music and stuff."

Jake nearly choked on his wine. "You're merding me. Arts at the Olympiques?"

"It's true. Paris wanted to prove that it was the world capital of culture. It was a bit like your Nolympics. In 1924, you could win a medal even if your only physical skills were squeezing tubes of paint and smoking."

"No, it's not the same as the Nolympics. Art takes talent, Paul. Poetry is a skill."

Not everyone's poetry, I wanted to say, but restrained myself.

"What about pétanque, was that at the 1924 Olympiques?" Jake asked.

"No."

"Shame. Comment ça va, your campaign for 2024?"

"It's looking promising. You know my old boss Jean-Marie, the ultra-patriotic politician, he's backing the campaign."

I had watched another of Jean-Marie's ads. It was subtitled in English, very well in fact, though not by me. I'd decided to stay well away from that hot political potato, and keep my name clear of his.

In the new ad, Jean-Marie was standing outside an old brick warehouse, holding a sledgehammer, saying that he personally was going to strike the first blow to make sure *pétanque* would be an Olympic sport. This, he told us, was the building that he was donating as Paris's 2024 *boulodrome*, its *pétanque* stadium. Then he looked us all in the eye and declared "Vive la pétanque! Vive la France!" before swinging his hammer and knocking a suspiciously large chunk of brickwork out of the nearest wall.

"Well, I know that Jean-Marie is a merde raciste," Jake said, summing the guy up pretty accurately, "but I guess he can make things happen, so chin to that."

We clinked glasses again, though this time Jake's was completely empty, so I went to the bar to get him a refill.

People were starting to populate the party boat, which was a converted cargo barge. The deck area had been fitted with glass walls and a roof, and laid out with café tables. At one end of the deck there was a bar, at the other a stage.

Everything about the décor was black and white, as if the

barge was dressed for dinner in a tuxedo and dress shirt. Black metal floor, white tablecloths, black curtain around the stage. The largest splash of colour in the place was a red-and-white banner that Jake had fixed above the stage – "Nolympiques 2024".

It was like any ordinary cabaret venue except that the floor swayed dangerously every time another boat went by. The River Seine is very narrow as it divides into two channels to flow around the Ile de la Cité, so the current runs fast and the passing boats were creating quite a bow wave. In the evenings there is a whole flotilla of *bateaux mouches* cruising up and down the Seine, so just walking to the bar felt like surfing. I was sure the tables were screwed in place, and the glasses weighted so they didn't fall over.

As I was waiting to get served, I saw Jake's two male Nolympic chums arriving – the older American with the long lank hair and the young French nerd. The narrow gangplank was bucking wildly under their feet. They were bulky guys, and walking wasn't one of their most developed skills at the best of times, so they were clinging on to the handrail, boarding one small step at a time.

I kept an eye on them until they had managed to grapple on to the deck, just in case any lifesaving was needed, and they must have thought I was taking the pee, because neither of them greeted me with much warmth when they finally made it to the bar.

"Something to drink?" I offered. Now that Marjorie's *pétanque* fee was creeping closer to my bank account, I was feeling generous.

"An IPA," the French nerd said.

"Vin rouge," the American grunted.

I ordered their drinks and asked them if they were intending to speak from the stage tonight.

"Speak?"

"Parler?"

I thought maybe I ought to hire them for my translation business. They were like each other's subtitles.

"You'll see. Tu verras," they told me, one language apiece, and I left them to it. I preferred to get back to Jake before the translation twins killed all my sympathy for the Nolympic cause.

I hadn't revealed much to Jake about the political and financial shenanigans going on around the whole *pétanque* campaign. I certainly hadn't breathed a word to him about the Martin family's corrupt property dealings or my attempt to blackmail Elodie into ordering Ambre's solar panels.

But I did tell him that I was keener than ever on getting it together with Ambre, and even confessed that I wasn't really sleeping with her. This, predictably, horrified him.

"Allez, Paul, you are like the man who opens the bottle of Chablis and does not want to drink."

"But I do want to drink, Jake. The whole bottle. It's just that she doesn't have the time right now."

"Time? Who needs time?"

Fortunately, Cécile's arrival cut him short.

Cécile was to be the star comedy turn in tonight's pro-anti-Olympic event, and she was buzzing. She grabbed Jake in a tongues-flying embrace, and I heard metal clatter against Jake's teeth. She was pierced and energetic, a dangerous combination.

"Salut, Paul," she squealed, and I was afraid she was about to knock one of my molars out with her prehensile tongue, but she confined herself to slobbering on my cheeks.

"Wo!" she squealed again. The floor had bucked upwards, and Cécile was in instant, arms-out, knees-bent ninja mode. She laughed and began a wide-eyed dance to the beat of the swaying deck. I guessed that her buzz wasn't all natural adrenaline.

"Hey, is there a dressing room downstairs?" Cécile said.

"You want to change clothes?" I asked. She was already kitted out in a black "Nolympiques" T-shirt. She looked ready to go on.

"No, man," Jake tutted. "She wants to rock to the rhythm of the River Seine. N'est-ce pas, chérie?"

"Oh oui," she rhymed. They locked tonsils again and began surfing as one towards the staircase that led below decks.

Well, I thought, if Jake ever wanted a real Olympic medal, there was one sport for which he was sure to win team gold.

The boat was crowded by the time Jake came on stage to introduce the evening's info-tainment.

All the tables were full, and people were lounging along the glass walls, silhouetted against the floodlit Notre-Dame. Alcoholic substances had been flowing generously, and the whole crowd would probably have failed an Olympic dope test. But then physical incapacity was a requirement for the Nolympics, so intoxication was not a handicap.

Jake's other Nolympic team members had turned up – the teenage pothead and the American yoga lady.

I was sitting down at the front, along with a couple of special guests, one of whom had promised to go on stage, despite my feeling that it might be disastrously counter-productive.

Jake walked, or swayed, across to the microphone stand, which was pitching about as if it was the mast on a tiny, wave-rocked sailing dinghy. He made a grab for the mic and got lucky first time. The audience cheered.

"Bonsoir Paree!" he called out. "Welcome to this soirée Nolympique on the Seine." This was greeted by another cheer, as well as a cry of "Parle français!" in an American accent. "Organiser les Nolympiques," Jake went on, "it's a contradiction in terms."

"Parle français!" It was the American guy again.

"Ta gueule!" a very French voice replied. Shut your trap. This provoked another cheer. Apart from Jean-Marie and a few people over the age of 75, the French really don't care about speaking their own language all the time.

"The Paris Olympiques are supposed to be all about inclusivité," Jake went on, doing his best to stay centre-stage while gravity repeatedly tried to fling him towards one riverbank or the other. "These new sports – skateboard, BMX, breakdance – they are supposed to be male and female, young and hip."

"Colonialisme américain!" shouted an American-sounding voice.

"But they are sports pour les élites! For example, the élite who can stand on a skateboard." With perfect timing, the rocking stage sent Jake crashing to one knee.

"Breakdance!" a wag called out, and Jake seriously looked as though he might soon be spinning around on his backside.

But he climbed back to his unsteady feet.

"Exactement," he said. "Breakdance is for the élite who can dance on their tête! These new Olympic sports are not inclusifs, they are exclusifs!"

He got another cheer, but it was half-hearted. Instead, the loudest sound was someone in the audience who shouted, in a strong French accent, "Give us your funny poem!"

Of course, this was what had made Jake semi-famous on social media – his obscene lockdown rhyme.

"Pas maintenant," Jake protested. "I have things to say, serious things."

"Funny poem!" the same French person called out, and the chant was taken up by the crowd. Soon the whole boatload was chanting what sounded like "Ferny pwem, ferny pwem!"

Jake stared at them for a few seconds, then lost his temper.

"Je ne suis pas un fucking jukebox," he yelled, apparently forgetting that no one under 30 knows what a jukebox is. Then he stormed, or swayed, backstage.

The crowd good-naturedly began to call him back, but the American yoga lady stepped into the breach. Her centre of gravity was heavy and low, so she hardly moved off centre as she glided across the stage and reached up for the microphone.

"Allez allez," she said like a kindly crèche assistant addressing a roomful of rowdy toddlers. "Nous allons faire du noga."

Everyone, me included, wondered what she was talking about. She smiled benignly at us.

"Noga, c'est le yoga Nolympique. No yoga – noga." She replaced the mic on its stand and, still miraculously managing to stay almost upright on the rocking deck, put her hands together as if in prayer.

"Allez!" she said, and we all followed suit, pressing our palms together.

She screwed up her eyes, poked her tongue out, and made a loud "Er" sound, like a kid who has just tasted black coffee for the first time.

"Allez!" she urged us.

She started up with the "Er-ing" again, making them louder and longer, her tongue poking out further with each gargling noise, her eyes goggling wider. We all did the same.

Soon the whole crowd was baying and grimacing like a pack of manic All Black rugby players.

"Très bien!" our teacher said, and started doing a new movement. Now her face was in repose and the only part of her moving was, alarmingly, her groin. She was thrusting her hips towards the audience and performing micro-clenches that provoked gasps and giggles.

"Allez!" she ordered, and I'm pretty sure that everyone, like me, started clenching under the table.

Then our guru pulled her grimace face again, and began "Er-ing" in time to her groin thrusts, and we all joined in.

"C'est le noga de Nora," she shouted above the cacophony. "Checkez-moi sur le social media!" She applauded us, or maybe herself, and then announced: "Et voilà un autre event Nolympique!"

On stage came the French nerd and the older American guy, rocking and stumbling in from either wing. They arrived one each side of Nora and stood still, their arms outstretched, trying to keep their balance, which was not easy on the rolling stage.

"Le no-board!" Nora announced, to laughs and groans. Every French person recognized the obvious pun on "snowboard".

One of the loudest groaners was Jake, who had appeared in the chair beside me, still looking annoyed at his failed speech.

"This is merde, man," he said. "She's kidnapped the show." I guessed he meant hijacked.

I had to agree that this wasn't helping to create a true alternative to the official Olympics. It was more like some hideous demonstration of the twin French loves of mime and English puns.

"Send on your guest," Jake urged me, as Nora et al attempted to make their way off stage, using a variety of techniques from shuffling feet to doggie paddle. "Tell him to speak now."

Jake was referring to Alain, whom I'd invited to come and talk about *pétanque*. When I suggested this to Marjorie, she was all for it. She had come along, too, to film Alain interacting with *le peuple parisien*. She wanted more evidence that there was real public support for the sport.

Alain, who by now had consumed three or four glasses of the boat's throat-stripping red wine, needed no second bidding to get up and perform.

He arrived on stage after a couple of stumbling false starts, his progress across the rolling deck made slightly more difficult because he had chosen to bring a pair of *pétanque* balls with him as props.

His appearance was greeted with spontaneous laughs. He was, after all, the funniest thing anyone had seen all evening. Here was a tipsily grinning man with a moustache as big as a rat and a horseshoe of grey hair, his sweaty shirt revealing a hairy navel, his khaki shorts threatening to explode, his fluffy cotton socks tucked neatly into leather sandals, he was rooted centre stage, trying his best to sway in synch with the microphone stand as he introduced himself. The name of his organization only added to the laughter.

But to his credit, Alain rode the laughs as he was riding the waves, and gave Marjorie and me, both of us filming from out front, some excellent footage of an impassioned call for France's national game to be recognized as such on the world's sporting stage.

If I had thought of it earlier, I would have done a remix of an old football song to accompany him. We could have had a singalong of "Pétanque is coming home".

By the end of his speech, Alain had the whole crowd chanting with him, "Viva la pétanka!". It was going to look great on social media, especially in contrast to Jean-Marie's self-serving political smarm.

This public enthusiasm, however, was Alain's undoing.

Carried away by the chanting, he decided that it would be a good idea to juggle his *boules*. It is never wise to start throwing turnip-sized lumps of lead from hand to hand in a crowded place, but performed on a pitching boat after several glasses of plonk, it was a genuine health hazard.

It came as no surprise when, after a single successful juggle, one of the balls flew into the audience to skittle through a table load of bottles and glasses, while the other ball hit the ceiling, bounced down on to Alain's forehead and ended up slamming with a sickening crunch on to one of his sandaled feet. The only merciful thing about it was that I'm pretty sure Alain was unconscious before he hit the deck.

Alain regained consciousness quickly, but for the first minute or so, all he could say was "Viva la pétanka". Marjorie and I assumed it was concussion and escorted him to the nearby Hôtel Dieu hospital, which was less than five minutes' walk away.

While Alain was being examined, we watched a live stream of Cécile on the barge. She sang her translations of Jake's Nolympic poem and a couple of his other gems, and they went down really well. For some reason, the vulgarity worked better in pure French. Maybe Latin-based swearwords are less brutal than Anglo-Saxon ones. There must be a potential thesis in it for a linguistics student: "Fucking *Putain*, a Comparative Study of Shockingness, Mother-*baiseurs*".

We also saw a fifteen-second film of Alain braining himself. This was an audience member's video that had quickly gone viral, portraying Alain as a victim of his clumsy juggling as well as France's love of puns. Sadly for him, the video's punchline – a caption, *"il a les boules"* – was French slang for "he is pissed off".

After Alain's head had been bandaged, he came to sit with us, waiting to be officially discharged. We showed him the film. His reaction to seeing the short disaster movie of his performance was Latin-based, but pretty brutal nonetheless.

29

Someone else had *les boules* about Alain's newfound fame. Elodie called me up next day, in ice-queen mode.

"Paul, can you not control this plouc you work with?"

"Alain, you mean? He just raised people's awareness of pétanque way beyond –"

But I didn't get to finish my sentence.

"Papa is furious. Your plouc has made us look absurd."

So that was it. Jean-Marie had recently elected himself *pétanque*'s public champion, the man with his finger on the *boule*, and now his big-budget self-promotion films were being out-clicked a thousand times over by a few seconds of a clown knocking himself out with a *pétanque* ball.

"Surely anything that attracts attention to the sport is good news for your father?" I objected. "You know what they say, all publicity is good publicity."

"As you say in English, bollocks."

I could see why she would think that. Hers was a family that did all its business in degrees of shadow. They chose their own publicity, carefully selecting the angle of light they wanted to shine on events.

The most annoying thing for the Martins was that Alain's film had appeared online the same night as Jean-Marie's own latest effort, during which he, in a computer-generated mock-up of his new *pétanque* venue, threw French tricolour *boules* with deadly accuracy, knocking the opposing team's balls – which were painted in the colours of the American, British and Chinese flags – out of the Olympic arena. We saw Jean-Marie accept the gold medal before ranting to camera about putting an end to

"Anglo-Saxon linguistic colonialism". This film, for obvious reasons, was not subtitled in English.

"Papa is investing a lot in this campaign," Elodie said. "He is taking risks."

"Yes, I saw that film of him with his sledgehammer, he looked like a real health risk."

"You English think you are funny, Paul, but you are not." Where had I heard that sentence before? "You must control your idiot plouc, and let papa lead this whole campaign forward, otherwise …" She paused for effect.

"Otherwise?" I asked, as I was obviously meant to.

"We will not be grateful."

Quite frankly, by that time I'd lost track of all the gratitude flying around.

It soon turned out that the Swiss were unhappy too, though not about Alain.

Marjorie summoned me to a Zoom meeting with our two friends in Geneva, Monika the tough German and Karl the amiable but sarcastic American.

Marjorie, Alain and I met as before at the incubator. Alain was wearing a yellowish peaked cap, in a failed attempt to hide the bandage wrapped around his head. The cap was too small and looked like a blob of mustard on top of a half-peeled potato.

Before hooking up online with the Swiss pair, Marjorie briefed us on the reason for our meeting.

"Monika and Karl are surprised, they say, that pétanque has been linked with the political campaign of an extreme right-wing political party. We must convince them that it is nothing to do with us."

She looked accusingly at me, the guy who had brought Elodie on board. I tried my best to look innocent while acknowledging my guilt. Fortunately, after lots of dealings with French girlfriends, it's an expression I've been able to perfect.

I had to maintain this look when the Swiss pair came on screen because Monika was in confrontational mood.

"What is this nonsense in the France Party's propaganda film with the pétanque balls and the flags?" she demanded.

"Qu'est-ce qu'elle dit?" Alain demanded, and I leaned across to translate while Marjorie explained to Monika that Jean-Marie's latest offering was "nussing to do wiz us".

"We agreed to support a compromise in which Paris would elevate the status of the French language," Monika went on, "but we did not agree to this outrageous nationalistic gesturing."

"Qu'est-ce qu'elle dit?"

I tried to translate while Karl the American chipped in.

"Attacking other languages with cannonballs is the epitome of non-diverse behaviour," he said, stroking his beard pityingly, like Father Christmas explaining to a child why it doesn't deserve a present.

"Qu'est-ce qu'il dit?"

I was kept busy with Alain while Marjorie continued to insist that "Jean-Marie Martin is not at all member of our campagne."

"Yes, I see you have been fighting your own campaign, Monsieur Fillon," Karl said, grinning and gesturing to his own fleshy skull.

Alain waved away my attempt to translate.

"Yes, I bang my ed, very comic," he said. "But you see the complete film of me? My speech? The public, they love the pétanka. They say 'Viva la pétanka, viva la pétanka!' This is the voice of the public, le peuple!"

Alain gestured to me to press home his point.

"Did you watch our full film of Alain's speech on the party boat?" I asked Karl and Monika. "You must have seen that the audience were really into what he was saying about pétanque. And they were a young, very mixed French audience."

Monika was mollified.

"Yes, yes, we watched it. That is why we are offering you another compromise." She smiled. After the puritanical Swiss disapproval, she was about to offer us some alpine milk chocolate. "If you can, how shall we say, discourage the continuation of the nationalistic campaign," she said, "we will recommend, very strongly, to the Paris 2024 committee that pétanque should be included as a demonstration event."

Even Alain understood this.

"Yes, yes, no prob-lemm," he said.

"Just for 2024, you understand," Karl added. "There will be no pétanque in Los Angeles."

This sounded like a code phrase used by French spies in a movie, but Alain dismissed it with a scornful puff.

"On s'en bat les couilles de Los Angeles," he said, doing the French thing of "beating his balls" to show indifference.

"LA is not their immediate concern," I mistranslated.

A few minutes later, we signed off the best of friends, and Marjorie turned to me, all smiles.

"So, Paul, now all *you* have to do is talk to your friend Elodie Martin and explain that her papa must stop his nationalistic merde," she told me.

My own smile fell as fast as Alain had done when he was plummeting face-first towards the stage.

We were still discussing exactly what I was going to say to Elodie, and how I was going to take evasive action afterwards, when Marjorie got a phone call. She listened gravely.

"We are going to Saint-Denis immediately," she said when she hung up. "The Paris 2024 people want to see us."

"You don't need me at the meeting this time," I said.

"They particularly want to see *you*."

Which didn't sound good.

Marjorie told Alain that he could go and rest in his hotel room, get something to eat, maybe. He was only too pleased to heed this advice.

"Best if you and I go alone," Marjorie told me. "If Alain gets angry, his skull will explode."

We taxi'd across the *périphérique*, into a neatly renovated ex-industrial area.

The taxi driver had grown up in Saint-Denis and chatted about how the area used to look. As a younger man he'd been here for raves at which chic Parisian kids had paid fortunes for saccharine tablets. Dead dogs used to float in the canal, and the people in his neighbourhood had thought that Paris was deliberately worsening the dereliction just outside the *périph'* as an extra barrier against the *banlieues*. But now it was all changing, he said, and soon Saint-Denis would be so shiny and glassy that it would blind Google's satellite cameras.

I half-listened while wondering how to avoid being kicked into satellite orbit by Elodie. Presumably she would be at the meeting.

The taxi went through a security barrier and into the campus I'd seen online – the hamlet of giant log cabins. Marjorie directed the driver to a building that sported a large gold-and-black sign, "Paris 2024".

After being X-rayed and interrogated at reception, we were given stick-on name badges and escorted to the upper storeys of the log cabin by a cheerful young intern, the same kind of suit-wearing hipster I often saw at the incubator.

He led us to a meeting room, an enormous, brightly-lit space that was taken up by a white table in the shape of the outline of the Olympic rings. It looked like a decapitated cauliflower.

Sitting at the table in two very comfortable-looking, high-backed office chairs were Héloïse and Louis, whom we'd met at the Eiffel Tower. Elodie wasn't there, but I assumed she would be along twenty minutes late, to remind us of her importance.

To my surprise, Héloïse said that the four of us would get straight into the meeting.

"Elodie isn't coming?" I asked.

"Non," Louis replied, and I tried not to sigh too loudly with relief.

"We thought you might ask that," Héloïse said, accusingly. "Monsieur Wess, you have been negotiating with Madame Martin and her father, n'est-ce pas?"

"No," I said, and everyone else in the room sniffed with French disbelief. "Not with Jean-Marie Martin. Only with Elodie."

"Explain, please," Louis said. (*S'il vous plaît*-sha.)

I began doing so in my most careful French.

"Elodie offered to promote pétanque as an Olympic sport.

In exchange, she asked me to correct a letter to a British film director. She wants him to make the film for the opening ceremony in Paris. She also mentioned that her father was interested in the pétanque campaign, and in the status of the French language."

"Interessé-sha," Louis repeated. He and Héloïse chuckled sarcastically. I knew why. In French, "interested" also means "with an ulterior motive". If you hear that someone is *intéressé*, it can be a warning that you're about to get ripped off.

"Elodie also asked me to do the English subtitles for her father's political films, but I said no."

"Very prudent," Héloïse said.

She explained that Jean-Marie's new *pétanque* venue was in fact a property scam. He was in the process of illegally demolishing a listed 19th-century wine warehouse near the Gare de Lyon, using patriotism and the Olympics as a pretext. He planned to build a temporary *pétanque* stadium and then, after the Games, to knock it down and make a fortune selling the empty site, which would be ten times more valuable than when it was occupied by the protected old building.

"We can't allow him to profit from all this," Héloïse said, "but in a way his scheme is advantageous for us, because he has gone one step too far. Now we can stop him." She pointed her joined hands, javelin-like, at me. "*You* can stop him."

"Moi?"

I'd been uncomfortable enough at the prospect of asking Elodie to have a word with her dad about toning down his French nationalism.

But Héloïse was implying that I should threaten Jean-Marie himself with legal action, which was an entirely different *pétanque* game. Scuppering a crooked property deal was the kind of thing that got you buried in the disputed building's foundations, wasn't it? This was France, a civilized country, but people here have been known to disappear discreetly, and not always of their own accord.

"Pourquoi moi?" I asked.

"You are an outsider," Louis explained. "If you prevent Monsieur Martin from building his new venue, we can present this as an *English* plan to sabotage pétanque. We can say that it is part of an Anglo-Saxon attempt to halt the campaign to make French the first language of the Olympics. No one will be surprised by that. You English are our best enemies." (*Ennemissha.*)

"But how do I do all that?" I asked.

"Simple. You tell Elodie that her father must end all his fraudulent schemes," Héloïse told me. "Otherwise you will expose him to the minister of housing. We will give you the necessary documents and the name of the person at the ministry whom you will contact. Or threaten to contact."

"Elodie won't believe me," I said. "I'm not the sort of person who can contact ministers. She will just ignore me."

"No matter," Héloïse said. "We will do the real work. Whatever happens, we will make sure that Martin's pétanque venue is not built and that he is fined by the city for ignoring building regulations. But he will blame *you*, and we will make sure that the French media do, too. That way, they won't be reporting on conflicts within the Paris 2024 team."

It all sounded very neat and cosy – for them.

The last time I'd blackmailed the Martin family, it had been in a way they understood – "I scratch your back, and you buy solar panels off the girl I want to sleep with." For Elodie and Jean-Marie, that was a perfectly sensible business agreement. If anything, I'd made myself and Ambre part of their scam, so I was on their level.

But now Héloïse was asking for a serious escalation in the blackmail – "Scrap your *whole* multi-million property game, Jean-Marie, or else." He and Elodie weren't going to be happy, to put it mildly.

"What if I don't want to do it?" I asked, wishing I knew the French word for scapegoat[5].

"Of course, you are free to refuse," Héloïse said. "But you

---

[5] In case any reader should need it: *bouc émissaire.*

admit that you have been working with Elodie on this opening ceremony film, the main object of which seems to be to get a parachutist to publicize her father's buildings. So if you refuse to help us, you might be accused of being their accomplice."

She let the threat hang in the air like the smoke from one of Jake's joints.

"But what about pétanque?" Marjorie asked. "If Monsieur Martin withdraws his support?"

"If Jean-Marie Martin withdraws altogether from any interference in the Games, then we undertake to argue in favour of pétanque as a demonstration sport for Paris 2024," Héloïse said. "I'm sure we will be able to convince our colleagues."

The winning trump card. Marjorie almost whooped. I guessed she was on a success bonus. I wondered if I was.

It looked as though there was no way for me to avoid going to see Elodie with a view to making her violently angry.

In truth, even worse than the prospect of facing her was a purely selfish fear: I felt certain that as soon as I scuppered her dad's schemes, she was bound to do the same for mine. She would take cruel pleasure in tearing up Ambre's solar-panel contract before my eyes.

I went to see Elodie that same afternoon, at her urban cottage in the fifth *arrondissement*. Just in case I was destined to exit the courtyard inside a newly-poured block of concrete, I made sure that several people knew exactly when I would be there, and I even made a video call to Jake as I walked up the long driveway towards Elodie's secret garden.

Jake told me that he had been ousted from the presidency of the Nolympics group. Nora the noga lady had staged a coup d'état. But he wasn't particularly bothered.

"Nolympics, no cry," he said. "I've got plans with Cécile. Des plans poétiques. Listen to this. We've written a new –"

"Sorry, Jake, going into a meeting, got to hang up."

I spared myself the gory poetic details. Besides, I was outside Elodie's garden gate and starting to hyperventilate.

I was still inhaling deeply when I sat down in her comfortable leather armchair and explained that, against my will, I was here to warn her that her family's property scams and power games were not going to work.

"Your Parisian colleagues intend to stop you taking over the committee," I said. "They know exactly what your dad is up to in the Olympic Village, and they've seen through his demolition job near the Gare de Lyon. I'm pretty sure they're going to try and prosecute him for ignoring building regulations. So, just between you and me, if you're planning to make an opening ceremony film, I think it would be wise to leave all your dad's buildings out of it."

It wasn't exactly what Héloïse and Louis had told me to say, and I sounded as if I was sympathizing rather than threatening. But I didn't see the point in getting Jean-Marie mad at me personally, and I didn't like being used as the English scapegoat. Scapegoats, like all breeds of goat, can bite back when provoked.

Elodie listened to me almost calmly, as if she had been expecting blackmail.

"What is your part in all this?" she asked me.

"I'm just the messenger boy."

"I don't believe you."

"I didn't *have* to come here and warn you," I lied.

"But you're enjoying this."

"You really think so?"

It must have been obvious from my demeanour that there were several million other things I would have preferred to be doing, including getting a root canal and having my nipples waxed.

"Yes, because you've always hated my father."

"Not *always*." Only since he fired me and tried to steal my tearoom.

"And you've always done your best to sabotage everything my family tries to achieve."

"Not *everything*."

But she wasn't listening to my objections.

"It's typical," she said. "It's as I predicted. You have proved yourself to be a gold medallist in the English sport of stabbing friends in the back. My father was right. As soon as you voted yourselves out of the European single market, he said that the suicidal economic damage of Brexit would turn the English back into the pillaging barbarians who had burned Joan of Arc."

"I don't think we'll be invading France again," I said. "Not unless the EU gives us the necessary work permits."

"You joke as usual, Paul," she said, "but you are forgetting how I tried to help you and your friend Ambre. And now you are burning me at the stake of your English perfidy."

It was a fine performance, although personally, I didn't see much resemblance between Elodie and Joan of Arc. Except, perhaps, the visions of personal grandeur.

"You make a great victim, Elodie," I told her, "but it's not *my* fault your dad is trying to defraud Saint-Denis and Paris while sullying the Olympic spirit with his nationalistic bollocks."

"All he was trying to do was defend the French language and culture," she said, like a lawyer claiming self-defence for a serial killer.

"Oh, yes, that's *all* he was trying to do."

She shook her head in well-feigned moral martyrdom.

"Well, it's too bad for your precious pétanque," she said, "and for your friend Ambre's contract." And then, after naming the part of my anatomy where she hoped Ambre would stick at least one solar panel, she told me in French to "fuck the camp".

I was only too glad to do so while still in possession of all my vital organs, so I got up to leave. But she wasn't finished yet.

"Oh, Paul," she called as I headed for the door.

I turned to see her holding up her phone.

"One thing you might like to know," she said. "I was me who sent those invitations to your friend Fleur." She paused for effect. "And who organized your presence in the advertisements for Meet-ologie."

Somehow, it all made sense. The petty yet efficient maliciousness of it was pure Elodie.

"Why?" I asked.

"At first it was just to annoy you, which is *such* fun." She smiled at me almost warmly. "Then I decided that it was necessary to distract you from more serious matters."

"I'm flattered," I said. "You think I'm such a dangerous adversary?"

"Oh, don't be flattered, Paul. Mainly, I just enjoy seeing you squirm. You English do it so well. You have such entertaining guilt complexes."

"Unlike the French?"

"Oh, we feel no guilt at all, that is our best quality. That's why you haven't heard the last of the Martin family. And who knows, maybe you haven't seen the last of yourself on French dating apps."

There was a sly glint in her eye.

I hoped there was one in mine, too, as I held up my own phone.

"One thing you forgot to ask me," I said. "Whether I was recording this meeting."

Her eyes narrowed, but she quickly regained her composure.

"What do I care?" she shrugged. "I haven't said anything incriminating. The stuff about Meet-ologie is meaningless. Pay a fortune for a lawyer if you think otherwise."

"It must be comforting to be so sure of yourself, Elodie," I said, trying to look as if I held all the aces, plus a few kings and queens.

I left the house as calmly as I could, and strode down the alleyway towards freedom. Only when I reached the street did I breathe easily. I had been terrified that she would actually ask the question: was I really recording?

Because the answer was no, and I'm such a shitty liar.

Less than an hour after I left Elodie's urban oasis, I got a message from Ambre. She forwarded a blunt email that she had received from Elodie, cancelling their contract. The cancellation was before the end of what the French call the *délai de réflexion*, the legal cooling-off period, so no compensation of any sort was due.

"Merde," was the only comment that Ambre added.

"There's nothing I can do to change her mind," I typed.

"No, I know," she replied.

"Merde," I concurred. It was a good description of things in general.

A couple of mornings later, Marjorie sent me a link to a news item. It was about Jean-Marie's arrest on the poetic-sounding French charge of *faux et usage de faux* – fake and use of fake. The Paris 2024 people had pounced already.

Fortunately for me, there was no mention of any English involvement in the affair. Yet.

I was just enjoying the sight of Jean-Marie getting into a police car while giving the TV cameras his most defiant face – a Resistance fighter going to the firing squad – when Madalena knocked at the door with a letter.

It was another large envelope depicting the France's best-known semi-naked lady, Marianne.

"Votre nationalité?" she asked.

"Let us pray," I said, though I doubted it.

And my doubts were confirmed in three or four crisply bureaucratic French sentences.

The letter informed me that although my interview had been a success, my application for nationality was turned down because of my *casier judiciaire*, my criminal record. It had been brought to the attention of the department (I could guess by whom) that I had previously been found guilty of contravening law number 94-665 of 4 August 1994 regarding the obligation to translate all commercial information into French when doing business in France.

This was of course a reference to my untranslated English tearoom menu. That old *chataigne*.

Such a contravention caused automatic disqualification from the process to become a French citizen, I was told. I could still apply for a residence permit, using all the documents I had sent for the nationality application – plus my three most recent monthly pay slips.

I hadn't received Marjorie's payment yet, and jobs in the

previous three months had been pretty sparse, so I knew that I might as well send in three sheets of toilet paper.

Oh well, I thought, at least Elodie's revenge was guillotine-like – swift and surgical.

Not painless, though, far from it.

Once Marjorie's money came in, I would probably have to spend it on a one-way Eurostar ticket back to London. Maybe I'd have enough left over to buy a sparrow nesting box for Ambre to remember me by. If she had time for memories.

It was all one big *merde*.

30

Unlike us Brits, who sold off all our heavy industry in the 1980s and 90s, France as a state still owns controlling shares in companies that make cars, aeroplanes and trains. So if you try to get in the way of the workings of the French administration, it owns several ways of running you over.

This was what I found out.

And I wasn't the only one.

Several months had passed. Jean-Marie was being well and truly rolled over by *La République*. His building site near the Gare de Lyon was still empty, though to be fair to him, it was providing a public service. The fences around it hadn't remained intact for long, and it was now performing valiantly as something the city needed far more than a *pétanque* stadium – a canine toilet. The neighbourhood's dog-owners were all taking their mutts there to lick each other's backsides and do their doings far away from the public pavements.

Jean-Marie's substandard Olympic Village buildings had been annexed by the town of Saint-Denis and finished off according to the strictest health and safety regulations. Jean-Marie had no doubt received a small fortune for his partial constructions, but it was precisely that, a small one compared to what he had been hoping to screw out of the system.

He had even been forced to change the name of his political party. The name "France" was already taken, he was told – by a country.

The last I'd heard, he'd been planning to change the party's name to "Jeanne d'Arc", his country's patron saint. But apparently someone told him that it wasn't a great idea because on election ballots, he would be listed family name first, followed by his party: "Martin, Jean-Marie, Jeanne d'Arc". And in French, *"marie-jeanne"* is slang for marijuana. The allusion might gain him a few votes, but he didn't want that kind of voter.

Elodie, meanwhile, had disappeared completely. After resigning from the Paris 2024 committee, she had vanished from the public eye. But then her secret garden in the Latin Quarter was a pleasant place to vanish to.

For whatever reason, my name was never mentioned in the media. Maybe France didn't need scapegoats, and it was just getting on with the job of protecting the image of the Paris Games.

I received a curt message from the naturalisation office when the time limit on applying for a residence permit ran out, but I was expecting that anyway.

Soon afterwards, another official letter was delivered. This one informed me that it was time for me to face *La République*.

My appointment with France was, fittingly perhaps, on the morning of the 2024 Paris Olympics' opening ceremony. I wondered whether, later that day, someone would be shoving the President out of a helicopter and then apologizing for forgetting the parachute.

Though, being French, they probably weren't going to opt for something as comedic as London had done in 2012. The opening ceremony was more likely to involve massed ranks of schoolkids debating a philosophical paradox, or the re-enactment of a *banlieue* riot set to music by Jean-Michel Jarre.

My own ceremony that day was to be much simpler. I was told that I had to "present myself" at an official building in central Paris to hear the French verdict on my character.

The *salles publiques* (reception rooms) of most French institutions feel like revolutionary courts. They are often decorated with frescos celebrating some popular uprising or other. It is made very clear to you that you are *chez la République*.

The person presiding often wears a tricolour sash of office, even if the rest of their outfit is a T-shirt and jeans. He or she sits on a wooden throne or behind an immovable desk. In a French town hall, even a wedding can feel like a kangaroo court.

Everything that happened to me was going to be done in a highly civilized and yet unstoppable way, symbolic of French bureaucracy as a whole.

So that morning I put on my most polished black shoes and my best tie, a souvenir from when I used to have a highly paid job. It was silk, in a rather startling shade of coral pink that I thought ambitious-looking at the time.

In my jacket pocket, I had a *convocation*, a document mid-way between an invitation and a summons, telling me where to report on what date. *La République* trusted me not to disobey.

Even though my appointment was in the epicentre of Paris, I decided to walk rather than take a crowded underground train. The influx of Olympic tourists had turned almost every *Métro* line into a permanent scrum.

I set off in plenty of time and strolled along the canal bank, which was bustling. Paris-Plages had been set up, with sandpits, deckchairs, pedalos, a swimming pool and, yes, *pétanque* pitches.

I crossed the Place de la République with its village of Olympic booths selling merchandise, sporting equipment, unsold tickets and some rather Nolympic food. The tall statue of Marianne herself in the middle of the square had been swathed in an Olympic flag.

I cut through the Marais, which had been pedestrianized for the duration of the Games. It was teeming with tourists browsing in clothes shops and Olympic pop-up stores.

The large open square in front of the Hôtel de la Ville, Paris's city hall, was covered in a selection of enclosures and marquees, all decorated with hoardings marked "*Paris, Ville Nolympique 2024*".

Yes, *Nolympique*. Against all odds and despite their own apathy, they'd made it happen. Without Jake, though. He was currently co-starring in a nightly cabaret on a Paris party boat. Joyous Franco-American vulgarity every evening from Tuesday to Sunday.

All over the Hôtel de la Ville square, people were queuing up to participate in Nolympic non-events. I saw a booth measuring the volume of people's shouts (or any other noise they cared to emit), a stage where two teams of kids were being timed as they piled green Parisian wheelie bins into an impromptu riot barricade, and a padded enclosure the size of a tennis court, in which the idea seemed to be that blindfolded people ran around and collided into as many inflated obstacles as possible. I watched a guy fall belly first on to a life-size, air-filled Gérard Depardieu and bounce right out of the arena, to the loud cheers of the spectators.

Humiliation was nothing new in this square, which was where Parisians were publicly executed before the Revolution. The Place de l'Hôtel de Ville lies just across the Seine from Paris's central court, the Palais de la Justice, though I doubt if condemned medieval Parisians ever felt that justice was being done when they were being hanged, broken on the wheel or – in extreme cases – quartered by four tugging horses.

As I entered the grand hall to which I had been summoned this sunny morning, I felt almost detached from events around me. This wasn't really happening to *me*, was it?

I saw Jake in the public gallery. It was hard to miss him. He was raising a bunched fist of encouragement at me and standing beside a girl with pink hair almost the same shade as my tie – Cécile. She nodded at me and smiled.

I didn't look around to see who else might have come to watch the proceedings. The room was airless, stifling, and I just wanted to get out of there as soon as possible.

A man in a black suit ushered me to sit on a hard bench in front of the wooden throne from which operations were to be directed.

After a few minutes, an official-sounding voice ordered everyone in the room to rise. I followed suit.

A woman stood before me, or rather I was before her. She wore a dark suit and a tricolour sash. I hardly listened to the speech she made, about the values of the *République* and the need to preserve and respect them if anarchy was to be avoided and France was to continue to prosper and develop.

Everyone began singing the "Marseillaise". I joined them but sang "mm mm mm-mm" over the bit about shedding impure blood – *un sang impur* – even though I had recently been informed that this wasn't racist. It was an 18th-century way of referring to the blood of French anti-revolutionaries who had murderous, and therefore impure, intentions.

After the anthem, I was called forward to the throne and told to sign a confession of sorts. A copy of this was given to me, and then, mercifully, I was allowed out into the fresh air.

In the square, beneath a massive banner on the façade of the Hôtel de Ville that welcomed the world to Paris in a hundred languages – in no particular order of supremacy – Jake grabbed my arm.

"Hey, mon ami, how does it feel? Not too bad?"

"It's almost a relief," I said. "Though I feel strange, weakened."

"It was inevitable," Cécile said.

"Yes, I suppose it was," I agreed.

Suddenly I was assaulted from behind, in a sort of rear bear hug. My attacker then released my arms and went for my head. Next thing I knew, I was being violently kissed on the lips.

"You made it," I said, as soon as I could breathe.

"Yes, I made time for you," Ambre said, laughing.

Perhaps I should explain.

The *convocation* that I had received was not to a criminal trial or a deportation hearing. It was a ceremony to mark the granting of my French citizenship.

This was why I had felt a kind of out-of-body experience. Before that day, I had only ever been English, which was by definition about as un-French as you could get.

Now suddenly I was half-French. Weakened in a way, suffering from diluted allegiance, but at the same time relieved. Now, no one was going to evict me from my home in Paris. And if I felt like it, I could go and open a Bavarian trattoria on a

Greek island or import Belgian baguettes into Bulgaria, and there was no longer a millimetre of red tape to hinder me. I didn't particularly want to do either of those things, but I was utterly free to do so, and it felt good.

How did I wangle French citizenship after being turned down because of my criminal record?

(That is a rhetorical question, and I am now partly French, so I am allowed to ask them.)

The answer is that the Paris 2024 committee, in co-operation with France's *pétanque* federation, put in a good word for me. To my astonishment, one day I received a letter informing me that citizenship had been awarded to me "for services to French sport".

In short, I had been elected a sort of knight of the grand order of *pétanque*, and, as an extra treat, a life member of FUCPET (though that was not something I would be putting on my CV).

Boules itself had enjoyed a similar happy ending. With Elodie and Jean-Marie Martin out of the picture, *pétanque* had been invited to Paris 2024 as a *sport de démonstration*. A *boules* tournament, without official Olympic medals, was to be held at the École Militaire. Marjorie was managing the event with, or despite, the help of Alain.

But what about Ambre? (Rhetorical again). Hadn't she dumped me after I scuppered her make-or-break solar panel deal with Elodie?

Well, strictly speaking, there hadn't been anything to dump, because we weren't in a relationship.

But in any case, thanks to my warnings about Elodie's reliability, Ambre and her business partner Lara had taken precautions. The instant they received Elodie's contract, they went running to France's national electricity company, EDF, and obtained financing for their venture. When Elodie later scrapped the deal, it didn't matter. With funding from a huge state-owned backer, they were well and truly launched. They had even got enough seed capital to take on new employees –

thereby giving Ambre a bit of free time.

And one day, when I went up to Ambre's room to give her a sparrow nesting box, I had received a lot more than a *merci beaucoup*. Ambre had shown me that gratitude could be far warmer, more unselfish and more exciting than anything the Martin family could offer. There and then, she and I had made as much noise as if I'd been hammering up a whole village of nesting boxes. And we had been making a delicious habit of it ever since.

"Alors," Ambre now asked me as we ambled hand-in-hand along the Seine riverbank, weaving our way amongst the Olympic hordes, "how does it feel to be French?"

"It's true what they say," I told her. "I do feel sexier, as if I could choose any woman in sight, and all I have to say to her is 'bonjour ma chérie,' and she will be dying for me to kiss her."

"You want to be kissed by any woman in sight?"

"No, of course not," I objected quickly. "I only want to be kissed by you."

"Oh Paul," she said, "you're not really French at all, are you?"

FIN

EPILOGUE

INT. PARISIAN INDOOR SPORTS STADIUM – DAY

In a large canvas marquee, an arena of fine gravel is surrounded by grandstands of plastic seating. All around the arena hang banners bearing the Olympic logo and the legend "PARIS PÉTANQUE 2024". The seats are packed with cheering spectators of all ages, many of whom are waving national flags of different colours and designs.

A TV camerawoman is standing in the centre of the arena as two men walk towards her. Both men are holding microphones.

One of the approaching figures is a bulky, moustachioed FRENCHMAN decked out in a blue blazer that is struggling to contain his ample stomach. The other is a younger, taller ENGLISHMAN wearing a dark suit and a tie of a rather startling shade of coral pink. He is the interpreter.

The two men's progress is accompanied by loud music. It is a guitar pop song. The words are indistinct.

Arriving at the centre of the arena, directly in front of the camerawoman, the bulky Frenchman raises one arm in the air as a kind of victory signal, causing his blazer, and then his shirt, to pop open. But he does not seem to notice the sudden baring of his hirsute navel. He begins to shout above the music.

FRENCHMAN IN BLUE BLAZER
(chanting into his microphone)
Viva la pétanka! Viva la pétanka!

> **ENGLISHMAN IN PINK TIE**
> *(into his microphone, deadpan)*
> Long live pétanque. Long live pétanque.

The background music swells. The tune is "Football's Coming Home". We can now make out the lyrics. They are in French: "Pétanque revient chez elle ..."

> **FRENCHMAN IN BLUE BLAZER**
> *(shouts into microphone)*
> Dans le bon sens, Paris a les boules!

He grins at the Englishman, who flinches and remains silent, because he doesn't know what to say – the Frenchman has clearly gone off script. The Frenchman repeats his announcement as a kind of challenge to the translator.

> **FRENCHMAN IN BLUE BLAZER**
> *(shouts into microphone)*
> Dans le bon sens, Paris a les boules!

> **ENGLISHMAN IN PINK TIE**
> *(hesitantly)*
> In a good sense, Paris has, er ...
> *(he gives a Parisian shrug)* No, I'm sorry,
> but that's an untranslatable French pun.
> You would not *believe* how many bloody
> puns I have to translate when I'm
> interpreting for the French. Practically
> every bloody sentence contains a pun ...

> **FADE TO BLACK**

Printed in Great Britain
by Amazon